W9-BLQ-643

BOOK SOLD
NO LONGER R.H.P.L.
PROPERTY

A French Wedding

ALSO BY HANNAH TUNNICLIFFE

Season of Salt and Honey
The Color of Tea

A French Wedding

A NOVEL

Hannah Tunnicliffe

DOUBLEDAY

New York   London   Toronto   Sydney   Auckland

This is a work of fiction. Names, characters, places, and incidents
either are the product of the author's imagination or are used fictitiously.
Any resemblance to actual persons, living or dead, events,
or locales is entirely coincidental.

Copyright © 2016, 2017 by Hannah Tunnicliffe

All rights reserved. Published in the United States by Doubleday,
a division of Penguin Random House LLC, New York, and
distributed in Canada by Random House of Canada, a division of
Penguin Random House Canada Limited, Toronto.
Originally published in different form in Australia by Pan Macmillan
Australia Pty Ltd., Sydney, in 2016.

www.doubleday.com

DOUBLEDAY and the portrayal of an anchor with a dolphin
are registered trademarks of Penguin Random House LLC.

Book design by Maria Carella
Jacket photograph: Mint Images/SuperStock
Jacket design by Emily Mahon

Library of Congress Cataloging-in-Publication Data
Names: Tunnicliffe, Hannah, [date]
Title: A french wedding : a novel / Hannah Tunnicliffe.
Description: First Edition. | New York : Doubleday, 2017.
Identifiers: LCCN 2016043650 | ISBN 9780385541848 (hardcover)
ISBN 9780385541855 (ebook)   ISBN 9780385542975 (open market)
Subjects: | BISAC: FICTION / Contemporary Women. |
FICTION / Family Life. | FICTION / Coming of Age.
Classification: LCC PR9199.4.T836 F74 2017 | DDC 813/.6—dc23
LC record available at https://lccn.loc.gov/2016043650

MANUFACTURED IN THE UNITED STATES OF AMERICA

1 3 5 7 9 10 8 6 4 2

First American Edition

RICHMOND HILL PUBLIC LIBRARY
32972000353732   RH
A French wedding : a novel
May 30, 2017

To my parents, Rob and Glen Tunnicliffe,

for all the love

Gwell eo karantez an dorn ewid madou leizh ar forn.

A handful of love is better than an oven full of bread.

—*Breton saying*

A French Wedding

Prologue

The spring sun finally splits through clouds, casting a pale white light upon the small crowd. Several glance up from their conversations. A gull rides the thermals closer to the ocean, like origami flung into the sky. It hovers and dips, assessing the scene below: people gathered in soft-colored dresses or pressed shirts and trousers, drinks in hands, the welcome sunlight striking off the golds and ambers inside thin glasses. An earnest-looking woman in a pink dress offers canapés on a silver tray. The guests move slowly to seats in rows, reticent to break off their chatter. They lean over to kiss cheeks and grip hands, so pleased to see one another, so pleased to be here for this. In front, a teenage boy with a violin looks toward the girl at the end of the aisle, her blond hair dyed blush at the ends, and clears his throat. She is his cue, which sends nerves through his stomach, fizzing like champagne.

The guests, sensing, settle and quiet. The garden gives a sigh of fragrance, a scent that is pink and purple and heady, from the lilacs and hyacinths and roses in full and marvelous bloom. Then the violinist starts to play, notes soaring up and around heads. The singer, in a long dress embroidered with flowers and with a red rose tucked above her ear, joins him in song. In the crowd a baby squeals a reply.

The bride is at the end of the aisle now. All eyes slide toward her. She wears a cream silk dress that floats down to her toes. Most hold their breath, some feel tears at their eyes, and others stare, mesmerized. She steps over the soft grass, a loose bunch of flowers in her right hand. The sun, grown confident, seems to shine out of her as well, as though she might just burst with joy into a thousand sparkling splinters. At the front of the aisle she pauses, passing her bouquet to a friend. When she takes the hands of her lover, those close enough notice how she grips them till her knuckles pale and hear when he says, "You are so beautiful," in a fragile kind of whisper.

They cling to each other, faces glowing, radiant. Hope—no, proof!—that it can be done and it can be good.

Deux ans plus tôt *(two years earlier)*

JULIETTE

Juliette wakes to the scent of dying roses: pink when they were given to her, now browned the color of summer skin, petals peeling away like sunburn. She is late, later than she wanted to be, on this day of all days. She blinks at the clock and leaps out of bed, swearing, *Merde, merde, merde.* She brushes past the drooping blooms, scattering more petals over the unmade bed and onto the floor like wedding confetti.

In the shower she washes quickly, hair knotted in a messy bun. She dries hastily and poorly, the towel thin and needing replacing. Brushes her teeth. Frowns at her face, which is too pale and too lined from so many nights in a kitchen. Makeup spread with a fast, light hand—too much and it will settle in the map of her skin—rivers and borderlines. Mascara. Blush to fix the problem of looking tired and wan. She brushes out her hair; it has grown down past her shoulders, a little frazzled at the ends, like her nerves, but unnoticeable once twisted up.

Juliette puts her thumb through the first pair of tights. She swears again and inspects the nail, which is short and ragged. She is more careful with the second pair; she takes her time, though it makes her heart jostle in her chest, impatient. Dress on and boots and then out the door with handbag slung over her shoulder swinging like a pendulum, her phone in her hand. She sends her restaurant manager, Louis, a quick apology as she rushes down the stairwell: "Pardon! Je serai bientôt là. J."

Her boots sound out *clip! clip! clip!* on the stairs as though they too are scolding her.

A neighbor, Madame Deschamps, opens her door as Juliette hurries past it. She gathers her robe around her and steps backward. Juliette gives her a polite smile but madame simply clutches at the pilled gray-blue fabric and stares. Juliette has no time to stop and exchange pleasantries, her boots marching her down the staircase, that ancient curling spine, and out the front door onto the street.

Outside, the morning light is gray and flat, and the world smells of concrete and dog piss and baking from half a block away, which Juliette cannot help but lift her nose to. She knows Henri is at the boulangerie, covered in sweat and flour; knows that he has propped open the back door to let in some air, no matter the scent of it, to feel its cool caress on his prickling pink skin. Juliette knows he will be having an espresso, dark and sugarless, relishing it like it is a kiss and telling any staff who comes near him, *"Foutre le camp!"* until he is finished, until he is revived. Juliette is welcomed, of course; they talk of flour and yeast and life without cigarettes and Henri's dog, who is his world and has a bad leg. If she weren't running late she would join him now, pull up a plastic crate and sit with him to mourn the cigarettes and praise the dog. But not today.

Juliette moves past stallholders setting up for the market, some calling out to her, some simply nodding their heads. Boxes are being opened and vans idle with loads of fish and crab, early spring berries, bunches of sweet lemony sorrel, chocolates, cheeses, oils and vinegars in thin green bottles, flowers with sweet-smelling heads the colors of confectionary. Juliette sidesteps a groggy tourist with a camera strapped around his neck.

It is only a short walk to the Place Monge Métro station, a block and a half. Juliette retrieves her ticket well before she reaches the entrance marked by the curved metalwork sign, the letters curled like tendrils, the stairs below it sprayed with spiked black curses and insults. Juliette presses her bag closer to her side out of instinct. This is the Fifth Arrondissement. This is Paris. A person can never be too sure. Juliette is the only one on the platform when the train rushes in with a sickly, warm wind. She boards and sits, suddenly feeling the pinch of her new boots. She had not worn them in properly. When she bought them she had wanted something pretty, something fresh for today. New boots to make her feel new— new and special and worth writing about, even if her hair is not perfect, or her nails, or the lines on her face, which declare that she is past forty now and so very tired.

A man on the seat opposite lifts his head from his paper and smiles at her. "Juliette!"

His hair is thick and silver, his lips full and twitching.

"Leon . . . ," Juliette replies, trying to sound cheerful.

Leon is chef and owner of La Porte Blanche, formerly Le Sel, a restaurant in the First Arrondissement. He rises and slips across the aisle to settle into the seat next to her. A woman in a bright-colored headscarf watches them, her face blank. Her dress is covered in flowers and leaves—orange, brown, black, and yellow—vivid but silent. Juliette wishes she were sitting across the aisle and next to her instead.

"I knew it was you," Leon says, tipping his head proudly. "You look nice. *Très jolie.*"

"*Merci,* Leon," Juliette replies.

Leon folds up his newspaper and places it in his bag. "Early start?"

Juliette nods.

"You work too hard."

Juliette knows it is strategic discouragement rather than concern. Leon is not Juliette's friend; he is her competition.

"Ah! Today is a big day, no?" Leon remarks.

"How . . . ?"

Leon taps his forehead. "I know. I hear these things. Interview with . . . ?" He grins, knowing.

"*Gault et Millau,*" Juliette mutters. She had been avoiding saying the name of the famous restaurant guide aloud, as though it might bring bad luck. Leon's smile is broad and satisfied.

"Dusollier?"

"*Oui,* Dusollier," Juliette confesses.

"Hmm," Leon says. "She's a tough nut to crack."

"Yes, I heard," Juliette replies, suddenly feeling less than *jolie,* wishing she'd had that haircut, which she had booked for last week. Juliette missed a lot of appointments lately: dates with friends and doctor visits; she hadn't been to the dentist in eighteen months and knew she needed a tooth filled.

"You've met her?" Juliette asks, although she's not sure she wants to know more.

Leon says, breezily, "Of course."

They stop at a station, the train filling, passengers rushing to seats. The shuffle of feet and jackets and bags, the smell of sweat and perfume both. A pregnant woman is left standing and those in seats avoid her gaze. The aisle between Juliette and the woman in the floral dress is filled by another woman peering into a handheld compact and applying lipstick, purse tucked under her arm, and a young man with a skateboard. He glares at Juliette.

"You'll be fine," Leon offers, patting Juliette's knee, his hand lingering a moment too long. He leans toward her and murmurs, "Dusollier's bark is worse than her bite. They're all like that, aren't they? The critics. They just want to feel important."

Juliette nods.

"You know what the trick is?" Leon whispers.

Juliette doesn't reply. His face is too close to hers and he smells strongly of aftershave. Bumping into Leon like this is far from ideal; she tries to avoid him at every opportunity: industry events, openings, when he comes to her restaurant, Delphine, to try her menu. It isn't just that he is a competitor; it is much more than that. Around Leon, Juliette feels secrets, like snakes, in her stomach—feels them squirming in that sideways way that snakes move.

"You've just got to make them feel special. See?"

Juliette glances at Leon's hand on her knee, at the gold band and then at him sharply. His hand is gone by the time she meets his eyes, but it is enough. The train jolts and passengers stagger. The woman with the floral dress looks through the gap at her. It is comforting to Juliette that she is there, watching.

"I see. *Merci,*" Juliette replies tersely.

"You'll be fine," Leon says again, smooth as melted chocolate spread out to be tempered on a counter.

Juliette straightens, emboldened by the headscarfed woman, by Leon's unwelcome touch, the warmth of which she can still feel on the top of her knee.

"How is your Celine?" she asks coolly, the name somehow slick and silver. "And the girls?"

Leon's smile is tight. "They are well."

"You must say hello to them all for me."

"Yes," Leon replies carefully.

Juliette looks to the window, the train slowing and her station coming into view. Brakes yowl in protest.

"This is my stop," she explains, gesturing with insincere apology.

"Of course." Leon is stiff in his seat.

Juliette blinks twice at the woman across the aisle as though she can read Juliette's mind, as though she can understand her unuttered gratitude, though for what Juliette is not exactly sure. She stands as the train brakes too fast and swings toward the lady with the purse, lipstick now applied.

"*Bonne chance,*" Leon says sleekly. "For the interview."

"I'm sure I'll be fine," Juliette replies quickly.

The fork-tongued snakes inside of her hiss and spit venom.

AMELIE DUSOLLIER CONTACTED Delphine one month ago. She had spoken first to Louis. He had covered the mouthpiece and jumped up and down in excitement. He was sprightly, Louis, thin, with dark circles under his eyes and a long, straight nose. "*Gault et Millau!*" he had mouthed before Juliette took the phone.

Juliette's head had been awash with new words and ideas, ingredients to be pieced together like a jigsaw. Juliette felt more like a matchmaker than a chef at times. She could never be completely sure what would marry together and what would not. Of course Jean-Paul—the man who first took her to bed, who first kissed her pressed up against a counter and took her hands and showed her how to cook and make love both, the two activities now firmly intertwined in Juliette's psyche—

would not have made such a fuss of it. He would have said, "What grows together goes together." But Jean-Paul was not a chef; he did not have a restaurant to run, the likes of Leon to compete against, or a point to prove. Jean-Paul had simply caught fish and women, his two occupations. *Wakame. Kombucha. Umami.* These were the words peppering Juliette's thoughts the morning Amelie Dusollier called. Juliette had been experimenting with Asian flavors—sweet and sour and pickled and crispy fried—ingredients Jean-Paul would never have heard of.

"Dusollier," the woman had said on the other end of the phone, her first name superfluous to explanations.

"*Bonjour,*" Juliette answered sweetly. "Juliette. Of Delphine."

"*Oui,*" Amelie Dusollier replied crisply. Leon was right. Critics and reviewers did like to feel important. They made nothing tangible of their own other than words. They poured no money into ventures that could thrive or shrivel to nothing. They took no risks. Yet they could make or break a restaurateur with a single review. And they knew it.

Amelie Dusollier's schedule and deadlines were set well in advance. She'd booked the interview, the tasting, and the photographer with Juliette many weeks ago. It had seemed like a long time to prepare, to get the new menu set and tested, to buy new boots and get a haircut. But Delphine still had to be run and time flew—like Juliette, up the stairs of Le Métro, into the brightening Paris morning.

Juliette pauses briefly to check her phone and there is a reply from Louis: "Sans probleme." She glances to the sky and gives thanks for Louis, as though he might have fallen out of it. Perhaps he had. The two of them are a good pair. Though Louis manages the front of house, he has an intuition for the kitchen that is rare; Juliette has him taste every dish she adds to the menu. Plus, he is good at hiring staff, he is good with numbers, he is sweet with customers but not too sweet. He is organized and discreet. Comfortable, tactful, and diplomatic with employees, he never loses his temper or drinks too much or too late with the team. His personal life is as quiet and organized as he is: one boyfriend, one cat, one small apartment, and penchants for Japanese whiskey, British gin, and the American ceramicist and decorator Jonathan Adler. He could be as discerning and stern with his opinions too:

Never wear a black scarf (it drains your complexion).

Don't rent if you can buy.

No drinking before noon.

Be wary of a person who sells insurance.

Never date a politician. They are worse than those who sell insurance.

Juliette wonders if Louis invents his life-rules based on doing the opposite of whatever she does. His neat life makes hers look disheveled, just like her flat, and crowded with problems.

Juliette's boots step over the cobblestones, pinching, as she reviews the things she needs to do before Amelie Dusollier arrives. She has given her chefs handwritten lists and they should be well rehearsed. She hopes their whites are truly white and pressed and that her best waitress, Fleur, did not argue with her boyfriend last night, since that leaves her face sour. She hopes the peonies she bought have opened a little more. She hopes the cutlery is speck- and spotless and the tablecloths are creased crisply, most of which Louis should have handled before she gets there.

Unlike Louis, Juliette does sometimes lose her temper and drink too much and too late with the team. Perhaps because she is a chef in her heart and these are things that chefs do. Or perhaps because she is her parents' only child, or because she is a woman and feels she has much to prove. Or perhaps because she works excessively, obsessively, and it is easier to stay at Delphine and drink than go home to her apartment with the browning roses and the clothes left on the floor and the bed that is so half-empty it feels vast and cold to touch.

A cyclist almost crashes into Juliette. His head is turned and looking the wrong way. He screams at Juliette as though it is all her fault.

"Putain! Fils de salope!"

Juliette opens her mouth to return the insults. She grips the phone in her hand, dying to throw it at him. Then the phone in her hand rings. She slows to stare at the screen. It reads "Dad." She lets it ring twice more. Slowing. Deciding. Stopping. She is so close to Delphine.

"Papa?"

"Juliette!"

"Hi, Dad."

"Morning, love. How are you? Where are you?"

"Almost at the restaurant," Juliette replies. Frustration prickles at her.

"Oh, good. Good . . ." He sounds distracted. Juliette shifts her weight from one boot to the other, regretting not getting them stretched, but mainly regretting answering the call. "Are you okay, Dad? Is it Mum?"

Her father's voice comes back clear and present now. "Oh no, darling, I'm fine. We're fine." He clears his throat. Juliette hears a voice in the background; she presses the phone closer to her ear.

Her father says, "I was calling about you! Your big day!"

Of course he had remembered about the *Gault et Millau* interview. Juliette's father remembered everything. He had been at every ballet recital, every school play, and every prize giving. Not that it was hard to win a prize in Douarnenez. It was a fact of such a small population—prizes were statistically probable. But Juliette's parents never regarded Juliette's achievements casually. In their eyes Juliette was a star, a beaming light, a source of perpetual pride. Somehow this made Juliette feel terrible instead of wonderful, made her notice and rue her imperfections, her hidden parts, her confusions and errors with even sharper judgment.

"Thanks, Dad," Juliette replies. She taps one foot and then steps back to let a person pass her. She moves under the eaves of a jewelry shop, the shutters still closed.

"How are you feeling about it?" Juliette's parents had moved from England to Brittany before she was born, but her father's British accent is strong even over the phone.

"Fine, fine. Yeah, lots to do . . ." Juliette says, hearing the pleading in her voice. *Let me go. Let me go now.* She stares in the direction of Delphine.

"Darling?" the voice in the background calls. It is reedy and longing. Dislocated.

Juliette's attention snaps to the phone. "Is that Mum?"

"That's great. We just wanted to wish you luck—"

"Darling? Where . . . ?" the voice murmurs.

"Dad?" Juliette frowns. "Dad, is that Mum? Where are you?"

"Don't you worry about us, sweetheart—"

Juliette hears a groan that washes over her like an icy ocean wave. It is full of pain. Everything else seems to vanish. Delphine. Amelie Dusollier. Paris. Juliette grips the phone as though it is a life buoy. There is only her and the phone, the two voices at the other end.

"Dad? Are you at the hospital?"

"Your mother is getting the best care."

"What is it, Dad?"

"It's nothing to worry—"

"Tell me what it is, Dad."

Juliette's father sighs and Juliette suddenly wants to cry. *Not today. Not now.*

"Pneumonia."

"Darling?" The voice is her mother's, but it sounds alien. Whispery and urgent. Detached and begging. Like a ghost's. Juliette squeezes the phone so tightly her hand hurts, as though trying to crush it, as though replicating the feeling in her own chest, the vise around her heart.

"Dad? How bad is it?"

Juliette hears her father's breath but he does not reply. At her mother's age, pneumonia would be bad enough, but added to her cancer it makes an equation that Juliette cannot bear to think about. A woman, walking swiftly with a skinny gray dog on a lead, steps too close to Juliette under the eaves. The proximity brings Paris rushing back. The light, the noises, the smells of the morning and the city assault her. She blinks and draws breath, as if coming up from under a wave. She thinks, urgently, of that other place, of the sea air, the quiet split by gulls' cries, the awful smallness of her village, and her mother's face, laid against hospital sheets thick and starched like the tablecloths at Delphine.

"I'm coming."

"No—" her father protests.

"I'm coming," Juliette says again.

As soon as she hangs up Juliette calls Louis. She's already walking in the other direction, away from Delphine rather than toward it, jogging across streets in the boots that hurt, narrowly missing traffic.

"I'm sorry."

Louis's voice is quick with concern. "What is it?"

"Maman."

THE DOOR TO Juliette's parents' cottage is red and shiny, the color of British postboxes and telephone booths. On either side hang baskets with flowers falling over the edges and green buds that will produce many more. Sweet peas and geraniums and pansies in yellows and purples. All her father's handiwork. Juliette needs to take her boots off. Her father struggles with the key and then has to lean his shoulder against the door to get it to open.

Inside is a time warp. Juliette's father climbs the stairs, the walls of which are lined with photographs in wooden frames, mostly of Juliette, colors faded to amber and peach and brown. School photos and family photos in which the three of them make a little trifecta, a pyramid, Juliette in the center of each one. Her first Holy Communion, Juliette looking like a tiny bride with stiff ringlets, her mouth pinched and cross. Her feet throbbing, Juliette pauses to sit on the bottom step and wriggle off her boots.

"I'll put the kettle on," Juliette's father calls out from the top of the stairs.

"Okay," Juliette mumbles in reply.

In Juliette's parents' opinion, the solution to every problem lay at the bottom of a teacup. If in doubt, put the kettle on. In an act of rebellion Juliette had started drinking coffee at the age of eleven, the blacker the better. But these days, she accepted the milky, sweet cups of tea with resignation. Perhaps her parents were right; perhaps tea would make it all better. A miracle was needed. Rituals were to be obeyed.

The hospital had smelled of antiseptic and decay, one insufficiently masking the other. Not the decay of lovers' roses, but the decay of flesh and blood and skin and bone. The smell of waste and loss. The smell that was so opposite to freshly baked bread, to pan-fried fish, to softening garlic or chilled wine—the scents that were all aliveness and joy. The smell of the hospital made Juliette's appetite vanish, made her stomach turn.

Her mother is sick, sicker than Juliette imagined, much sicker than when she last saw her, though perhaps her parents had been keeping the dire nature of things to themselves, as they tended to do. The pneumonia had ravaged her in a short time, her father explained. The nurse who came in to change dressings, to empty and refill things, and who seemed to know her parents better than Juliette did, who patted Juliette's father's shoulder so kindly that it sent a bolt of guilt straight through Juliette, seemed to agree with her father about that. They had all looked toward Juliette's mother as she inhaled so audibly, in such a labored way, as though to demonstrate the point. She sounded like she was trying to breathe underwater.

Juliette climbs the stairs in stockinged feet. Her soles ache and pulse with each step. The balls of her feet and the side of her right foot are the worst. She passes a pile of newspapers on the middle stair. The kettle is bubbling by the time she reaches the kitchen. She glances around at the mess: bills, newspapers, notices, general detritus. Counters are covered in odd things: screws, seed packets, library books, a comb.

"Dad?"

He has his head in the fridge and is moving things around, muttering to himself. "I had some . . . Oh, your mother's jam, I should . . ."

"Dad?"

He lifts up a bottle of milk and peers at the date. "Is it the sixteenth?"

"Twentieth."

He opens the lid and sniffs anyway, uncomfortable with waste.

"I don't take milk," Juliette offers.

"Sorry, love," he apologizes. When he leaves the bottle on the counter, Juliette picks it up and puts it in the rubbish for him. The smell of rotten food coming from the bin is strong. When the tea is made they take their mugs to the dining table. Juliette's father has to clear more piles of papers to make room for them.

"With your mother gone, I know it's a bit untidy . . . ," he says absently.

"How long has she been in the hospital?" Juliette doesn't add *this time*.

Her father looks to a pile of papers and picks up the newspaper on top. "Not long. A couple of days? It is Wednesday, isn't it?"

"Yes, it's Wednesday."

"We went in at the end of last week."

"So more than a few days then."

Her father waves the paper triumphantly. "I was going to show you this!"

"Dad, we're talking about Mum."

He pushes it over to her side of the table. It is Douarnenez's local newspaper. Over the years, Juliette's name had been in it a few times—once for representative gymnastics, when she was twelve; twice for high school exam results. Her mother had clipped the articles. They were probably still in the house somewhere, maybe in a tower of papers in another room. Her father leans over the table, twisting the paper back to face him, flicking through to find what he is looking for.

"Ah! There."

He prods at the page.

A VENDRE. BOULANGERIE.

"A bakery for sale? Dad, I have Delphine."

Her father pulls the paper back toward him. "Oh, I know, I didn't mean . . . It's Stephanie's. Do you remember her? Stephanie Jeunet?"

"Yes, I remember—"

"I saw it and thought of you. Knew it was around here somewhere. It's only a week old I think . . ." He checks the date at the top of the page. "Yes! Only a week. She hasn't sold, I am sure of it."

"Dad, I live in Paris."

"I know, love; just thought you might be interested. Have a read. You never know."

The paper comes back over to her side. Juliette gives it a polite glance. Of course she knows the bakery, of course she remembers Stephanie Jeunet. Juliette had been to Stephanie Jeunet's bakery hundreds of times. Stephanie had tried to teach her mother how to make *kouign-amann*, the pastry that came from and defined Douarnenez: the humble, soft, buttery layers made sweet and chewy with caramelized sugar. Maman could never master it, but Juliette took to pastry like a duck to water. When she had been younger she had dreamed of owning a bakery. Now her plans were bigger, more significant. Juliette had outgrown that dream; she had outgrown Douarnenez. Above the For Sale notice for the bakery is a tiny one-line advertisement requesting a housekeeper and chef for a property outside of the village. Juliette peers at it, curious. Very few wealthy people or vacationers have properties outside the village.

"You don't need to keep these things, all these papers."

Her father looks around the room. "It needs a little spruce-up."

"It looks like a bomb went off."

Juliette's father looks confused. "It's not that bad."

Juliette shakes her head. "Are you hungry? I'll make dinner."

"You aren't going back to Paris tonight?"

Juliette's heart sinks. She had switched her phone to silent but had still heard the vibrations of calls and messages, her phone buzzing like an angry insect in her handbag. She had ignored it.

"Not tonight, Dad." She sighs.

Her father's face breaks into a broad, hopeful smile. "Yes, I could eat. That would be lovely."

IN THE HOUSE Juliette finds cheap wine, bottled clam juice, old onions and potatoes. Not ideal and not enough to make a meal with. Because it's too late to go to the shops, Juliette goes out to ask a neighbor if she has anything to spare.

Capucine Reynaud's home is homage to all things Breton, with large chestnut armoires and a grandfather clock that is too tall and grand for the house. On her bedroom door hangs her grandmother's Sunday dress, traditional black with blue and red birds and flowers painstakingly, perfectly stitched, the threads thick and unfaded. Juliette glances at the line of family photos in the hall: most are black and white, with faces that have noses and lips and eyes that are so familiar.

Juliette's mother had taught Capucine Reynaud English for many years. Not that her English became any better for it, but she adored Juliette's mother, as did so many in the village. Madame Reynaud pushes parcels of fish and octopus and mussels into Juliette's hands, gives her fresh heavy cream and a handful of eggs that will make up for the things she has to combine them with. Then she urges Juliette out into the garden and tells her to take whatever she likes, plucking dark spinach leaves for her as Juliette takes some chervil and breaks off sorrel. The green and lemon scent of the sorrel fragrances Juliette's palm, helping her to forget the dreadful hospital smells.

"Is your mother still unwell, Juliette?" Madame Reynaud asks at the gate.

"Unfortunately, yes."

"Is it getting worse? The cancer?"

"No, it's pneumonia now." Juliette wishes to be somewhere else. "But she'll be okay."

Capucine Reynaud knows death—her husband, her nephew—she can tell that Juliette is not telling the truth and gives her the look Juliette dreads. Pity. Sincere, heartfelt pity, which is somehow worse than disregard.

"Thank you so much for the food. The fish and mussels . . ."

Madame Reynaud waves away the thanks. Capucine's youngest son, Paol, is a fisherman. He probably caught the fish that morning.

"She's so young . . . ," she murmurs, tutting.

Maman isn't, of course; she is in her early eighties now, but Madame Reynaud, perhaps only five or ten years her junior, is a picture of health. She still gardens, walks swiftly and easily, helps to sew the costumes for her granddaughter's ballet concerts.

"I should go. Papa . . . ," Juliette says quickly, kissing Madame Reynaud on her soft brown cheeks.

JULIETTE'S FATHER SITS at the dining table while Juliette prepares dinner, keeping out of her way, as she prefers. Juliette gently cooks the seafood in wine and clam juice, letting the sweet steam bloom in her face before setting it aside. She takes the salted butter from the pottery dish her mother keeps it in and makes a roux in a big pot with which to cook the onions and sauté the greens. She glances at her father doing a crossword puzzle with glasses at the end of his nose, sounding out words and counting letters to himself. He looks years older like that—body curved over the table, face pinched in concentration. Juliette cannot bear to think of him aging so fast; she turns back to her soup instead, adding the herbs, more butter, and the egg yolks mixed together with cream; stirring, tasting, breathing it in as though it might clear out all her other thoughts—thoughts of Delphine and Dusollier, her father's face creased like a walnut over his paper, her mother slipping, slipping from life's grip.

By the time they are ready to eat, the sky is properly dark and Juliette is suddenly starving. They eat in silence, spoons clinking the sides of the bowls. Juliette's father pours her a glass of wine.

"*Merci.*"

"You seem a bit edgy, sweetheart."

"It's been a big day."

"You missed the interview because of us."

Juliette shrugs, feeling both guilty and bitter. What kind of daughter begrudges a mother her illness, her cancer? "I'm sure it can be rescheduled," she says, knowing it cannot be. A great review in *Gault et Millau* was going to be Juliette's proof: Proof that the huge investments she had made in time, money, and heart were all worth it. Proof that she has her life firmly in hand, that she is something worthwhile.

"You work too hard," her father says sadly, reminding her, for a brief moment, of being on the train with Leon this morning.

"You always say that."

"You do."

Juliette tries not to be irritated. "It's my life, Dad."

"Well . . ."

She looks up from her bowl. "Well, what?"

"Nothing." Her father seems to shrink a little.

"What were you going to say?"

"You said, 'It's my life.' I was just going to say that, you know, it's not your life. It's your job. It's your work."

Juliette lays down her spoon. "It's not just a job. Delphine is my dream. My passion. It's what I want to do."

Juliette's father nods. "I know, darling. It's just you said your 'life.' We worry about you, your mother and me." He tips his head as though Maman were right beside him.

"You don't need to worry about me. I'm a big girl."

As she says it, Juliette feels suddenly tiny, not as big or capable as she is trying to convince herself and her father. She longs for the person she knows so well—skin and body, voice, breath—who knows her in those same ways. Who makes her feel desired. Who makes her feel less small and less lonely.

"Yes, but you're our girl."

"Dad. Please."

"We love you."

"I know, Dad, I know." The exasperation is evident in her voice. She regrets it but she resents them both for it too. There'd be no need to be cagey if they weren't so loving, so smothering. She wishes they didn't need her so much. She pulls at the neckline of her dress. Sometimes she feels as though she cannot breathe in Douarnenez, in this house. Juliette eats faster, pulling the tiny mussels from their black shells and scooping mouthfuls of the salty, creamy soup, flecked green with sorrel, into her mouth. Once finished, she takes her bowl to the sink. She feels hot and claustrophobic. She missed her interview. She is worried about Delphine, worried about the messages, unchecked, on her phone. She wants to be in Paris, away from here. Anywhere but here.

"It's so easy to get caught up in things," Juliette's father continues. Juliette wants to cover her ears. She turns on the tap too quick, so the water gushes out noisily. Still she hears her father say, "To lose sight of the big picture."

She turns it hard the other way. "Christ, Dad!"

He looks up at her, alarmed.

"It's not just a job, okay?"

"I wasn't—"

"Delphine means something to me. I've built my life around it."

"Juliette—"

"It's doing well. It's doing really well." Juliette tries to sound sure. "It's mine. My sweat and tears. There's no shame in that!"

"Of course not."

"I'm proud of it."

"We are very proud of you, darling," her father reassures her. "We always have been, we always will be."

"I know." Juliette feels suddenly deflated. She holds on to the edge of the sink. "Sorry."

Her father brings his bowl to the sink and pats her back. They aren't a very demonstrative family. Maybe it is their Britishness. It suits Juliette. She doesn't want to be held or cradled or covered in kisses by her parents. Her father's hand on her back speaks volumes—volumes that can, at times, feel like a huge weight.

"We love you."

"Thanks, Dad."

"But, sweetheart . . ."

It is rare for Juliette's parents to disagree with her.

". . . there's only one thing you should build your life around," he says softly.

JULIETTE SENDS HER father to bed and does the dishes. He doesn't protest, simply kisses her on the forehead and shuffles to his room. The washing up soothes and distracts Juliette from looking at her phone, which has continued to vibrate. She cannot bear to listen to the messages and hear Louis's panic and confusion, the thought of which fills her with dread. When the dishes are finished she wipes her hands and stands with her back leaning against the sink, taking in the cluttered dining room. She tries to remember the last time she was in Douarnenez and is sure, for a brief moment, it was only a couple of weeks ago. But then she counts back weekends—the busy time for Delphine—that she can recall by the guests who had come in, by the ways she had found herself in the mornings—often fully dressed and asleep on top of her sheets, on her sofa, once on the bathroom floor. She is part of Paris now—her life, her lover, her friends, and her work—all embroidered upon it, bound together, thread and cloth. Juliette counts back eight weekends and then stops counting. It cannot possibly have been that long since she last visited.

The last time Juliette visited, her mother had been in the house, wiping and sorting and tidying. Maybe there had been too many things then, memorabilia and photos and those porcelain statuettes her mother loves. But during that visit the cottage seemed more ordered. Now it appears shabby and old, like it is ready to give up. Juliette rubs her eyes. She cannot remember if it really had been any different or whether it was simply her mother's presence that had made it seem so. Even in her illness, Juliette's mother has always been so luminous. People assume she is in her early sixties, which hasn't been true for two decades. Without her mother, Juliette notices her father is doddery: the mumbling over the crossword, the way he shuffles when he walks. Juliette wonders when he'd last seen a doctor himself.

There's only one thing you should build your life around . . .

The last time Juliette had seen her parents her mother had asked about her love life. It was the standard line of questioning. Juliette had been bold enough, stupid enough, giddy enough to grin. She had wanted to mention her lover but Maman would ask too many questions. Questions that Juliette didn't want to answer, questions that would lead to answers Maman wouldn't approve of. The grin had said enough. Her mother imagined other circumstances, cleaner and simpler circumstances. She had been happy. Which later made Juliette wonder if even a grin could be a lie. A white lie at least.

———

She goes to the dining table and picks up the paper her father left on the top of the pile. "For Sale. Bakery." She tries not to scoff. It is cruel to scoff. Stephanie Jeaunet worked day in and day out in that place and there is no shame in work like that. Baking had been Juliette's first curiosity and introduction to cooking, the experience of making *kouign-amann*, of cooking the breads and cakes for the saint's days, birthdays, and Christmas. At fifteen Juliette took orders for her *bûches de Noëls* and large gingerbreads made with honey and delivered them, wrapped in cellophane with big red bows, to neighbors' houses on Christmas Day. But now Juliette has Delphine. Delphine is hers. She is Delphine. Juliette glances at her bag, neglected phone inside, left by the top of the stairs. She hopes she still has Delphine. She still owes the bank a lot of money—it isn't really all hers yet—and the *Gault et Millau* review had been crucial. As devoted and passionate as Juliette is about the restaurant, the truth is that the industry is a cruel master. The demands are relentless. The costs and expectations high. There is no room for error or disorder, or for a personal life that isn't neat and exact as a ledger. It requires someone in total command. Even Leon, outwardly cool, possessing a skin that seems to be Teflon-coated, has mess and disorder he keeps hidden: a marriage that is far from perfect, things that need to be secret. Juliette knows about those kinds of secrets.

Juliette looks back at the paper in her hand. There is only one page for job vacancies and businesses for sale in Douarnenez. Juliette scans the listings again: bakery, mechanic shop, children's clothing store; waitress, apprentice plumber, the chef/housekeeper position she'd noticed earlier. She screws the paper up in her hand, making the words inside disappear, before dropping it to the floor. Stupid tiny town.

There is no growth here; everything and everyone is in a state of disrepair and decay. It makes her feel unsteady. It makes her feel as though it might be contagious, that she needs to get out, fast, or she'll succumb to it too.

Juliette moves to the sink and reaches for the roll of gray trash bags her mother keeps on the shelf beneath. She takes one to the dining table and sweeps the piles of papers into it, then steps back. On the table is a shining patch where the papers once stood, clear of dust. Then she grabs a stack of letters and bills by the phone and shoves them into the bag too. A line of photographs, mainly of Juliette as a teenager— sullen and unsmiling—go in. Magazines, old newspapers, plastic lids, a blurry photograph of their long-dead cocker spaniels, loose coins, a pair of broken scissors, trousers with a tear in the pocket and a needle waiting in the fabric. Juliette fetches another trash bag. And on and on and in it all goes till the space looks five times bigger and clear and Juliette can breathe better. The clock on the wall ticks audibly; it is now close to midnight. Juliette is panting a little. Finally she sees the paper she screwed into a ball on the floor and she pushes that in and ties the top of the sack. It takes all her strength to drag the bags down the stairs, nearly hooking her handbag up with one of them, and out the front door. She can feel the soft weight of the magazines and hear the glass-and-wood clatter of the photo frames as she bumps them along to the edge of the curb. When she straightens, the cool night air fills her lungs. Above her hundreds of stars glitter in the black cloth of the sky. Juliette stares. The night sky never looks so clear in Paris.

WHEN JULIETTE WAKES it takes her a moment to remember where she is. Her hand moves to the other side of the bed, loneliness—dark, cold, and liquid—filling her stomach. Then she looks around for her own bedroom, her things. She stares at the blue floral pillowcase and then the thick brown carpet and, on it, her handbag, the top spread open, her phone facing up to her. She picks it up and scrolls through the messages. Fourteen of them, mostly from Louis, none from the person she longed for, who had been in her dreams. The one who makes her feel warm and misplaced and guilty, as though she shouldn't have those kinds of thoughts in her childhood bedroom.

Juliette gets to her feet, glancing down for a moment at the old T-shirt and leggings she had pulled on in the dark.

"Dad?"

There is no reply. Juliette knocks gently on the door to his room. The door is unlatched and swings gently open. The bed is unmade, the blinds drawn closed.

"Dad?" Juliette calls out again. She wonders if her father has gone to the market to get food. He would do that if he thought it might make her stay longer. He would buy her favorite fruits, fetch a fresh loaf of bread, and collect a broad, sticky wedge of *kouign-amann* in a brown paper bag. From beyond the closed blinds Juliette can hear a truck in the alley outside. A phone, once cream, now aged to yellow, rings in the kitchen.

Juliette puts the receiver to her ear. *"Bonjour?"*

"Juliette?"

"Is that you, Dad?"

"Oh, good, you're still there. I'll be home soon."

Juliette feels a sting of guilt that he assumed she might have already left, escaped. She rubs her eyes with her free hand and realizes the sound outside is the garbage truck grumbling up the narrow lane toward the cottage. It must now be late morning.

"Where are you?" she asks.

"I'm . . . I'm at the hospital. You're not going anywhere, are you, love?"

Juliette ignores the question. "Why didn't you wake me?"

"I went early. I got a call. I didn't want to wake you. You seemed so tired."

"Dad, you should have—"

"Just don't leave yet, okay?"

The tone of her father's voice, the urgency, does something to Juliette's inner workings. Her breath catches in her throat. The sudden silence stretches thin and brittle, like toffee, about to shatter.

"What is it?" Juliette whispers.

"I'll be home soon," her father says again, attempting firmness. There is pain in his voice. Heartbreak. Grief.

Now Juliette hears everything—the garbage truck growing louder, her breath, the sounds of the hospital in the background—beyond her father's labored breathing, the sound of her own heart beating.

The garbage truck.

"Juliette?"

Juliette drops the phone so it bounces on its cord and races down the stairs. Photographs of herself, her child self, her young self, watch as she passes, a blur of unbrushed hair and too-big T-shirt and leggings that have faded from black to gray at the seams. Juliette yanks at the door and bursts out onto the street. The men look at her, momentarily distracted, gloved hands gripping gray plastic sacks.

"*Arrête!*"

Juliette tumbles onto her knees.

"*Pardon?*" one asks.

"*Arrête!*" she begs again, lifting up her palms, grazed and starting to bleed. And then in English, "Stop! Leave them! Leave the bags!"

The two men glance at each other.

"It's not rubbish!" Juliette sobs, still in English. "Leave it. Please leave it."

The men lower the bags, placing them beside her. They stare. Juliette covers her face with her blood-flecked hands and cries:

"It's not rubbish . . . It's not rubbish . . ."

Le Weekend

VENDREDI (FRIDAY)

Chapter One

MAX

He is probably driving too fast, considering he isn't on an autoroute, but he likes these back roads better. And he likes driving too fast. He likes the thrum of the engine coming up through the soles of his feet, through his legs, into his crotch. He likes gripping the steering wheel with just one hand, the wind biting the elbow of his other arm hanging out the window. This car, slick and red as lipstick, purrs.

Max is going to be late. The others will all be there soon, just as he had asked them to be, waiting for him. He can see them on the lawn, staring back at his country house, Juliette fetching them long, cool glasses of Pimm's with fresh garden mint stuffed in. They will be travel weary but impressed. Eddie and whoever he'd said his new girlfriend was—the American one, Betty? Nina and Lars, bless them. Their kid, though she probably wasn't a kid anymore. Hot Rosie and her awful husband, Hugo . . .

Helen.

Max had missed her earlier call but listened to the message. The deep, soft whir of Helen's voice, edged by the effects of cigarettes and New York, saying she was looking forward to it, that frankly she needed a break. Telling him she'd be there by nightfall and that later she'd be picking up her sister, the half sister technically, Soleil. Max found it hard to pay attention to the details. Something shifted inside him at the sound of her voice. Something uncoiled.

Max rubs his eyes. He has been touring and drinking too much. He's been operating on about five hours of sleep a night and it is no longer enough. The cocaine takes the edge off and keeps him awake, but he'll lay off it after today; he has promised himself.

Max turns the music up even louder till he feels the blood pounding in his ears and blinks away tiredness. His eyes, those strange khaki-colored eyes, the color of dark bay leaves, of swamp water, are his father's eyes. Not that he ever tells anyone that.

Helen is the only one of Max's friends who knows about his father, his family. The whole lot of it. He can count on one hand the number of people who know much about his childhood. Him and his dad, Helen—that's already three fingers. The other two are for social workers.

It never works to try not to think of something once you've started thinking about it. Max knows that from thinking about Helen every single day of his life since he can't even remember when. Actually, that isn't true. He does remember. It was summer. Helen was sitting next to Rosie on the grass in the common area outside one of the lecture blocks. She wore a long skirt hitched up to her thighs and she was laughing. Rosie's hair was white blond and cut just like Debbie Harry's on the Blondie record Max's dad owned, while Helen's was long and tangled at the back, dark as Christmas pudding, the kind other people's families ate. She wore swingy earrings that moved when she did. Her thighs were the color of cream.

Max watched her for longer than was socially acceptable. She must have felt his eyes on her. He remembers her getting up and walking over, barefoot. He remembers not being able to look away and grinning like a young boy, which he never did. Especially not when he was a boy. She asked him for a light and he pulled a green plastic lighter from his pocket. "I'm Helen," she said.

Helen.

Helen.

Dear Helen.

Max has said her name in his head about ten million times since that day. He knows the texture of it in his mouth without even having to say it aloud. He knows how it would feel to call it out in the middle of lovemaking or to say it in a whisper into the pale shell of her ear, among the darkness of her hair. Max shudders. He feels himself growing harder and presses down on the accelerator.

Helen.

Max wills himself to stop thinking about her. It is stupid. It is always stupid. This is the hopelessness of trying not to think about something once you have started. His thoughts tip to the other end of the spectrum, like an hourglass suddenly turned.

Dad. Fucking Dad.

See? It's impossible.

It didn't start right away. It started when his mother left, when he was six and a half, or at least that's how Max remembers it. His mother had been there, he tried to remember— she was a pretty murky, fuzzy kind of memory now—and then she wasn't there. A snap of the fingers. A vanished mother. It was Max's fault his mother had left; his father told him that often. And because of it his father beat him. It was one of the few reliable aspects of Max's life. His dad had always been sullen, angry, but after that the rage poured out onto Max. His father beat him on the back, on the legs and stomach. He avoided Max's face. He kicked him down the stairs and once held his head in the kitchen sink until Max was half drowned. There had been a used-up tin of baked beans in the dirty water. Max's father stomped on him; threw him against walls, doors, and the table; and whipped him with his belt. Or the cord of the toaster. Or the kettle. He called him names the kids at school hadn't heard of yet.

One night Max's father threw him out into the street. Max was twelve. For a brief moment he was elated, freedom like a bright taste in his mouth. Then he realized he was coatless and it was the middle of a London autumn, almost winter. He walked only half a block, the impossibility of leaving smacking at him, before turning around and trudging back to that wretched green door, then curling himself, shivering, on the doormat, waiting for his dad to let him back in. Max's very worst moment of cowardice.

Max swerves. *Christ. Was that a cat?* Photographs of his mother, so few of them. Grainy ones with rounded corners; she seems to be looking past the camera. Perhaps she has already spotted her other life, the one she is going to escape them for. A photo of her at the seaside pulling windswept hair away from her mouth, wearing an orange-and-white-striped swimsuit. Another of her on a couch, holding Max as an infant. She has on a pale blue dress and black eyeliner and looks, somehow, emptied out. *I don't want this baby. This isn't my life.* There had been no one to tell Max why she left, exactly, and where she had gone. His recollections were strange and mixed up, and sometimes his brain pieced memories together out of those few photographs. Hadn't they been to the seaside together? Eaten ice cream out of cones? Hadn't she worn a yellow swimsuit, not an orange-striped one? The truth stuck too fast to fantasy.

Have we passed Rennes?

Passed?

Passed.

Past.

It is pointless to think about his mother, to wonder. What kind of woman leaves her child? What kind of woman leaves her child with a monster? It was a devil's trade: Max's life for hers. Max will probably never see either of his parents again, if they are still alive; will probably never live in England again. Paris is his home now and it suits him. The sky and slate roofs the same color, the lumps of still-soft dog shit on the pavement, the smell of coffee, baking bread, caramel, cigarettes, and urine. The women neat, with woolen coats, pretty scarves, slender legs in panty hose. Lips like ripe cherries. Paris will do.

That woman, his neighbor Claudine, the social worker with the cat she calls Pedro, would probably have something to say about all that—about his family, about the women—not to mention the coke. She likes to talk. She sings jazz in her spare time and knows her greats—Ella Fitzgerald, Billie Holiday, Nina Simone. She is always carrying bunches of fresh flowers. She likes those tall, strong-smelling white ones with the blossoms that look like popcorn. Her apartment was an inheritance from an aunt, she tells Max, happily handing out details about her personal life to anyone like leaflets she's got plenty of. She smiles too much. Yes, Claudine would have plenty to say about Max's personal life. But Max cannot trust a social worker, particularly one who smiles too much and lives with a man-cat for company.

———

The sign ahead reads SAINT-ALLOUESTRE.

Max rubs his eyes again. He needs glasses but he won't go to an optometrist. Helen has glasses she uses for reading now, round tortoiseshell ones. Everyone Max screws these days is in their twenties. They have skin lovelier than velvet, heavenly and unmarked. No pubic hair. Smooth all over. Narrow waists, hollow bellies. They don't get old. Helen, on the other hand, is getting old at exactly the same rate as Max. She has lines around her eyes. The skin on the back of her hands has thinned, is becoming papery. But. Oh. All Max wants is to stand in the dark with her. In the dark they will be young again. Then he will run his thumb over her soft lips, unbutton her shirt, peel off her trousers. He will press her against him, sweet skin, full breasts, all of her against all of him. Feel her head on his chest, take in the Helen scent of her, lift her face to kiss her so deeply she can hardly breathe. Lift her onto him, carry her to where they can lay themselves down, fill her up till her head brims with stars.

"*Helen.*"

"*Max.*"

Helen will exhale his name in a whisper that moves through him like a current, reaching the very tips of him. Perhaps he will cry. Who wouldn't? The sound that completes a person. Helen saying his name and making him *finally* feel so whole, so alive, that he fears running over, like a drawing escaping its edges.

"*Max.*"

The night suddenly bright. His head filled with stars too. Startling. Shining. Bursting . . .

A car horn blares like a wounded beast, tearing a large rip in his thoughts, causing him to swear and swerve and bump up against a curb that is closer than he had thought. His head swivels to catch sight of the car headed in the opposite direction, righting itself; the arm out the window, the middle finger raised; the driver cursing. Max's heart races, his breath is ragged. He flicks on the turn signal, braking and pulling to the side of the road and bumping over the grass. He blinks and then laughs.

Max glances at the passenger seat to make sure the small velvet box is still there. It has rolled into the crease of the chair, the closed mouth of it turned up to him. Max smiles. His plan is safe and so is he.

Max closes his eyes for a nap, to sober up. To pull down the screen on the past, his childhood, his father. He drifts into fantasies of Helen. His future. A new decade: his forties. Sleep strokes at his body and his mind.

He still has an erection.

LONDON, 1995

Max very nearly didn't make the gig. He'd been drunk or hungover or both. But he got there, getting to gigs being one of the very few things Max could be relied on for, and that was the night there was the record producer in the crowd. They'd almost had a break like that before but it had turned to nothing—all talk and no action, no contract, no cash. Still, it had piqued Max's interest. It made him think it was possible and encouraged him to get to gigs despite being wasted, getting over being wasted, and all the increasingly fewer shades in between. It made him curious just to turn up and see. Besides which, playing music and performing made Max feel the most like himself. There weren't many things like that.

There was a big crowd that night. The band had been getting larger and larger crowds, but there was always the memory of playing to just a handful of people, the unease that it might happen again.

The guys were there, the usuals. Helen, back from a trip to India, her long hair in braids. Lars and Nina, the odd couple. Lars—tall and lean; Nina—short and plump. Him fair, her dark; laid-back contrasted with frank and earnest. Good old Eddie, of course, distracted and disheveled as always. Rosie was going to call in later; she had a date. Max couldn't help but look out for her in that mass, her small, precise frame and blond hair, the way she made everyone else look a little messy in comparison. They weren't close, Max and Rosie, had never really been close, but he felt better when they were all there. Rosie was dating a doctor, Helen said. Helen also said the guy was an "uppity prick," while Nina reported he was nice enough. Max had never met the bloke but agreed with Helen nonetheless. Helen knew her way around uppity pricks. She was an expert.

Everything came together that night and that wasn't just the booze talking, though it always helped. The band was getting along really well, best they ever had. The crowd was into it, which didn't always happen. They were all one energized mass, moving together like a school of fish, a murmuration of starlings. And within it, the guy from the record label Parlophone, watching and listening. Not that they knew it at the time. When Max squinted and put his palm up against the lights, he was looking only for his friends' faces—Lars was the easiest to spot. Not only was he the tallest but his smile had a wattage unmatched by anyone else.

Afterward, when the band was all wet with sweat and sucking on beer bottles like hungry babies, all of them backstage and stoked, fucking stoked, the Parlophone guy introduced himself. He wanted to see them in his office next week. His name was Bob, a name that proved he must be a suit, that he must be for real. Besides, Bob knew his music. Bob talked about the Jacks like he'd been at all their rehearsals, had listened in when they'd made decisions about including this or excluding that. Bob said they sounded like David Bowie and Chrissie Hynde had had a love child and that child had been raised by Keith

Richards and Stevie Nicks, said they seemed to be the only ones not doing the Britpop thing. He had them nailed. And he wanted them; Max could see it in Bob's hungry eyes. Max knew when a person wanted a piece of him. It was what made him so good with women. Bob gave them a business card each. He wrote down "Wednesday, 2:30 p.m." on the back of each one with a black Biro that left ink on Max's sweaty fingers. After Bob said good-bye they all fell apart laughing like it was the funniest, stupidest thing they had ever seen or heard. But they knew it was something. Max knew it was for real, knew it in his bones.

Max told the guys he would catch up later at the bar they always went to when everywhere else was shut. Jostling through the crowd was easy; it was broken up now, a thing of many parts. Max felt pats on his back, an arm around him for a moment, and heard a guy roaring something in his ear he didn't catch but grinned at anyway. They had done good. Everyone was happy with them.

"Max!"

Helen ran to him with her long, silken skirt moving like liquid around her legs. Her skin was browner than usual, her eyes shining. Max let her cling to him, allowing himself a moment to breathe her in, the scent of her skin made up of patchouli, soap, and smoke.

"Good to see you, kid. How was India?"

"Amazing."

"I want to hear all about it."

"I'm going to bore you senseless," she warned.

Max kissed her cheeks, leaving slick patches of sweat. "Never."

Lars next, slapping him too hard on the back, palm as big as a plate. "Brilliant. Fucking brilliant." His eyes were wide and he looked wasted, but that was just Lars, high on music and pride for his friend. Nina, still on her stool, gave a thumbs-up and a smile that said all that Lars had just beaten into Max's back.

Eddie collared Max. "Look at you!"

Conversely, Eddie was wasted. He wrapped his arms around Max's slippery waist and jigged him up and down. Laughter came out of Max in wheezy spurts. "Put me down, you arse!"

Eddie did as he was told, then pushed a warm beer in a plastic cup into Max's hand. Max welcomed it down his throat. He wiped his mouth with the back of his hand and looked around at them all.

"Guy came to see us. After. Record label guy," he said in purposeful staccato.

"What?"

"He what?"

"Who?"

"Parlophone," Max replied.

Helen shrieked; Max caught her in his arms, beer spilling over both of them.

"Shit, mate, shit . . . ," Lars said, shaking his head.

Laughing, Nina got off her stool to give him a firm hug. "Holy, Max. This is really happening, hey?"

Max shrugged. "Looks like it."

Eddie was swearing and doing fist pumps. He almost stumbled into a guy standing by the bar—a big guy with lots of tattoos. Lars yanked Eddie upright by his shirt and made apologies.

Helen shifted into the spot underneath Max's arm, which he slung over her shoulders. She fit perfectly there. Max felt the tiny hairs that had escaped her braids tickling his nostrils as he kissed her head. Everyone was laughing and talking. Max felt as though the blood in his veins was bristling and sparkling, more alive and vibrant than ever. Felt like his body was made of bright particles, gold dust, assembled for a moment in his form, but for how long, who knew? Felt radiant. Felt invincible. He squeezed Helen closer to him and tried to commit the moment to memory like processing film in the darkroom.

Max felt a finger in his side and turned to see Rosie.

"What did I miss?"

Helen peeked out from Max's wing. "Max might have a record deal!"

Rosie checked Max's face, his smile unshakeable. "Get out."

Max nodded.

Rosie laughed. "Well. That is news."

Max put down his beer and drew Rosie in under his other arm. With her there they were complete. The half dozen of them, all together, as they should be.

It always surprised Max that of the entire memory (which, despite the coke and alcohol flooding his system at the time, Max remembered so well, so vividly) the part he recalled most perfectly was the one that came with the smells of the venue—beer, sweat, smoke, dust, and dark—and the sounds—the Cure played loud through the crackling speakers—and the solidity of bodies under each arm—blond hair near his face, Helen's smooth, tanned arm under his calloused fingers. It was the memory that bore Rosie's earnest face rather than Helen's. It was when she said in his ear:

"Max. You deserve it."

Chapter Two

JULIETTE

The kitchen has the best light in the house, especially now, as it moves from midday sun into afternoon light. It falls through the windows in brilliant puddles, shadows cast by the leaves of the linden tree outside, and it moves. Dances, in fact. Over hands and spoons and the worn gray flagstones. Over the bread dough Juliette has made. It is her favorite room in the house. It smells of yeast and flour and a warming oven, but also the stone of the floor, the metal of the taps, the plaited tress of papery pink Roscoff onions, and the copper of her favorite bowls. Even the cast iron and roasted, salted butter scent of the *billig*, the griddle used to make *crêpes de blé noir* or galettes, that sits on one of the counters. Most people wouldn't be able to distinguish these things, but to Juliette they are as familiar as the salty-sweet perfume of a lover's skin. The kitchen is her sanctuary.

Max didn't update this part of the house—a slate-roofed stone cottage now with a huge extension of blond wood and expansive windows. Other than its appliances, the kitchen is original. The small windows with warped glass don't have

huge modern blinds that whir down when remote controls are
pressed. The thick, worn wooden beams are a rib cage in the
low ceiling. Here the spring light is exactly as it should be
in west Brittany, Finistère, the end of the world—sweet, the
color of chamomile tea, and dappled, not hotly bullying its
way into the room.

Juliette presses her palms on the floured bench top and
looks out the stone-framed windows at the garden. It is bor-
dered by flowering rhododendron bushes, spring flowers in
toothy whites and girlish pinks, established trees that Max left
standing, as well as a gnarly and ancient apple tree espaliered
on a fence. In the center of the lawn is the girl who arrived
this morning with Max's friend Eddie. Beth. An American
with long red hair. She has pulled one of Max's white lounge
chairs into the sunniest part of the garden and is arranging
herself upon it, magazine between her lips while she scoops
her hair into a bun on top of her head. Juliette squints to
make out the pattern on her white bikini—tiny pink raspberries topped with green leaves like winter hats. Eddie comes
by now to lean on the back of the chair. Juliette barely caught
Eddie's name as he rushed to shake her hand before striding into the house, looking around, pointing out the size of
everything—huge!—dumping his bag, with fat percussion, in
the lounge. Juliette went to the list she'd taped up inside the
pantry, on which she'd written "Eddie and ??" (Max couldn't
remember the girlfriend's name). She added "Beth." Then, in
her mind, not on the list: *American. Red-haired. Young. Bikini
with raspberries.*

Eddie is English and from London like Max. His voice
reminds Juliette of her father's. It makes her feel nostalgic.
Juliette watches Eddie smearing sunscreen on his face, up to
the line of his thick dark hair. He has very pale legs, which
poke out from a pair of white shorts that look brand-new, the

fabric almost matching the shade of his calves. Juliette notices the small crocodile logo on the back, by the pocket. Eddie turns, sees her, and waves. Juliette lifts her palm, now covered in flour. He isn't so bad looking, she decides. It isn't fair for Juliette to judge the color of a person's legs. She has spent the last year here in Douarnenez, gathering seaweed from the beach, cutting lavender, raking leaves, and washing windows, her skin browning from Parisian milk white to Breton café au lait. Even her hair has lightened, now more chestnut than brown, made noticeable from the haircut: short, curls by her ears, and a tiny fringe. She will never again have to lift and twist it, as Beth does, and tuck it into a pleated white chef's toque. Juliette might never wear a toque again. Thinking of toques reminds Juliette of the bread, which she needs to punch down and divide. She pulls the bowl toward her and removes the cloth. The dough rises above the rim in a luscious curve.

"Was it Julie?"

Juliette turns to see Eddie inspecting the fruit bowl. He picks up an apple.

"Juliette."

"Right! *Juliette*. So French." Eddie grins with dimpled cheeks. It makes him look like a boy despite the five o'clock shadow and the glinting gray strands in his hair. Max told her Eddie is the manager of a whiskey bar in a boutique hotel. Juliette can imagine it; the customers would love him.

"I am French," she says.

"You actually *are* French? From here?" Eddie sinks his teeth into the apple. "You don't sound French."

"My parents were from England." She is getting used to the past tense now, though it still makes her pause a moment.

"Ahh. So you are a bit English."

Eddie looks so pleased with himself that Juliette laughs.

She shrugs, although she wants to say, *Non. Je suis Bretonne,* which she has come to realize means even more than being French. She thinks about sinking her hands into the soft, swollen dough on the bench but doesn't want to turn away so quickly as to be rude.

"Max said he got himself a French chef from Paris."

"That's me, then. I was the French chef from Paris," Juliette says, smiling. "Now I'm the Breton girl who keeps the windows clean."

That has them both looking out the window toward Beth. Eddie steps closer, apple in hand. He looks down at her bowl.

"Bread," Juliette explains.

They are now standing side by side, the gardens and lawn ahead of them, Beth and her chair in the middle of the view, dotted appropriately, as she is, with raspberries.

"Beautiful," Eddie murmurs. Juliette is unsure if he means his girlfriend or Max's house and gardens. Then he says, "He should have had us here earlier. This place is amazing."

Juliette nods. She doesn't explain that Max rarely has guests. Sometimes he brings a girl, someone he seems wholly unattached to, who might attempt small talk with Juliette in the morning, the conversation pocked with awkward silences. For the most part Max comes solo. He drives from Paris through the night or early morning, sending Juliette a quick message en route so she has just enough time to throw on a coat and wobble over on her bike from her parents' place in the village. She keeps things in the house she knows he likes—*andouille de Guémené,* the famous smoked and dried pork sausage; her version of piccalilli relish with local cauliflower; as well as hard cheeses, preserved sardines, and tins of handmade crackers and *sablés*—in case he arrives before she does. She orders at least two dozen Cancale oysters if he is staying more than one night, more if he has company. There are always champagne, salted butter, and cider in the fridge; liqueurs, gin, whiskey, buckwheat, and Saint-Malo potatoes in the pantry.

"You've known Max a long time?" Juliette asks Eddie out of politeness, knowing that he has. Max had described each of them to her, clearly his five favorite people in the world. It was the most animated Juliette had ever seen him.

"We went to Camberwell together. It's an arts college in London." Eddie has almost finished his apple. "Well, *we* went to college—Lars and Nina, Rosie and me—Max did more drinking . . . and less classes."

Eddie holds the apple core by the stalk. Juliette remembers the rest of the names from stories she has been told and the list Max dictated to her.

> Rosie and Hugo.
> Nina and Lars and their kid, Sophie.
> Eddie and ?? [Juliette had remedied the blank, of course.]
> Helen.

Eddie laughs. "To be fair, none of us studied very hard. Mainly we were partying or trying to get laid." He glances around till Juliette opens a cupboard and shows him the rubbish bin. "Thanks." He wipes his hands on his shirt. "Then Max went and made a life out of that."

Juliette nods. Max Dresner, the guitarist for the Jacks. The man who dated both of the Marceau twins. Party boy. Musical genius. Rogue. A man the press loved to write about because he fit a formula—good-looking man with bad behavior. But Juliette knew that Max was more complex and compelling than what was written about him.

"I forgot Helen," Eddie says. "You've heard of Helen, right?"

Juliette nods again. Max had told her about Helen. His voice quickened when he spoke of her. Her wildness and compassion, her beauty, the rareness of her.

Eddie gives a little laugh. "Fortieth birthday party . . . reunion . . . It's really nice. I'm not complaining." He mumbles, "But Max probably just wants to see her." He glances back to Juliette's bowl. "Sorry, you were in the middle of something."

Eddie leans over. The light from the window accentuates the swollen curve of the dough. Juliette has the urge to run her fingers over it, to feel the firmness, the resistance, to tap against the gases that have made it rise. It seems too intimate to do so in front of a guest; her fingers twitch against the bench top. Beside her Eddie now lets out a hoot. Juliette follows his gaze out the window.

"That's my little lady!"

Beside Beth's chair is a bundle of fabric covered in tiny raspberries, fallen beside her magazine. Her palms face up to the sun; her eyes are covered with big dark glasses. And her breasts, high and rounded as Juliette's dough, are exposed to the light, nipples the pale brown color of fallen rose petals, the surrounding skin creamy and unmarred.

Eddie is laughing hard. "That girl has no shame."

Juliette shrugs and smiles. "It's okay, Eddie. You're in France, remember?"

"HAS EDDIE'S BIRD got her baps out?"

Juliette is cutting the now-baked bread into thick pieces. She already has a plate of cheeses, sliced andouille, and crudités of spring carrots and the local green cauliflower with a Mingaux cream cheese. She pauses, knife in hand, as a man comes into the kitchen. The sun is lower now, turning clementine and getting in her eyes.

The man claps his hands together, his face a hundred happy creases. "Sorry!" He laughs. "I thought you were one of the girls. I'm Lars." His height means he almost has to slouch due to the low ceiling.

"Juliette," she says. "I work for Max."

"Aw, you poor thing." Lars shakes his head in mock sympathy. He has ruffled sandy-colored hair. When he blinks, Juliette notices that even his eyelashes are blond.

"It's not so bad."

"Well, you're braver than most."

Lars holds out his hand, which Juliette shakes. His hand is covered in pale freckles and his fingers are long like the rest of him.

"Welcome to Douarnenez," she says, offering him the plate of food.

"Thank you." He beams, piling cheese onto bread.

Two women follow Lars into the kitchen. They are the same height, but the first one is dark-haired and heavier than the other, who is blond and wearing sunglasses. The dark-haired woman's face is soft and round; she too shakes Juliette's hand firmly.

"I'm Nina."

"She's with me," Lars adds.

"Rosie," the blond woman says. She is carrying a basket and on one hand wears a rose-gold ring with a large stone the color of jadeite.

"I'm Juliette. I work for Max," Juliette says again.

"You poor thing," both women say together, and then laugh at the same time. They don't look at all alike—Nina dark, confident, and plump; Rosie blond, polite, and trim—

but they somehow seem like sisters. Max had described them to Juliette over the phone. *Nina—publisher, top girl, smart as hell, she's with Lars. They have a daughter, Sophie, and Lars is a stay-at-home dad. He'd do anything for those two. Rosie—jeweler, talented too; unfortunately she's married to Hugo . . .*

"That's what I said," Lars cuts in. He slips his arm around Nina's back.

"Who's here?" Rosie places the basket down on a bench top. "Is Helen going to be late? When's her flight in from New York?"

"Tonight," replies Lars. "Where's Hugo gone?"

"He's getting luggage from the car."

"Who has the boys this weekend?"

"My parents."

"That's the way," Lars says comradely, lifting his hand to high-five Rosie. "So for now it's us, you and Hugo, Eddie and . . ." Lars looks to Juliette.

"Beth," Juliette offers.

"Right. Beth McBaps."

Lars gestures out the window and the two women quickly crowd in. Juliette steps out of the way. She should probably get the bread to the outdoor table before it gets cold. It tastes so good warm, with a generous smear of Guérande salted butter.

"Bloody hell," says Nina.

"She's got no top on," Rosie murmurs. She tucks a strand of hair behind her ear.

Juliette glances outside and then back to the blond woman, who has a tiny frown on her lips. She recalls the next part of Max's description. *Rosie and Eddie were a thing once. Nothing too serious. But sometimes I wonder . . .*

"She's a firecracker," Lars says admiringly.

Nina swats him. "How old is she?"

"Midtwenties maybe?"

"Stop staring," Rosie scolds.

"There's just so much . . . boob," Nina says. She turns to Juliette with a wry smile. "I bet you've seen worse."

Juliette recalls the girl who came down to breakfast still tipsy from the night before, and the one who couldn't find her shoes; Juliette lent her a pair of old slippers that had been her father's and that she kept at the house to wear when she did chores. Gorgeous, giggling, smooth-skinned, half-naked girls. Girls smitten with Max, clinging to him like a bean plant to a stake.

"Topless is okay in France," she says.

"Yeah, girls—topless is okay in France," Lars pipes up.

Both women give him withering glares.

Lars picks up the platters with the bread, cheese, and crudités. "Do you want these on the table, Juliette?"

"*Oui,*" she says gratefully. "Please."

When Lars has left, Rosie plucks two bottles from her basket and sidles closer to Nina, who is still standing at the window. Juliette busies herself, going to the fridge to take out a large tray of whole silver-bellied sardines.

"Are you alright?" Rosie whispers.

"I'm fine. Truly," Nina says. "Stop fretting."

"I can't help it."

"Well, you'll have to. Sophie is with us and this is supposed to be a nice weekend away. If anything, you can help me with her. She's . . . having a hard time."

"You can't blame her, Nina."

Nina glances over at Juliette. She is salting the sardines and doesn't meet Nina's gaze. The years spent running a restaurant and hearing the most personal conversations means Juliette knows how to be invisible. She's seen it all—fights and confessions, breaking up and making up. There isn't much that shocks her anymore. Delphine had been known within a circle of high-ranking politicians and businessmen as the place to bring your mistress. It had been small, dark, intimate, and safe. Juliette's ex met her there too, feeling bold enough, at times, to reach for her under the tabletop, to slide a hand smoothly up her thigh.

Nina lowers her voice. "We're not telling anyone. Not even Sophie, remember? We don't know anything yet. Don't say anything, please. Not even to Hugo."

The door opens and a thin man with glasses steps in. His back is ramrod straight, and he pushes his glasses up on his nose to survey the kitchen. "Talking about me?"

Rosie's face brightens a little too much. "Hugo! No. Do you mind putting these bottles in the fridge?"

Hugo is almost as tall as Lars, but his hair is dark and thinning, the creases in his face running in different directions.

"Anything else?"

"Sorry?"

"I've been getting instructions all the way from Paris."

"Don't be silly."

Hugo's voice rises: *"Don't be rude. Stop here so I can take one hundred photos of lavender. Don't say anything inappropriate. Don't be too smart."* Hugo pauses to lift his eyebrows to Nina. "Hey, Nina."

"Hey, Hugo."

"I did not say that." Rosie glances from Nina to Juliette and back to Hugo. "Just take these, would you?"

Juliette gestures outside. "There is a drinks fridge in the bar, by the deck. This one is full of food, I'm afraid."

Hugo takes the bottles, then steps over to Nina. She

lifts her head as he kisses her on the cheek. He looks over at Juliette. "Hi, I'm Hugo, husband who does as he's told." Rosie sighs.

"I'm Juliette. I work for Max. It's a pleasure to meet you."

Hugo nods. "Do we put our things in any room?"

"Yes." Juliette had anticipated Max being here by now to show guests to their rooms. "There are four double bedrooms and one twin single upstairs. Please help yourself."

She doesn't mention the little bedroom off the original hallway. That is hers. Max offered her one of the bigger, modern rooms, especially when it was just him and her in the house, but Juliette refused. She loves the "Blue Room," as she has named it. The duck-egg-colored walls are thick and warped, the floor made of stones just like the kitchen, partially covered with a braided rug she transplanted from her parents' cottage. It's small but cozy, nostalgic somehow but none of the memories are hers or her parents'. The walls block out both sound and light like a womb. The only window, dressed with wooden shutters on squeaky hinges, contains old glass, which makes the view wobbly.

Nina starts ticking off on her fingers. "One room is Max's, I presume. Then one for Eddie and what's-her-name . . . Boobs . . ."

"Beth," Juliette supplies again.

"Beth. You and Hugo. Lars and me. That's four. Where is Helen sleeping?"

Hugo snorts. "Are you kidding? In with Max, if he gets his way."

"It hasn't worked for him so far," Nina says. "Juliette, is it okay if Sophie sleeps on a couch?"

"Yes, sorry," Juliette replies. "I put spare linen at the top of the stairs. There is a day bed in the music studio or she can sleep in the lounge, whichever you think is best. The studio is further from the rooms, so you might not be very close to each other."

"Oh, she'll be happy with that," says Nina.

Hugo adds acerbically, "Max will be thrilled too. Thought we weren't bringing kids."

"Jesus, Hugo!" Rosie cries out.

"You get up on the wrong side of bed?" Nina asks.

Max had described Hugo last of all. *Hugo . . . he's a fucking twat.*

"It's been a long drive. My wife has been battering me with instructions on social graces."

Nina smiles sweetly. "Maybe you need them."

DESPITE STILL MISSING Max and Helen, Juliette prepares dinner. Tonight's menu is sole and silver-bellied sardines; a salad of beetroot, pink grapefruit, goat's cheese, and mint; and spring asparagus with almonds and a lemon dressing. Max had asked her to keep the meals very casual, so she set a table outside with simple silver cutlery, tea lights in glass jars, a pile of paper napkins, and two little wooden bowls with flakes of *fleur de sel* and black pepper. Already there is a craggy pile of shells in the bin, the group having tasted its first Breton oysters, which Juliette served with lemon cheeks as a starter. In the kitchen, Juliette pan-fries sole fillets in a little butter, making mental notes about her guests and their eating habits. Eddie and Nina are enthusiastic about food; Hugo is more of an academic. He informs everyone that you shouldn't eat oysters in a month without an *r* in it and explains that Cancale is the most famous village in Brittany for them. Rosie eats only a little and then becomes distracted in conversation. Beth, now dressed in a short, swingy summer dress with pale blue and white stripes, is curious but tentative. All of the group, barring Beth, drink a lot of Muscadet wine, direct from a wine supplier from Quimper.

Max's friends, gathered around the candlelit table, are polite but informal, much like a family. Eddie and Lars laugh and chat while Nina and Rosie have their heads close together, talking in cozy whispers. Beth and Hugo hang off to the side, looking down into their drinks or out to the night sky. That is the hazard of old friendships: extras and in-laws get left out. Lars, in charge of the music, selects old stuff—the Smiths, New Order, the Stone Roses, R.E.M.—for the dinner's sound track.

Juliette turns the fish fillets over one by one. She wonders if the group will find the food too plain. She has become a traditional cook over the past year. She uses ingredients directly from Douarnenez whenever she can—sardines and other seafood, spring vegetables, local yogurts and cheese. She has given up being experimental, exotic, or avant-garde; it no longer appeals to her. Now she cooks as she learned to from Jean-Paul—same name as the pope and the fashion designer, though he was neither pious nor stylish. Jean-Paul had been a local fisherman in his thirties when Juliette was still in her teens. Juliette had been in awe of him—his age, his disregard for convention, for rules. He'd been on oceans and seen cities with names that sounded like spices. Juliette always complained that Douarnenez never changed, that it was suffocating—*un filet de pêche*—but Jean-Paul had just laughed. "Maybe you'll want that one day, Juliette. A place that never changes, that is exactly as you left it."

Despite his travels, Jean-Paul was thoroughly Breton. He smelled of the sea, of iodine and salt and rope, like a winter oyster, and aside from his calloused hands, his skin was strangely soft and smooth. He was a magnificent, intuitive cook. Juliette thought of him often, especially when cooking fish, even though he had died some years ago. She had learned a lot from Jean-Paul. About cooking. About herself. If she closes her eyes she can imagine herself back in his tiny, clean, galley-like kitchen. The smell of hot butter and the relenting garlic; the sound of the sea and gulls calling. Juliette opens her eyes. She removes the sole from the pan and piles the fillets onto a large platter, taking them out to the group.

The salad and grilled sardines, accompanied by pink onions and herbs, are already on the table. Juliette passes around plates.

"*Manger*. Please, eat." She notices Eddie leans over the fish while Beth, beside him, holds her plate to her chest. Hugo takes two pieces of fish and Rosie chews a spear of asparagus. Juliette goes over to Beth and curls her hands over the back of her chair. She whispers, "It's sole. It's very mild. There should be no bones; I think you'll like it."

Beth glances up at her, lips parted, and whispers, "Are we waiting for Max?"

Beside her Eddie chuckles. "You could be waiting awhile. Probably bumped into a groupie on his way here."

Lars lifts his head and laughs.

Nina leans toward Beth. "Ignore them. We've learned it's best not to wait for Max. He, ah, sometimes gets distracted by—"

"Women," Eddie says, grinning at Juliette.

Juliette straightens, letting go of the back of the chair. "Is there anything else I can get for you?" she asks the group.

"More lemon?" Hugo asks.

"They're right there," Rosie says, pointing to a bowlful of lemon cheeks.

"Oh, right," he mumbles.

"Anything else?" Juliette checks.

Heads shake. Before she leaves the table, Juliette watches Beth swallow a mouthful of fish. On top of the bar is the plate Juliette made for herself: a piece of fish and some bread. It was arguably the best fillet of the lot, the one she imagines Paol Reynaud, whom she bought most of her fish from, had thrown in for free, just for her. She is almost inside when she spots a figure at the edge of the patio in the dim light. Her pale blond hair hangs over her back in one piece like cloth. She wears a gray sweatshirt that is much too big for her. Juliette pauses for a moment. The girl is focused on something in front of her, on the grass. Juliette moves slowly and lowers herself down next to the girl, but not too close.

"It's a pretty night."

The girl looks to the sky and nods. It is close to being a full moon, the night sky deep blue rather than black, the stars golden rather than silvery. The light has faded to gray green at the horizon. There are no gull cries but the air is sea-scented. Juliette takes a forkful of fish.

"Have you eaten?"

The girl's head twitches. Now that she is closer, Juliette notices that the ends of the girl's hair are dyed black irregularly, as though dipped, a handful at a time, into an inkpot. Her fingers, gripping the ends of her sleeves, have nails that have been chewed right down.

"Did you want—" Juliette starts to ask.

"I get carsick," the girl explains quickly. "I'm not hungry."

"No problem," Juliette says. She eats more of her fish and balances her plate on her knees to tear the bread in half and mop up the sweet, briny juices. She allows a long silence.

"You're Juliette," the girl says, finally filling it in.

Juliette smiles and nods.

"I'm Sophie."

"Nina and Lars's daughter."

"Yeah."

Sophie stares down at her lap. Juliette begins preparing the dessert in her head. She has homemade apple sorbet ready in the freezer, but perhaps she could douse it in Lambic, cider brandy. Max would approve of that. She is saving *kouign-amann* for Saturday, Max's birthday night, when they are all together to celebrate. Max hadn't wanted a formal dinner or fuss, but Juliette planned to treat him with his favorite dishes all the same. "Whatever they say, Juliette, forty is *not* the new thirty," he'd pronounced with a grimace. Juliette hadn't told him she'd already celebrated hers.

Despite Max's job, his familiarity with the press, he is quite private. He has few close friends, no family Juliette has ever met, and a tendency to seek out desolate places. He told her he'd found this cottage after a photo shoot in *la ville-close*, by the marina. After the shoot was over he'd just started to wander. And kept wandering, at times along the cliffs and foreshore. Juliette imagined him with his head full of thoughts and music, dark jacket on and cigarette between his fingers, assessing the sea and beaches she knew so well. It must have taken a couple of hours traveling along the coast to reach this part of Douarnenez, to find the old stone cottage among the overgrown grounds.

The places that sold quickly and appealed to out-of-towners were in *la ville-close*, not out here like this cottage. They were the small places like her parents' home: in town, sandwiched between others, nestled in the heart of Douarnenez. Her parents said they paid too much for it back in the late sixties, but it is worth ten times that price these days.

It is officially Juliette's home now.

Not long after her mother died, Juliette's father had

become ill. Truth was he'd been ill for a long while but had been ignoring it to care for her mother. Juliette should have noticed, but she hadn't been around often enough, and his poor health looked so much like tiredness, like sadness, that it wasn't clear to either of them. Not until it was too late. Now only her parents' things, their detritus, and a thousand memories remained in the house.

After her father passed, Juliette had called the agency about the housekeeper position. She commenced just as Max was completing the renovation before his next tour. Everything felt clean and modern, unlike Juliette's ghost-filled home. Max had directed the renovation himself, right down to the inset brass door handles, all-white bed linen, and jute floor rugs. The kitchen, apart from the addition of commercial appliances, was relatively untouched and in need of kitchenware and crockery.

"You do it," Max had urged her, which Juliette understood to be a compliment. Max had dined at Delphine; he trusted her. "Choose whatever you like and use this for the bills." He had flicked her a silver-colored credit card.

Light reflects off something in Sophie's lap and Sophie tips her head up quickly.

Juliette peers over. Sophie's lap is full of empty oyster shells, some of them broken.

"Do you mind if I have . . . ?" Sophie asks.

"Of course I don't mind," Juliette replies. She studies Sophie's face. The teenager's cheeks are pink and her eyes are glazed. A tired and hungry face—Juliette knows it well.

"Did you want to try some oysters?" she asks carefully.

"Oh. No. I don't eat them," Sophie says, and then pauses. "I'm collecting the shells. It's a . . . hobby . . . or I don't know . . . something, of mine."

Juliette places her empty plate down beside her. She moves closer in order to see. Sophie turns her body ever so slightly toward Juliette, presenting the collection of shells in her lap. Juliette notices other things then. A broken eggshell—a wild bird's, not a hen's; it is tiny and pale green and has spots the color of coffee grinds. Two feathers. Then something shining—a bent fork.

"I didn't get that from here," Sophie says hurriedly. "It was on the side of the road, when we pulled over for . . . a bathroom break." She meets Juliette's eyes. "I don't steal."

Juliette nods. "Cool collection," she says instead.

"I guess it's just rubbish."

A memory floods her: her palms bloodied, garbage bags at her knees, the men watching and fearful of her pain, her desperation.

"Not if you don't think so," she replies, her voice soft.

Sophie's cheeks flush a darker pink. Silence falls between them. Juliette considers a strategy.

"Hey . . . do you think your parents would mind . . . ," Juliette whispers, leaning nearer, "if you have a tiny bit of alcohol?"

Sophie blinks and lifts her chin. "I'm *fifteen*," she says, as though it were fifty.

Sophie's face reminds Juliette of herself in the photographs in her parents' home. The girl so restless in her own skin. Sullen and confronting; challenging and hoping; wishing to be somewhere else.

"I'm making sorbet with cider brandy tonight," Juliette replies. "I mean, I didn't think it would be a problem, but I thought I'd better ask."

Juliette stands up and brushes the front of her pants, picking up her empty dinner plate in her other hand.

"It's quite a bit of cider brandy, actually. Don't tell?"

Sophie nods.

"*Bon*. I'll bring you some better cutlery."

She directs her gaze at the bent fork in Sophie's lap and then watches as a tiny smile graces the girl's face. Juliette quickly feels guilty for telling Sophie not to tell her parents. Secret keeping should be her business, not Sophie's.

IT IS MIDNIGHT before everyone returns to their rooms. They—Sophie included—had eaten their desserts, then another cheese platter of washed-rind Port Salut, creamy Saint-Paulin, and soft cream cheese served with fruit. They'd groaned from fullness, and Eddie joked that Juliette was part of an underground group that fattened up British people like foie gras geese to serve their body parts to diners in Paris. Nina and Rosie were tipsy, and Hugo suggested Lars should stop topping up their drinks. That had all three of them, Nina, Rosie, and Lars, roaring with laughter until Hugo said he was retiring to bed. Beth fell asleep on Eddie's arm, right at the table, and then Sophie left too, her odd, broken collection tucked into her sweatshirt. The remaining few got along better with the exclusion of Hugo, Beth, and Sophie. Nina, Lars, Rosie, and Eddie sang to the music Lars chose and leaned against one another and clinked their glasses together in toasts to various things that became more and more idiotic.

From Rosie: "To Brittany!"

From Eddie: "To Max's big, fuck-off house!"

From Lars, drumming on the table: "To the Jacks!"

Then another, before Rosie punched Eddie's upper arm and they all looked at Beth, still sleeping: "To topless birds!"

From Nina: "To Juliette! For feeding us like kings!"
They were as drunk and stupid as teenagers.

With everyone finally in their rooms, full and happy,
Juliette gives the table a final wipe-down and stacks the chairs
in three piles in case a late wind comes through. Then she
stands on the deck and listens to the sound of the waves. *Roar,*
shh shh, roar, shh shh. These are the moments Juliette imagines
sharing: a warm hand in hers, darkness and silence between
them, and the distant sounds of the sea.

A breeze rocks Juliette on her heels. She can feel breezes
better now that her hair is short and wonders why she didn't
cut it earlier. People say it suits her, even older women in the
village who still wear their hair long, plaited and pinned atop
their heads. Juliette feels more like herself with it short, but
then some things you learn about yourself later than you
expect. She had cut it herself one night, thinking of her father
clipping the dogs after lavender oil baths. Juliette's mother
hated him washing the cocker spaniels in the bathtub, but
her father wouldn't wash them outdoors, he was too besotted
with them. Juliette had snipped her hair using a small pair of
silver scissors she'd found in her mother's sewing kit after her
father had died. Her mother must have had them sharpened
regularly, because they made quick work of it.

Closing her eyes to the breeze, Juliette remembers the
two of them before either was ill. Sitting in bed together,
sharing a newspaper and drinking tea. Walking the dogs, one
each. At the dining table listening, enthralled, to Juliette's
stories of life in Paris. Juliette can see her mother's face. Her
funny, crescent-shaped eyes, her wide forehead and pointing
chin. Laughing at some joke Juliette has made. Skin covered
in freckles, as it had always been, for as long as Juliette could

remember. Even her hands had always been freckled. And warm when her fingers laced with her daughter's, soft when pressed against Juliette's cheeks, comforting against her back. Juliette imagined a kind of invisible thread that bound her parents both to each other and to the earth. Once her mother's bonds were severed her father's had started to fray. It had taken only a matter of months before he was untethered too.

Juliette blinks. She is tired. She walks back to the kitchen, thinking about tomorrow's preparations. When she opens the kitchen door there is a woman seated at the bench. Her back is to Juliette and she has a bottle at her elbow. She is dressed in cropped black trousers, a light jersey or maybe cashmere top, and patent leather ballet slippers on her feet, which are crossed at the ankles. Juliette clears her throat. The woman's dark hair, cut in a shoulder-length bob, swings as her head turns. Juliette glances at her right hand: there is a ring much like Rosie's on it, but with a dark stone, and a cigarette between her fingers.

"Shit. Sorry. I'm smoking."

Juliette looks at the bottle. It is one of Max's favorites: tequila with a gold label and a pale, bloated worm in the bottom.

The woman smiles guiltily. "I gave this to Max a while ago . . ."

Her eyes are as dark as her clothes, her lips bare, a pink gray. Before Juliette can speak, she does.

"I don't suppose you usually let people smoke in the kitchen. Max tells me you're a proper chef."

"Max is kind. *Was* a proper chef," Juliette corrects her, rinsing the cloth and then laying it over the tap by the sink.

"I'll only smoke this one, I promise. I didn't know my way around and didn't want to wake anyone up."

Juliette nods. She thinks of Henri, the baker, and of their

conversations on the plastic crates in the early morning as the rest of Paris was just waking: lamenting the loss of cigarettes, reluctantly acknowledging the sensitivity it returned to their taste buds, commiserating over strong coffee and croissants still so hot they flaked and fell apart in their fingers. The tequila bottle is pushed toward Juliette.

"I got it from a small town in Jalisco. It's supposed to be famous. Will you share it with me? I think it's called something stupid like 'Big Cock Tequila.'"

The two women stare at the label on the bottle. It has a picture of a rooster on it. Juliette considers. She is probably too tired to start more preparation work now.

"Max got a kick out of that," the woman says, smiling and blowing smoke toward the floor, away from Juliette.

"I bet he would have," Juliette says. *"D'accord."* She lifts the bottle to her lips. The tequila is dry and sour and hot going down her throat. She coughs and laughs, the woman laughing back. One of her front teeth is slightly crooked.

"I don't drink much tequila," Juliette says, wiping her lips with the back of her hand. Lately she has been drinking a local *chouchenn,* a honey wine, in the evenings, made by the beekeepers who have a stall at the market.

"Probably a good idea." The woman nods. "Some of the people I met could have done with drinking a little less tequila."

"What took you to Mexico?"

"Work. An artist. I have a gallery," she says, tapping cigarette ash into a saucer. "He does very large-scale sculptures." She looks into the distance. "They're beautiful pieces. He uses a lot of collected material and the colors are vivid. His village is so small it's barely there. They make tequila, that's about it. Now, though, a lot of them are helping him with his art. It's changed the place. I've only been twice, but the difference . . ." She breaks out of her stare to glance at Juliette. Her voice is soft and deep, affected by the smoking, but not raspy. Buried in her accent, something about the way she makes vowel sounds reminds Juliette a little of her mother's voice. Her mother, who had laughed so easily and charmed everyone in Douarnenez despite her dreadful French.

"It's really quiet here. New York is never like this. There's always noise."

"Paris is like that too," Juliette replies. Juliette thinks of the apartment near rue Mouffetard with windows that opened out to the street and the constant noise, day and night: pigeons arguing, lovers drunk and shouting, motorbikes, laughter, high-heeled footfalls, delicate autumn rain. Someone else lives there now.

The woman is still. "Did it take you a while to get used to . . . ?"

Juliette notices the misgiving in her voice. "It can feel lonely at first," she replies.

The woman nods slowly. She is not just a beautiful woman; she is a girl too, with fears barely below the surface.

"I'm Juliette. I work for Max."

"I'm Helen."

Juliette takes the hand Helen extends, as she is now used to doing, and finds it to be cool and smooth, not unlike the satin of an oyster shell.

"Juliette," Helen says softly. "Max has told me all about you. Was I the last to arrive?"

"Yes. I can make you something to eat, if you like."

Helen straightens and stretches. "No, don't make me anything; I'm not hungry. I ate on the plane." She picks up the tequila bottle and drinks from the neck, not spluttering as Juliette had.

"Did the rest of them treat you well?"

"Oh yes—"

"Even Hugo?" Helen raises one eyebrow.

"Yes," Juliette replies politely. "Everyone is very nice."

Helen smiles, crooked tooth showing. The imperfection is charming, childlike somehow. "They are, aren't they? I wish I'd got here earlier. We haven't been together like this for a long time. Maybe Rosie and Hugo's wedding . . . No, it can't be that long. Max got most of us to Paris for the Disque d'Or award but I think Rosie was pregnant with Patrick . . ."

Helen's soft, rolling voice is soothing. Juliette stifles a yawn. "Sorry, I—"

"No, I should go to bed too. I've got to pick up my sister tomorrow morning. And you must be exhausted."

"It has been a long day," Juliette admits.

"Where am I sleeping?"

"Bedroom right at the end of the hallway upstairs, past the bathrooms. Sophie is down that end too, in the studio."

"Oh, dear little Sophie, how old is she now?"

"Fifteen."

"Fifteen . . . ," Helen says, drawing breath. "How did that happen?" She stands up. "Thanks for letting me have my smoke. Outside from now on, Scout's honor." She makes a gesture with her fingers against her chest, then laughs loudly. "I don't know what that was, I'm no Scout. See you in the morning?" Helen asks.

"I'll be here."

Just before Helen leaves the kitchen, one hand on the door, she turns back, frowning. "Hey, where is Max?"

Juliette glances at the wall clock before looking back to Helen. Officially, it's now the next day. Very late, even by Max's standards.

"Not to worry," Helen reassures her before Juliette can reply. "He's always late. He'll get here."

But what is more worrying is that Juliette isn't all that concerned about Max. She's more disconcerted by the way Helen's slight, shadowed outline fills the door frame and how her pale fingers curl around the brass handle.

Samedi *(Saturday)*

Chapter Three

ROSIE

The clear morning light creeps over Rosie's skin. Here they are, so close to England, and yet everything feels immediately different. Even when she is only half awake. The soft, pure light reminds Rosie of the spring afternoon picnics she'd had with her boys when they'd each been little. Dragging a blanket, sometimes just a towel, into the garden to share their sandwiches and strawberries, to throw crumbs to sparrows. Those had always been the best days, those picnic days, when Rosie planned nothing and time seemed to slow right down. She had been so busy when the boys were young, wondering, at times, whether they would ever grow up, if she would be changing nappies and getting up for night terrors for the rest of her life. But then they'd suddenly grown, and the baby days had vanished.

That was why Rosie had so longed for Patrick, her last. As challenging as those days had been (again, for the third time), they had been full. Full of work and joy combined. Full of wet baby kisses on her cheeks and the sound of heavy, learning footfalls in hallways. Picnics with strawberries and sandwiches and the warmth of the sunshine on her skin.

Rosie turns her head to her husband. She can no longer sleep in—too many years of getting up too early for the boys—but Hugo is fast asleep. His mouth is open, his legs spread. Hugo has never had to make himself smaller in bed. Sometimes Rosie misses the tiny single bed with the thin quilt they had kept in the nursery. She slept on it for years in the end, accompanied by the sweet, milky scent of a baby. Of course there was no use for the bed, or a nursery, once the children had grown out of being babies. Hugo had made the room a study, the single bed sent off to a school garage sale fundraiser. A wife should sleep in bed with her husband; Rosie agreed it was right. Plus, the boys no longer really needed Rosie to sleep next to them. Sometimes that thought made her heart physically ache.

Rosie looks to the closed door. She had heard Helen come in last night, but hadn't gotten up. She had heard, through the floorboards and the thick countryside silence, murmuring in the kitchen—too faint to wake anyone else, but Rosie was a light sleeper, her ears acutely trained for whimpers and whispers. Lying in the dark, Rosie had tried to make out words, but hadn't been able to. Rosie and Helen were less close than they once had been. Rosie and Nina caught up often, but it was different with Helen. You never knew when she would make contact or simply appear, a surprise visit from New York, normally on the way to somewhere else. At college the three of them—Rosie, Nina, Helen—were like points on a tripod, making one another steadier.

Rosie first met Helen in a life drawing class: Rosie, determined and anxious, and Helen, unkempt and apathetic. Rosie had reason to be anxious; she knew, pointedly, how much the course and materials cost. Helen had no clue. Rosie wanted something out of it, and Helen, at least at the beginning, just seemed to want to run away from home. It wasn't really Helen's fault; they came from different worlds. Rosie's dad was a butcher and her mum stayed at home with Rosie and her three brothers. Conversely, Helen's dad was a wealthy businessman—his pugnacious face was often a cartoon in the papers—and her mum looked like a royal. A royal with breast implants. But still, Rosie and Helen were closer then. They accepted each other as they were; they made each other laugh.

Rosie had been convinced she was the one who now had things sorted. Rosie was the grown-up. She had a husband and three children. She had a beautiful home. She was on the PTA and her bake stand at the school fete made record profits. She went to the gym four days a week and looked good, she knew, younger than her age. She had given up smoking a long time ago; her skin thanked her for that. She had more in her fridge than a bottle of wine and a hardened lump of Parmesan cheese. She grew vegetables! Rosie did not envy Helen's life—her New York life—with her gallery, the bars she went to, the men she attracted like moths to a flame. Rosie didn't wish for late nights, to sleep in, to be able to wear silk without the risk of someone putting his peanut butter–covered fingers all over it. Plus, despite all the men who flocked to Helen's flame—artists, of course, with tortured souls, beautiful bodies and thick heads of hair; entrepreneurs; a race car driver once; musicians, quite a few of those—Helen had never maintained a relationship longer than a few months. It was as though she just couldn't find what she was searching for—despite their money, looks, and talent. Rosie thought she was being stupidly fussy; she told Helen once too, to which Helen had just laughed. Helen didn't seem to care. She didn't seem to want the normal things like marriage and kids. That bewildered Rosie. Their lives were in such stark contrast. When Rosie was knee-deep in Legos or stepping in a puddle of pee left on the bathroom floor, Helen was in Guatemala, inspecting a three-story-high art installation, or drinking a whiskey sour in a Chelsea jazz bar.

And yet, they did love each other. It was something about being such old friends. They were more like family than friends. Whatever happened they had their pasts in common. Plus, it was Helen who encouraged Rosie to make Fleet a small business rather than just a hobby, after Rosie sent her the ring with the stone the same color as Max's eyes. Rosie had had so much more practice since then that although it wasn't her best work, but she was still fond of it. Helen had loved it. The women Rosie was friendly with nowadays, who had children the same ages as the boys and who were on the PTA and possessed similarly abundant vegetable gardens, were sweet but indifferent about Fleet. One of them had been honest with her eventually; she said the pieces were too costume-like, too rough, see? Rosie understood.

Rosie hears the sound of a shower being turned on, the water slapping against a floor, then a person filling the space in between. Hugo turns, still sleeping, toward her. She studies the softness of his skin, loose under his chin, and the lines that usually frame his mouth erased by the gentle hand of sleep. Hugo looks less like himself and more like her sons when he is sleeping. His sternness is gone, his trenchancy. Rosie has taken to staring at Hugo when he is sleeping more and more these days, looking for someone or something that isn't there when he is awake.

Sometimes, when they go to Hugo's medical conferences

and all the other wives are there, rapping manicured nails against champagne glasses and laughing so widely, Rosie wonders if she has been living someone else's life. It almost makes sense; she had been nursing a baby for much of the last twelve years, sleep deprived and stumbling through the days like a zombie. Only now that Patrick is older does it feel as though a fog has cleared, that she can have a life for herself, can have Fleet. But Rosie had chosen this life. She chose Hugo. Rosie still remembers the moment in the pub when Hugo had said he was a surgeon and Rosie told him her father was a doctor. Rosie hardly ever lied, not if you didn't count the little lies you have to tell children about the tooth fairy and whatnot. Back then, in that pub, Rosie had felt herself lying and didn't flinch for a second. She *leaned into* it. Hugo had been so handsome, so nonchalant, so knowledgeable. His voice had that delicious, fancy edge to it, like Helen's. He didn't look anything like the guys whom Rosie was used to. Not like Max and Eddie had been back then, always crumpled and smelling and laughing maniacally, acting like boys. Hugo was a gentleman. Hugo would look after her. Rosie saw what she wanted and reached for it. Rosie was culpable for all this, more culpable than Hugo.

Rosie turns the other way, toward the wall. The sun is growing in strength now. She closes her eyes and listens to the sounds of the house waking up in its heat: the creaking and groaning like an old lady with sore joints. The cottage, if you could still call it that, is stunning. Max had done a good job with the renovation. The modern, floating oak-board staircase; the large windows; and the inset brass handles. Rosie was hesitant to say it, but it was very grown-up. Max had taste, she had to give him that, in design and music and young women. Those were Max's specialties.

Rosie hears muffled voices in the hallway. She recognizes

Nina's whisper and lifts the duvet from her body. When she opens the door and steps out, Nina is showered and dressed, smiling at her.

"HOW DID YOU sleep?" Rosie asks her friend.

"Not too bad. Feeling a bit hungover. I need a coffee. You?"

"Fine," Rosie lies. "It's nice being out here, away from the city, don't you think?"

"It really is," Nina agrees. "It's so quiet."

When they reach the kitchen, Nina surveys the clean, empty counters with hands on her hips and then goes to the espresso machine on the bench opposite the kitchen windows. "Do you think I'll be able to get this thing going?"

"If anyone can . . . ," Rosie replies, hopping up onto a stool and watching Nina stare at the knobs and dials.

Nina doesn't function well without her morning cup of coffee. She carefully removes a part from the machine.

"Did you hear Max come in last night?" Rosie asks.

Nina is searching through cupboards now. She shakes her head.

"Isn't today his actual birthday?"

Nina triumphantly holds up a large foil bag of ground coffee, the top folded down and secured with a clip. "Yes, it is, I think."

"The first of us," Rosie says. "Do you worry about it?"

Nina scoops out some grinds with a spoon and adds them to the part of the machine she has removed. She shakes her head. "Turning forty? Not really. I think about Sophie more. Who she is talking to online, who her friends are, finishing school . . . why she is so angry . . ." Nina pushes the part back into the machine. "Do you worry about it?" she asks, pressing a button. The kitchen fills with the sound, the rage, of it working.

Rosie thinks about it a lot. She hadn't expected to; being the youngest of the group she still has over a year before she will face it. For Hugo's fortieth Rosie had planned a surprise dinner with workmates, parents, and some of their friends at a local restaurant. Three courses, speeches, white flowers as centerpieces. It had been very fitting. Everyone told Rosie she had outdone herself. Rosie had bought Hugo gold cuff links and four fishing rods, one for him, three for the boys. They hadn't been out with them yet though. Hugo preferred fly-fishing and he wasn't sure the boys were up to that.

Rosie thought of turning forty mostly when she was in the bathroom, staring at her reflection. The lines, the softness, the thinning eyebrows, the hairs above her lip. Rosie pulled her cheeks and stomach taut, turned to observe the sag of her arse. When the boys had been little she had no time to notice the years dashing by. Now the boys got themselves ready for school and made themselves breakfast, and the house was quickly empty and quiet, too quiet, despite a few city noises—garbage bins being emptied or retrieved, dogs padding past the gate, joggers close behind, bikes, cars, robins in the tree out front. Rosie began to see herself in reflections in doors, wineglasses, wing mirrors . . . everywhere.

The coffee is now coming out of the machine in satisfying dark spurts. Nina lifts a full cup to her face and breathes in.

"I'm worried about you," Rosie replies, diverting the subject.

Nina gives a soft smile. "Oh, Rosie, I'm going to be fine. I'm always fine. I come from hardy stock."

She raises her eyebrows at Rosie. Nina isn't slim like Rosie. She hates the gym. She sends Rosie YouTube videos of people falling off treadmills.

Nina is hardy. Everyone would agree with that description. But Rosie remembers the time Nina wasn't so hardy, after Sophie was born. She had bled too much, had needed transfusions, and had to stay at the hospital for a week. And then, when she came home, Nina hadn't been hardy at all. She'd been pale and thin, too thin for a woman who had just given birth, and teary too, which wasn't like Nina at all. Lars and Rosie took turns looking after her and Sophie, as though they were both babies. Rosie cooked and brought over dinners; Lars fed Sophie bottles and soothed her and changed nappies. Rosie did the grocery shopping when the cupboards were empty; they both ferried cups of tea and tucked Nina into clean sheets. It took months for Nina to get back to her normal self. Although Lars had proposed to Nina and Nina had said yes, after Sophie was born all those plans seemed to dissolve. Becoming a mother had almost broken Nina.

Nina blows on the top of her coffee and reaches out to pat the top of Rosie's hand. "This is supposed to be a holiday, remember?" She takes a sip of her coffee. "If you want to worry, you can worry about Max. He's easy to worry about. He's so late, he's probably drunk somewhere with some poor young thing . . ."

Rosie rolls her eyes. Poor young thing indeed. Max isn't sweet to the women he sleeps with. He doesn't call them back, he forgets their names, and yet they continue to flock to Max without him even trying, knowing, somehow, that he may not care about them but he will know how to sleep with them, how to make them feel good and disposable all at once. It never ceases to amaze Rosie how many women

Max manages to sleep with, how many women seem to want exactly what little he has to offer. The funny thing is that as careless as Max is with the women he sleeps with, he is loving and kind to the women he is friends with. Helen especially. Max and Helen are so close they sometimes seem not to have to speak, already knowing what the other is thinking. When they are together they are always laughing. They light one cigarette and share it. They go to art galleries, get drunk, and argue about Francis Bacon, whose work Max loves and Helen doesn't. At college Max made tiny sculptures out of wire for Helen that filled her bedroom—even a plant holder once, from a coconut shell and a bedspring—and wrote notes in her textbooks for her to find, like "Fuck you and your existentialism" and "Helen Barnett has great tits." Things that would have annoyed Rosie no end had he written them, in pen no less, in her textbooks, but which sent Helen into peals of laughter. They were love notes. Max adored Helen.

People said that Rosie and Nina were "peas in a pod," but the real peas were Helen and Max. From different worlds and yet made the same way, broken in the same way. They had never been a couple, never slept together as far as Rosie knew, and yet they were a pair. A set. Of course Rosie was sure they had nothing to envy. Just two lost and fractured drunks still acting like teenagers. They had no plan. They never had plans. But even without having seen them yet, Rosie suddenly has the uneasy feeling she has been wrong, that they might have something Rosie no longer has.

That if anyone is lost it might be her.

❧

BRIGHTON BEACH, 1995

They weren't supposed to be a couple. Not in Rosie's mind, anyway. Not that she'd told Eddie that, as they lay back against the stones digging into her skin. It was June but the weather was dreadful. That's England for you. That's Brighton for you. The grubby ocean scent in the air, the stink of the wet wooden boards of the pier, tobacco, and sweat—Eddie's of course. Eddie was not part of Rosie's plan and yet here they were. Again. He passed her the smoke.

"Supposed to be summer. Almost. Weather's crap."

His hair was too long. His jeans were too short. His sweat smelled of onions and brine.

"It's crap," Rosie agreed.

Eddie rolled onto his side, looked her up and down, and gave her a grin. "You're a picture, Rosie."

"I need a shower."

"You look good without one."

Not long and they'd be done with study and Rosie would be somewhere else. With someone else. Not under the Brighton pier, sharing a smoke with Eddie.

"Is Max going to class these days?" Rosie asked, still lying on her back.

Eddie looked out toward the sea. There were seagulls nearby arguing over something, probably a cold chip. Their cries struck the air like slaps.

"Not much," Eddie replied. "I don't think he's worried. He's getting good gigs."

"He won't finish his degree?" Rosie shivered from the cold.

Eddie shook his head. "Doubt it."

"He should finish."

"Think he's happier with his music."

"He spends too much time arsing about. He's almost finished." Rosie tried not to sound scolding, but failed.

"He's happy," Eddie murmured.

He reached over and touched Rosie's hair. The gel had lost its hold. The strands were limp and gritty.

"I like it like this," he said.

"Dirty?" Rosie sniffed. She hated the sound of her voice. Too much like her mother's when she was looking at herself in the mirror.

"Short," Eddie replied.

Eddie and Rosie had first kissed at the pub, a night Max had been playing. It wasn't on purpose. It was cider. Rosie never drank cider but Helen did. The cider made Rosie feel weird—that was her excuse—so when Eddie started chatting with her he suddenly seemed appealing. Maybe it was because Max wasn't with him and Rosie wasn't sure about Max. Max was reckless and blunt, he took too many chances, and he made Helen wild. Max was the kind of person Rosie's mother warned her about and Rosie was inclined to agree with her mother about that kind of thing. But with Max onstage and occupied with the band, Eddie was on his own. He asked Rosie questions. He seemed interested. It felt good to have someone interested. Then he leaned in too close and his lips were just there and he was, well, handsome enough.

"Are you cold?" Eddie asked, fingers now on her bare shoulder. She should have brought a jacket.

"A bit," Rosie conceded.

"Take my jacket."

"No, I'm fine, thanks."

Eddie's kindness bothered Rosie because she was supposed to be breaking up with him. Eddie was sweet, but he wasn't what Rosie had in mind. He wasn't clever or ambitious; he wasn't focused. He didn't even have many opinions on things, was affable in almost every situation. Rosie's brother Simon had met him; they'd instantly gotten on like a house on fire, discussing music and soccer and the best local *breweries. Simon said that Eddie was a "great guy, a really decent bloke." But Rosie wasn't after just another great guy or decent bloke. She wanted a man. A proper, grown-up man.*

"Eddie—"

"Oh, Rosie, you are fucking freezing, just take the jacket," Eddie interrupted.

"I don't need it," she replied, shivering.

"If you don't take the jacket I'm going to smother you with something else."

"I don't want it, Eddie!"

"You were warned . . ."

Eddie hoisted himself up and rolled on top of Rosie, squashing her further into the bed of gray stones.

"Ow! Jesus, Eddie!"

"I told you . . ."

Eddie was laughing and his breath was close to her face. She could smell the smoke and the salt and grease of the chips they'd shared before.

"The stones . . . !" Rosie protested, her voice muffled.

Eddie was now sniffing at her neck. "God, you smell good, Rosie."

"Get off me!"

"You smell like roses," Eddie said.

"I do not. I smell like fags and booze. Get off!"

"No, you smell good. I swear."

Eddie started kissing her—small, peppering kisses below her jaw growing bigger and more generous as he reached the top of her collarbone. Rosie felt her body, all muscles and bones and resistance, betraying her.

"Eddie . . . Come on . . ." But Rosie's protest was halfhearted at best. Kisses were pressed along her collarbone. Rosie felt her head tip back, just a little, encouraging.

"You are so cold," Eddie murmured, slipping his hand, softly and slowly, up her top.

Rosie's voice vanished, along with her intentions, all the explanations she had practiced—"It's not you, it's me"; "It was always a casual thing"; "You'll find the right girl, Eddie"—melting in the wake of those kisses, in the heat of Eddie's breath against the base of her throat, in the creeping desire of his hand moving toward the worn silk of her gray-white bra. Rosie breathed, heavily, against Eddie's hair, felt her eyes closing, her hips lifting. Eddie's fingers moved inside the cup of her bra, skimmed her nipple, closed over, took possession. Rosie had such small breasts. Some of the men she'd been with, the smart, going-places ones, had told her so.

"You are brilliant. God you are brilliant," Eddie whispered on her skin.

Eddie wasn't good enough. He wasn't part of Rosie's plan. But he was impossible to break up with.

Chapter Four

MAX

Helen in a green satin shirt that makes her breasts look like slinky hillocks you want to lay your palms upon and a black skirt, worn with shiny black heels. Looking whatever it is that is beyond beautiful (*radiant* comes close, but *fuckable* is all Max can honestly think of). That hair, swinging; that soft, wet mouth, open, laughing. Max tugs her away from everyone, pulls her into a closet, which smells of dust and lemon-scented cleaning products but muffles the sounds—the chitchat and *har har har* and *clop-clop* of shoes against gallery floors. Her breath hot on his face, her breasts rising and falling. The fragrance of her neck, her skin. Undoing the buttons on her shirt, yanking up the skirt, pushing down the underwear. Feeling her warm and damp against his fingers, *dear God.* Her mouth on his, tasting of her cigarettes, of red wine. Her hand pushes down into his trousers, urgent, searching for . . . finding . . .

Max sits up too fast. His head hits the visor. He rubs his forehead and groans. It takes him a minute to figure out that he is in his car. Sunlight floods in rudely through the front window. Did he crash? Max looks out the side window at a grass verge and then blinks at the front of his car, checking for damage. He scans down his body. Legs, crotch, torso, all still intact. Then he remembers where he is headed and reaches for the box on the passenger seat, rolls it in his fingers. He spots his phone and touches the screen but it remains black. Dead.

Max laughs. He must have pulled over to sleep on his way to Douarnenez. Like an old man. Shit. He *is* an old man. Forty. Today! And while forty isn't *old* old, it is old enough and it makes Max feel slightly sick. Like he is sliding, faster and faster, down a cliff and at the bottom there is nothing—a void. Not even the smash of body against ground but absolutely nothing. A gray nothing that is dull and damp and hanging. Worse than a used dick. The thought makes him check his own. Still there.

Max reaches over to the glove box, digs under the warranty and an old map, and pulls out the small bag. He dips his finger into the powder inside and rubs it on his gums, blinking fast. He has the fleeting image of a woman's soft, concerned face, that neighbor and social worker, Claudine. She wore her sobriety like a shiny enamel pin.

"You might survive it, you know," she'd said to him once.

"What?"

"Life."

Max had been confused and Claudine had laughed.

Max frowns. An old man? Fuck that. He starts the car, shifts the gearstick, and pushes down too hard on the accelerator, imagining that green satin shirt.

THE HOUSE IS a marvel. The old half, the cottage, with stone as gray as Breton clouds, masking the new half at the back—glass and exposed wood, brass and copper details. Like a butterfly emerging from a chrysalis. Magic. Max loves it every time he sees it, as though it is a new thing. It's the kind of home you see in *Architectural Digest*. He isn't sure the locals like it very much, but Max doesn't care for their opinions. He pays Juliette to keep everything and everyone sweet, and she does a good job of it too. Plus, she makes a mean *kouign-amann*, the exterior cooked crisp and colored toffee brown, the inside soft, layered, and sticky.

When Max pulls up there is a van and three cars parked out in front as well as Juliette's little blue Renault, which looks more like a toy than a car to Max and has to be older than Max himself. Max cannot tell if Helen's rental car is among the ones parked but gets out quickly and strides to the front door, pushing it open. He hears conversation coming from the kitchen.

Max spots Rosie first. She's wearing pink flannel pajamas with elephants printed all over and she's talking to Nina, who's dressed in a navy linen dress and sandals. Juliette is by the bench. She's cut her hair. She looks over and smiles.

"Happy birthday, Max."

Both Nina and Rosie wheel around, and Rosie squeals, "Max!"

She gives him a firm hug and Max remembers just how small Rosie is. Short and wiry, like a kid; you wouldn't guess she'd had three of her own. Nina kisses his cheeks and Max inhales her perfume. Gardenia and something else, she's worn it for years and years. She gives a gentle smile that makes Max want to curl up next to her and tell her all his secrets.

"Happy birthday," they say together, then laugh.

"My gorgeous, gorgeous girls," Max purrs, pulling them both toward him. "You too, Juliette, feel free to join us," he says, glancing over.

She's cutting a brioche loaf and stacking the slices onto a large plate. There's a jar of jam on it too, with a bone-handled knife beside it.

"You seem to have enough . . . ," Juliette mumbles, blushing.

"Never enough," Max jokes.

"Where were you?" Nina asks. "We were all waiting."

"We called you all night," Rosie adds.

"Phone was dead," Max says dismissively, not mentioning the old-man nap. "What did you do without me? Go to bed early without any supper?"

"Exactly," Nina replies.

"I fed them. I promise," Juliette says.

"She did," Rosie says, nodding. "Her cooking is incredible."

"Do you want a coffee?" Juliette asks Max.

"Fuck yes."

Rosie returns to the barstool she had been sitting on. Nina reaches over to the brioche and drops jam onto a slice.

"Nice place you've got here, Max."

"Thanks, Nina."

"How you feeling about the big four-oh?"

Max restrains a grimace. "Fine. Good. They say forty is the new thirty."

"Yeah, but that's bullshit," Nina replies drolly.

Max laughs. "I missed you."

"You know where I am. You just pick up the phone and call me. Or, better yet, buy me tickets to Paris. Heard of the Eurostar?"

"Have *you* heard of the Eurostar?" Max counters. "You could come see me."

"I'm not buying train tickets to come see you when I don't know where you are from one week to the next. You could be touring New Zealand for all I know. I mean, you invited us here and then turned up late."

Max reaches out for Nina's cheek. "I'm sorry, Mumma Bear. Will you forgive me?"

Rosie laughs but Nina pretends to be annoyed. "No."

Lars comes into the kitchen. "Max!"

"Lars, mate!"

They hug each other tight and then Lars rubs Max's bald head, ruffling hair that isn't there. "Need a cut, mate."

"Yeah, yeah. The girls don't seem to mind."

"Bet the girls love it," Lars says, winking, his blond eyelashes catching the light.

Nina shakes her head. "How old do you have to get before you stop calling us all 'girls'?"

"Do we offend you?" Max asks, grinning.

"I don't mind it. Makes me feel young," Rosie says, fingers wrapped around a teacup.

"It's so belittling," Nina grumbles.

Lars goes to her and kisses her head. "How you feeling about the big four-oh?" he asks Max.

"Your girl just asked me that."

"First cab off the rank," Lars says warningly.

"You'll all catch up soon enough."

"Not for a while . . . ," Rosie mumbles into her tea.

"You cut the path, Max, we'll follow your lead," Lars says.

"God help us," Nina replies.

Max inhales, puffing out his chest. "Well, I'm not planning on changing very much, mate. Am thinking of keeping up the same diet and exercise regimen . . ."

"Which is?" Nina asks.

"Booze, smokes, drugs, and shagging," Lars answers, and they all laugh, including Juliette, who is facing the window.

"That's it," Max agrees. "I'm going to write a book about it. You interested in publishing it, Nina?"

Nina grimaces. "*Rock 'n' Roll Method to an Early Grave?*"

Max laughs. "Ouch."

Juliette passes around the fresh bread and jam and serves Max his coffee. Rosie pats Max's arm, leaving to get changed. After a few sips of coffee, Max clears his throat.

"Where's Helen?"

Lars grins. "Was wondering how long it'd take you to ask that."

"Picking up her sister," Juliette says.

"Oh, right." Max nods, remembering the message on his phone. His heart sinks.

He tries not to feel disappointed. But his body aches for the dream that vanished too fast this morning. The silk shirt, the scent of her skin. Max shudders, tries to shake it off. Disappointment is a pathetic wimp of an emotion. Useless. He has a brief memory of his father's breath on his face. *Don't give me that face! What have you got to be sad about?*

"How does Helen suddenly have a sister?" Lars asks.

"I don't think it's a real sister," says Max. "She's her dad's daughter."

"Half sister," Nina says.

"No, not even. Her dad married that Spanish woman, what was her name?"

"Oh, that's right. The one that looked like that actress . . . what *was* her name?"

"Anyway," Max says, "she had a daughter before they were married. Soleil. She and Helen were close; Helen practically raised her for a few years. Then her dad and what's-her-name—"

"Mariposa!" Nina supplies.

"That's it. Mariposa and Helen's dad split up. It was pretty messy."

"As all his splits are," Lars says grimly. Juliette is stacking dishes into a dish drawer but glances over when he says that. "Sorry, Juliette, we're being so rude."

"*Non*. It's fine."

Nina turns to Max. "How old is Soleil now?"

"Not sure. Mid-, maybe late twenties? Helen hasn't seen her for a while. She said something about Soleil having a hard time."

"Hard time?"

Max shrugs, chews on a piece of brioche, suddenly starving. The sweet, buttery bread dissolves in his mouth. "You'll have to ask Helen. You know what I'm like on details. Fuzzy at fucking best."

"Helen said she should be back by midday," says Juliette. "Soleil is coming by train. The nearest station is over an hour away."

Max nods, distracting himself from his own impatience by eating more bread and watching Lars finish stacking the dishwasher, with Juliette. He is nodding to some tune in his head.

"I'm going to the market later, if anyone would like to join me," Juliette offers.

"I will," Nina replies. "And I'm sure Rosie would love to."

As Juliette leaves the kitchen, Max reaches over to Lars, now drying his hands on a tea towel, and shoves his shoulder.

"It's good to see you."

"You too, mate. You too. I watched the Jacks' Tokyo tour online. Bloody brilliant. I can't believe you're still making music. You know, that it's your job."

"Still making music," Max echoes.

"It's brilliant."

Max grins but feels uncomfortable. Lars had been a talented bass guitarist too; he probably could have been something and someone, but that would have meant leaving Nina and Sophie for long periods of time and that was never going to happen. Sophie had been a surprise. Lars had stayed at home with her while Nina pursued her career in publishing. He'd had odd jobs here and there since—in retail, hospitality; he did carpentry every now and then, but he never charged enough and took a long time getting it absolutely perfect. Plus, Nina's work took her away often, to book fairs and writers' festivals; it was easier for Lars to be at home. Watching Lars's eyes shine, talking about Max's music, his work, makes Max feel both great and terrible at once.

"How is life with you two?" he asks.

"Three," Nina says drily. "We have a teenager," she reminds Max. "She takes up a lot of emotional space."

"Where is Sophie?" Max asks.

"Probably still sleeping."

"Probably out taking photographs, more like," Lars says. "We bought her a camera."

"Thought it might make her more sociable," adds Nina. "Give her a hobby she could talk about."

"She talks," Lars mutters.

"She's obsessed with that thing."

"She takes really good pictures. You have to see them, Max. Even Rosie agrees."

"Pictures of dead things," Nina says.

"Dead things?" Max asks.

"Yeah, rats rotting in the gutter, birds. She wants us to buy her a cow skull for her birthday."

"I think it's an antelope. Something with those horn things . . . ," Lars says.

"She likes macabre stuff. She's 'dark.'" Nina uses her index fingers to make quote marks.

"Wasn't her mummy into Siouxsie and the Banshees at her age?" Max teases.

"Yeah! That's right," says Lars.

"Oh, stop it. They weren't that dark," Nina scoffs.

"They were. You said your mum used to have a fit. The makeup you wore . . . the hair . . ."

Both Lars and Max are laughing.

"Okay, okay, settle down. I wasn't asking for skulls for my birthday . . ." Nina scowls.

Max imagines the indomitable force Nina must be at work. She's bold. She has gravitas. It's no wonder Lars acts as though everything is gonna be all right; with Nina at the helm it will be; she'd make sure of it. The secret is that Nina is soft and loving underneath all that: the intelligence, the wit, the drive, and the sarcasm.

"Sophie's a good girl, really, mate," Lars says to Max. "Stubborn as her mum and a bit of a creative, I guess. She's even been talking about Camberwell, can you imagine? Anyway, we're really lucky."

Nina looks down at her hands against the bench top.

Max notices the midmorning light spilling in from the kitchen window. He rarely spends much time in the kitchen; it's Juliette's domain. Now he observes that it has the prettiest light in the whole house, gentle and dappled as it falls through the leaves of the linden tree. Out on the lawn he notices a couple leaning against each other, holding hands. The woman is wearing floral-patterned shorts and a white sleeveless blouse with tan sandals. Her thick red hair is tied up with a silk scarf. The man scratches the back of his head.

"Eddie. There's the bugger," Max says. Lars and Nina follow his gaze. "Is that his American girl?"

"Girl . . . ," Nina tuts.

"Had her tits out yesterday," Lars adds.

"Huh. Is that right?"

"It's *France*. Women go topless in France," Nina says.

"Are you going to go topless, Mumma Bear? Get the jugs out?" Max asks with a laugh.

Nina says drily, "There is something really disturbing about you talking about my breasts while using the term *Mumma Bear*."

Lars laughs loudly. "Yeah, mate, that *is* weird."

Max raises his palms in mock surrender. "I've been in France too long. See? It's made me kinky."

"You needed no help," Nina says.

"I better go meet this one. She sounds like my kind of girl . . . ," Max mumbles.

As he leaves he hears Nina muttering, "*Eddie's* girl."

Chapter Five

JULIETTE

Hugo, Rosie, Nina, and Beth squeeze into Juliette's father's old Renault. The tiny car is easier to park than the van she hired at Max's request, and Juliette is a creature of habit. Instead of joining them, Lars opts to go for a run, Sophie is out taking photographs by the beach, and Eddie and Max sit out on the deck, slapping their knees, laughing till they cry. Helen and the almost-not-quite-sister haven't returned yet.

Hugo, taciturn, sits in the backseat next to Beth, with Rosie on Beth's other side. Nina is in the front seat next to Juliette. The car rumbles over the driveway and turns onto the street leading to the center of Douarnenez. They twist along the coastline, the headlands punctuated with pink thrift and plum-colored heather. Juliette winds down her window, the cool spring air bustling out the musty leather seat scent that reminds her so much of her dad.

Nina and Rosie are murmuring to each other about Sophie, so Juliette turns her attention to Hugo and Beth.

"Where are you from?" Hugo asks Beth.

"Kentucky."

"Oh. That's a nice part of the States."

"Sure is."

Juliette can hear the smile in Beth's voice. She has a slow, steady, pleasant way of talking. It makes her seem a bit older than she is. So far she isn't anywhere near as brash as Juliette guessed she might be, the topless American.

"Full of horses, I hear," Hugo replies, his accent polished and clipped.

Beth laughs. "Not the useful kind though—that's what my daddy says. He's not keen on horse racing."

"What does he do?"

"He's a preacher."

"Oh. Well, that's a noble profession," says Hugo.

"He's a noble guy, I guess. Also kinda suffocating. It's better that I live here and he lives there."

"Fathers can be difficult," Hugo murmurs.

"You're right. I have a lot of brothers and sisters though, so he is kept busy being difficult to them. I'm one of eleven."

"Eleven?"

"Yeah. Eddie was freaked about that, I think. Worried I might wanna drag him off to church."

"Don't think you'd have much luck there," says Hugo.

Beth laughs again. Juliette glances in the rearview mirror. Beth has those teeth all the American tourists in Paris seem to have—perfectly white and straight, like cubes of sugar in a box.

Soon the village comes into view. The stone buildings huddle around the marina, where boats bob in the water, masts moving like metronomes. Some of the cafés are open, tables and chairs out in front, a few people sipping coffee or reading the paper. The sun isn't yet high in the sky; the waitstaff wear long sleeves and the village is still waking up. Juliette slows the car as the streets narrow. They drive past shop fronts and doors painted black and blue and red. A dark-haired woman pushes a pram across the road with her young son trotting beside it.

"This is such a beautiful place!" Rosie says rapturously. "Nina, can you imagine a Fleet studio here?"

"Fleet is Rosie's jewelry business," Nina explains to Beth and Juliette, adding, "She's amazing."

"I'm a mum mainly," Rosie says.

Juliette concentrates on maneuvering the car around a pothole.

"What do you do?" Hugo asks Beth.

"I'm a hairdresser."

"Ah."

"And you?"

"I'm an orthopedic surgeon." He gives a small, funny laugh. "So we both make cuts."

"Hugo!" Rosie reprimands from her side of the car. "That's unnecessary."

"It's my job."

"It's okay—" Beth tries to interject.

"Make cuts . . . it sounds horrible," Rosie mutters.

"Last I checked, *it* actually paid the bills."

Juliette watches Nina give Hugo a pointed look. Hugo glares back. Rosie is frowning at Beth, though Juliette cannot decide whether it's because of disapproval or embarrassment due to Hugo's comment. She returns her gaze to the road ahead.

"Look at that tiny church," Nina says to Rosie, pointing out the window. Rosie follows Nina's finger and they resume their conversation about Douarnenez and its prettiness: the stone, the colors, the small windows, the smell of baking bread.

"It didn't bother me," Beth reassures Hugo, now staring straight ahead.

JULIETTE PARKS THE car down a side street, pointing out the narrow house nearby, her parents' fisherman's cottage. The stone cottage is close to others in a curled row, like the back of a sleeping cat.

"Juliette, it's so sweet!" Rosie exclaims. "When did your parents move here?"

"The late sixties. Before I was born."

"I can see why. It's charming."

"Just you?" Hugo asks.

"Oh, Hugo." Rosie sighs.

"Just me," Juliette replies quickly, trying to sound light-hearted.

"What is it like inside?" Nina asks, as though complicit in providing distraction.

"Oh, it's very small," Juliette says dismissively. She doesn't want to take them in. It is her hideaway, untidy and too filled with treasures and secrets. A place where the pause button has been pressed, everything in a kind of suspended animation.

"The markets are just down this street. They're not far," she advises.

She waits for them to gather up handbags and phones before locking the Renault and pointing in the direction of Les Halles. The small, covered market is unlike the gigantic, sprawling Les Puces or the quaint, open-air bookstalls by the Seine that they may have visited on vacations to Paris. At Les Halles the stalls are functional and neat, all fitting in one large room, with jars of meats or vegetables in orderly queues. It is busier and noisier in the summer, with greater numbers of tourists and extra stalls making *crêpes de blé noir* with cheese and ham, locals selling chocolate-dipped strawberries and gelato in cones. For now, in the spring, it is just bustling enough while still allowing the sounds of the village— someone practicing piano, dogs barking, a skateboard rolling against stones—to weave through. Juliette knows all the stall-holders by first name. She speaks to Marcel about his son, Anton about his bad knees, Elodie about the book Juliette has just finished reading that she must remember to bring next time so she can lend it to her. Strolling down the wide aisles wearing her tan-colored trousers rolled to the ankle and sage-green top with a high, wide-cut neck, Juliette speaks the language that comes most naturally, the language she thinks and dreams in. And she feels good. Even pretty. *Jolie.*

While the others explore, Juliette buys bags of food— leeks, cheese, duck, herbs, spring rhubarb, almost fluorescent-green cauliflower, more seafood, dark and glossy cucumbers, ropey andouille sausage, and olives lolling in shining, golden oil. She doesn't carry her purchases; rather she orders what she wants and the merchants keep the goods behind their stalls for her to gather when she is finished. They choose the best fruit for her, the firmest and brightest-eyed fish, the thickest bunches of sorrel. This is the reward for remembering names and sons and accidents and reading tastes.

Nina and Rosie join her as she approaches the last stall, a table covered in jars of honey in varying shades of sunshine, wheat, and ocher. Juliette glances around for Beth but cannot see her. Hugo is ambling behind, carrying a shopping bag of his own. Juliette has noticed him sampling cheeses and tasting wedges of fruit and pieces of sun-dried tomatoes.

"*Ça fait tellement longtemps que je ne t'ai pas vu!*" exclaims Odette, the woman who sells the honey, kissing Juliette's cheeks. Juliette smiles as Odette babbles about her recent trip to Africa. She half listens, half eavesdrops on Nina and Rosie's conversation.

"But the food was disappointing, I'll tell you that. I could not wait to eat my bread, my cheese. Oh, Juliette, the dairy is bad. Very bad . . . ," Odette is saying.

Rosie leans toward her friend, her hand wrapping around Nina's wrist. "You have to figure out what is going on."

"I will. But not now." Nina's arms are crossed.

"But . . ."

Rosie looks as though she is about to cry. Juliette shouldn't be listening but can't help herself. She tries to focus on Odette.

"Well, you know your *maman,* she was crazy about buckwheat honey. And your father crazy about those dogs!"

"Yes, yes, you're right. He did love them," Juliette replies.

"I was so sorry to hear . . ."

"Thank you. Yes, it has been . . ." Juliette feels herself flinch, still unable to summon the right words. If the right words exist.

"Did you want some buckwheat honey?" Odette asks kindly.

"Non, merci."

"I'll put a bottle of *chouchenn* in the bag, my dear."

"Thank you, Odette."

Juliette glances back to Rosie and Nina.

"I know you care about me, but I will be fine, Rosie. Okay?"

"I don't think—"

"You're getting obsessed with this. It's just another thing to think about instead of thinking about . . ."

"What?"

"I know you're unhappy. You've been unhappy for ages. And now that the boys are grown—"

"Nina, no. Do not say that."

"Oh, I love honey," Beth murmurs, suddenly beside Juliette.

Rosie and Nina turn to face them both. Rosie glances down at Beth's small shorts and the long, lean legs below them.

"Hi," Beth says cheerfully.

Rosie's lips purse. Juliette passes Odette a handful of bills. Hugo joins the group and looks around at them all. His cheeks are ruddy.

"Isn't this great?" Beth continues.

Rosie's hand slips off her friend's wrist.

"Right!" Juliette says brightly. "Are we ready to go?"

"*Oui,*" sings Beth.

"*Bon.* I'll pick up my things—perhaps you can help me, Hugo?—and then we'll head back to the car. Lunch is langoustine and artichoke *crêpes de blé noir*, leek tart, two types of salad, and *gâteau* Breton with berries." She ticks the items off with her fingers.

"Yum!" replies Rosie, her voice a little too high.

"*Mademoiselle! Excusez moi?*"

Juliette turns to a man calling out from a shop across the lane.

"*Mademoiselle?*"

He is holding a paper bag, standing in a stone doorway. Juliette waves. He is Pierre, the local pharmacist. Juliette hates to think of the many pills and tablets she has collected from him, particularly over the last year, her father's name in tiny black type on the white bottles. Pierre looks from side to side, reticent to leave the doorway, probably because he is solely in charge. He gives a hasty wave and holds the bag up high. Hugo jogs over. When he reaches the door, Pierre passes him the bag, pointing to Beth. Juliette watches them converse, Pierre even reaching out to pat the man's shoulder. Beth moves quickly to meet Hugo when he crosses the lane.

"Here you go."

Beth pushes the package into a handbag hanging from her shoulder. "Thank you."

"You speak French?" Juliette asks.

"Yes," Hugo replies. "I lived in Paris when I was a resident. It was a while ago."

"I didn't know that."

Hugo shrugs.

"That's cool," Beth says admiringly.

Juliette notices that Nina has wandered off toward the car, with Rosie trying to catch up to her. Hugo turns to Juliette and reminds her about wanting help with the groceries.

"Tu as besoin d'aide pour les courses?"

It's funny, Juliette thinks, that a person can seem to have a different personality when speaking a different language. She prefers French Hugo. His name, in her head, with the dropped *H*, seems like a completely different word.

SOPHIE WAITS BY the drive when Juliette pulls the car up to the house. She is picking at a lavender plant. Her lanky frame is draped in an oversized T-shirt paired with narrow gray jeans and black sneakers. Her hair hangs at the sides of her face like two curtains, threatening to be drawn any moment.

"Hey, Soph," Rosie says. "We got *pain au chocolat*." She waggles a bag out the window. Juliette watches Sophie give a false smile.

"Great," she says wanly. "Hi, Uncle Hugo."

"Hi, Sophie." Hugo is already up and out of the car, holding the door open for Beth, who clambers out, all legs. She holds her handbag close to her side and smiles at Sophie.

"You've met Beth?" Nina asks her daughter.

Sophie gives a weary look. "You introduced us last night, Mum."

"Oh, right."

Juliette remembers when everything her mother said or did was exasperating or odd or both. When, like Sophie, she used to chalk up every mistake. A never-ending performance review. She regrets it so much now.

"Where's your dad?" Nina asks.

"I don't know," Sophie says. "When I got back, everyone had vanished."

Beth and Rosie head into the house while Juliette goes to the car trunk and passes Hugo bags to carry inside.

"Is Helen back?" Nina asks Sophie.

"I don't know. I don't know what Helen looks like."

"Yes, you do. You remember your aunty Helen."

"No, I don't."

"She lives in New York. She owns an art gallery. Max and Helen are very close . . . She's a good friend . . ."

Sophie's expression is mutinous. Juliette grips the remaining bags and gently closes the trunk.

"Oh, Soph, you remember Helen—"

"No," Sophie interrupts. "Why do people always say that—'you remember'? Like saying 'you remember' is going to *make* you remember. It's so dumb."

Sophie's baby-soft blond hair shifts; the black tips look like feathers serving to warn the world she is no one's baby. Juliette glances away, beyond the box hedge lining the drive, beyond the apple trees, to leaves shaking in the distance. A disk of light among the branches momentarily distracts her.

"Well, she's a friend of ours and she's bringing her sister," Juliette hears Nina explaining.

"How old is she?"

"Helen's sister? Twenty-five, I think? Ish?"

"So I'm the only kid here."

"What, darling?"

"I don't get it. You know I could've stayed with Ella. Her mum said it was okay. What am I even doing here?"

"We wanted to have fun, as a family . . ." Nina's voice trails off.

There is that flash of light again. Juliette tries to make it out, wondering if it is a mirror hung in the trees to scare away the birds.

"Are you listening to me, Mum?"

"Sorry?"

"You aren't listening to me."

"I was trying to see . . ." Nina is looking into the trees too. Juliette makes out a pair of bare legs and shorts.

"Mum!"

"There's someone in that tree . . . ," Nina murmurs.

Juliette can see him now too. A boy. Or someone growing out of being a boy. His brown hair is thick and ruffled, his skin tanned to caramel. He wears a shirt rolled up at the cuffs. There is a glint coming from his wrist. The sunlight is reflecting off the face of a watch.

"I'm going inside," Sophie huffs.

"Sophie!" Nina calls to her back.

She wheels around. "Yes?" Her voice has a threat in it.

Nina raises her palms. "We'll have a good time, okay? Look at this gorgeous house, and the food is wonderful . . ."

Sophie's expression remains impassive.

"The beach is close by . . . we can go swimming," Nina gently appeals.

"I hate swimming."

"You *don't* hate swimming," Nina insists. "You love swimming. You had that green-and-white swimming costume . . . when you were little . . ."

"See?" Sophie says. "God, you think I'm a baby. You think I know nothing. And you're doing it again: 'You remember, you *love* swimming.'"

"But you *do*."

"No, Mum, I don't," Sophie says sternly.

Juliette bets Sophie pours out all her frustrations on her mother as though she deserves it, has *earned* it, somehow, for bringing her into the world. Speaking to her as though she is simply the most infuriating person on the planet. And Nina, usually so poised and in control, is uncharacteristically passive in her daughter's presence, trying to appease her, longing for her love.

"I hate swimming," Sophie adds.

"Sophie!"

Juliette watches the avian tips of Sophie's hair swish across the back of her T-shirt as she turns and Nina rushes after her. This is an argument on repeat. Juliette turns back to the trees and lifts her free hand to the neighbors' sixteen-year-old son.

"*Bonjour,* Etienne."

"*Bonjour,* Juliette."

LARS IS IN the kitchen when Juliette returns inside. He is at the counter eating, still wearing his running gear. Nina goes to him, fitting neatly under his chin.

"Sweaty," he warns. Nina shrugs and kisses him anyway.

"Sophie found you?" she asks.

"Came in, gave me a look like I was dead meat, and then left," Lars replies.

"Glad it's not just me she seems to despise," Nina says with a sigh.

Juliette starts putting food into the fridge. It's one of her favorite chores: returning from the hunt.

Nina drinks from Lars's water glass. "Says she doesn't want to be here. She wants to be with Ella. And she's cross because I told her she remembers Helen and she says she doesn't . . ."

"Huh?" Lars says.

"It doesn't matter."

"She doesn't remember Helen? No. She remembers Helen."

Nina raises an eyebrow. "That's what I said."

"I'll talk to her." Lars takes his glass back.

"How was your run?"

"Good. I took Eddie with me and we went down to the beach. It's incredible. This huge, wild beach, the gulls riding on the thermals; it was empty except for us. Beautiful. Eddie, on the other hand . . ." Lars laughs. "I thought he was going to expire."

Nina grins. "Last night's booze?"

"Guess so. I kept it pretty slow but he gave up halfway. By the time I got back here he was . . . well, he was like that."

Lars points out to the garden. Eddie is on his back in the grass, arms and legs spread-eagled, sunglasses covering his eyes. They all laugh.

"Bless him," Nina says, wiping her eyes. "He'll never change."

They watch Beth approach and lean over him. Eddie lifts his head for a kiss. Beth frowns, tests his forehead with her palm and strokes his hair.

"How long do you give it?" Nina murmurs. Lars has his hand against the curve of Nina's back.

"Not sure. This one seems different."

"You're an optimist," says Nina softly, leaning back against him.

"That's true," Lars says, and kisses the top of Nina's head.

"Look at you two," Helen's voice purrs from the door.

Lars and Nina open their arms at the same time.

"Hi, Juliette," Helen says over her shoulder as she floats into their embrace.

"*Bonjour,* Helen," Juliette replies, smiling.

"You are as gorgeous as ever," Lars declares, holding Helen at arm's length. She is wearing a long black dress with leather sandals and a necklace made of large, misshapen silver links.

"I need him around every morning," Helen says to Nina. "How are you?"

"We're good, sweetheart."

"I haven't seen your Sophie. Where is she?"

Nina lifts her shoulders. "Around, somewhere. She's *not pleased* with us. Me mainly."

"No?"

"Teenagers don't much like to holiday with their parents."

Helen raises an eyebrow. "No . . ."

"It's good for us to all be together," Lars insists.

"Yes, of course," Helen replies, patting Lars's arm fondly. "It's nice for *all* of us to be together. Took us long enough. When was the last time?"

"Rosie and Hugo's wedding?"

"That was years ago. Decades." Nina is shaking her head.

"But all of us . . . together? It might have been," Helen says. "How are they anyway? Rosie and Hugo. I walked past their room but it sounded like they were having an argument."

"What about?"

"Don't know. Rosie telling him he didn't have to know everything about everything and him saying she acts like he doesn't know anything about anything. I didn't get involved." Helen pulls a grape off its stalk in a fruit bowl beside them and pops it in her mouth.

Nina frowns. "You know them. They always argue. Maybe a bit more lately . . ."

Helen crunches through her grape. "Is Hugo still an arse?"

Lars laughs. "Tell us how you really feel."

"Well, he is an arse." Helen shrugs.

"He feels like a fifth wheel when we're all together. You and Max don't help that," Nina replies.

"I still think Eddie and Rosie . . . ," Helen murmurs.

"Ho ho!" Lars says, laughing. "Now there's ancient history."

"That probably weighs on his mind too . . . ," Nina muses.

"Hugo's an okay bloke, Helen. Bit stiff and all that, but he takes care of our Rosie," Lars says.

"He better."

"Be nice." Nina wags her finger, smiling.

"All right," Helen mutters.

"And whatever you do, don't mention Eddie and Rosie. It always sets Hugo off."

"Don't mention it? See, I told you there was something—"

Nina scoffs. "Helen Barnett, there is not *something*. There is *nothing*. It's ancient history, like Lars said. Eddie's got a girlfriend here."

"That one?" Helen nods toward the window.

"Her name is Beth," Lars says.

"We shouldn't make her feel awkward. Or Hugo," Nina instructs.

Helen shakes her head. "Awkward? Hugo? Hugo does awkward all by himself."

"You promised you'd be nice."

"Yeah, well, I might retract it," Helen says mutinously.

Juliette interjects: "Helen? Have you seen Max yet? He's been very keen to see you."

Helen turns. "Not yet. Where is he?"

"He was out the back," Lars replies. "But he might be having a shower now. He only got in a few hours ago."

"Why was he so late?"

Juliette shrugs, not mentioning that he'd stunk of alcohol and sweat. Helen laughs, her good spirits back.

"God love him. I'll find him. Soleil is putting her things in our room. She'll be down in a minute."

"The mysterious sister," Lars says.

"The very one," Helen replies.

Chapter Six

MAX

Max laughs to himself under the shower, thinking about Eddie. Messy, hopeful, and hilarious Eddie. Thank God for him. For still collecting Star Wars dolls (figurines!) in his late thirties, for tattooing a gecko on his arse cheek while drunk in Perth, for persuading his parents to continue paying for his health insurance. For being as useless at love as Max is.

Max doesn't keep in contact with Eddie enough, but it never seems to matter when they see each other again. It's as though no time has passed. They are still stupid; they are still just boys. They will always be boys. Being with Eddie makes Max feel better, makes him feel like less of a failure. The girls, Nina and Rosie, they're great, but sometimes they make Max feel like an anomaly. Like he hasn't quite got his shit together. But there is never any judgment with Eddie.

Helen manages to fit into both worlds. Rosie and Nina love her, but so do Eddie and Max and Lars. She is comfortable with any one of them. When she walks into a room no one looks away, not even Hugo. She's something to look toward, sure. But it is more than that. Helen makes people feel good, she makes people laugh, she knows how to light up a place. A couple of times she had appeared unannounced after one of Max's shows, and in those times Max felt like he was twenty feet tall, the best, the luckiest man on the planet.

The three girls had been practically inseparable at college. Helen had introduced Rosie to Nina and the rest of the group after Rosie and Helen met in a class. Max remembers the studious, pretty Rosie paired with bohemian and rebellious Helen. If Rosie was a rose, as her name suggested, then Helen was a fragrant, bright-tongued orchid. Nina fell somewhere in between them; she was as earnest as she was fun. She scolded them all sternly, when required, but had the fullest laugh. All three of them loved Tori Amos and Björk. They argued about politics, art, and celebrity gossip. They read and swapped *The Handmaid's Tale* and *Midnight's Children* and a dozen or so Danielle Steel paperbacks with well-worn corners and swollen pages. They drank cider from plastic bottles, Malibu and Coke, and cheap wine out of boxes. Rosie was competitive and giggly when drunk, Nina sleepy and sweet, Helen wild and affectionate. All three of them loved to dance.

Max's memories of that time are so vivid, as though the decade had been placed under a bell jar: captured, crystal clear, beautiful, and preserved. Why those years are so bright and perfect, and everything else since seems blurry and nondescript, Max isn't sure. It can't *just* be the drugs; Max used drugs back then too and drank a lot, if not more. These days he feels old and tired. He has even been growing tired of his work too, though he could not admit it to anyone. Playing with the Jacks was a dream job—how could he be sick of it? What would he do otherwise? There is nothing else Max is good at.

Max doesn't like to think that the memories in the bell

jar are his best years and there are only less great, blurry ones from here on out. No. It isn't going to be that way for him. He has a plan. A Great Plan. He is going to keep his life *and* make it even better. If life is a game, he is winning; he is streaks ahead.

Max gets out of the shower and hurriedly dries off. He pulls on underwear and a pair of shorts and walks into the hallway bare-chested, carrying his T-shirt. He notices movement in Helen's room and feels his face splitting into a grin before he sees her. He wants to run. He wants to shout, *Helen, I've got a great idea!* But when he steps into the doorway a small figure with dark hair in a huge bun, wearing loose trousers and a bright orange crop top, turns to face him. Her skin is soft brown, like a hazelnut. She meets his gaze. Green eyes, freckles across the bridge of her nose. She glances down at his chest.

"Sorry, thought you were Helen."

"You must be Max." Her voice is flat.

"Soleil?"

She nods.

"Nice to meet you," Max says, rearranging his thoughts. He gives his most charming smile.

Soleil blinks and then continues unpacking clothes. They're neatly folded in a pale blue suitcase, like one you might see in a show from the seventies. Max notices her bun is made of dreadlocks, thick coils curled around one another. Max had been expecting someone young and shy, vulnerable. Helen had said Soleil was going through a hard time. Young women going through hard times were Max's forte.

"This is your house, right?"

"Yes. You like it?"

"I think you ruined the landscape, to be totally honest with you."

Max suddenly wishes he had put his shirt on. He crosses his arms. "Okay."

"The old house must have been handsome as it was."

"It was falling apart." Max's voice is defensive.

"Old houses tend to do that. You're supposed to repair them, not bolt on something new and out of place."

"Out of place . . . Right."

"It's like Frankenstein's monster."

"Frankenstein's monster?"

Soleil pauses for a moment. "Your kitchen is nice though."

"Oh, well then."

They stand in silence for an uncomfortable length of time, the suitcase of clothes between them.

"Helen says you're a musician," Soleil says.

"Guitarist. For the Jacks." Max tries to sound humble but that doesn't work either. Fuck it. If being in the Jacks doesn't impress her nothing will. His house is like Frankenstein's monster? His house is gorgeous. Everyone loves the house.

"Like, more than one Jack?" Soleil asks.

"Sorry?"

"You said 'the Jacks.'"

"Yeah. *The* Jacks . . . Fuck, are you serious?"

Soleil's face clouds over.

"You've never heard of the Jacks?"

"Should I have?"

Max laughs but it's not the laugh he was aiming for—the wry but carefree one. The one that says, *You're hilarious, sweetheart.* Max's laugh comes out bitter and makes him feel old. He briefly thinks of coke—just a bump would do the trick—before reluctantly remembering his promise. Not here, not while he's with the others. He changes tack. "Helen said you were having a hard time."

Soleil crosses her arms. "Is that right?"

"You're not having a hard time?"

"Do I look like I'm having a hard time?"

Max throws up his hands. "I'm just making conversation."

Soleil shrugs. "You don't have to. Not on my account."

"I'll leave you to unpack then."

Max waits for a beat. No apology, no "thank you for having me." He shakes his head and slips on his T-shirt.

"Lovely to meet you!" he calls out behind him, when he is in the hallway. Something in his voice reminds him of being a kid, reminds him, dare he say it, of his father. The sarcasm that emanated from him like a stink when he was drunk. Arrogance and bitterness, believing the world owed him something.

HELEN MAKES MAX think of Elbow lyrics. Those are the songs he wishes he'd written. Poetry. The real stuff. Raw and honest and bleeding and hopeful. Asking her to back a horse that's good for glue, dreams of marriage in an orange grove, admitting he's too stubborn, selfish, and old . . .

She's the only thing in any room she's ever in.

"Max. There you are."

Her smile is wide and white, her hair shiny. She opens her arms and he steps into them, the perfect circle. She wraps him up and into her and laughs, and the sound is better than water against the shore, better than rain on a roof, better than any track he ever wrote.

She smells like cigarettes and soap and jam and flowers.

She smells like love.

"How are you?"

"Better now I've seen you."

"You old flirt."

"Easy on the 'old.'"

"Forty now, Maxie."

"Did you think I forgot?"

She holds him away for a moment. "Looking good for forty."

"No shit."

They are both giggling. When Max had needed family, Helen had been family. Sister, friend, aunty—always, always there for him. No matter how much he screwed up.

Lars walks past holding a platter. "You two found each other, I see," he says with a wink.

Max thinks of the box in his room and his Great Plan, and his heart starts to race. "We did," he replies.

Helen squeezes his forearms. "Should we help Juliette with lunch?"

"Yeah, let's do that."

"Then a walk on the beach and a smoke and pretend no one else is around?"

"Perfect."

Max wants to pull her back to him, to have all of her body pressed against all of his body, but he lets her go and her hand slips down his arm to his hand and he catches it. Her touch makes his skin feel warm and electric. Alive.

She leads him into the kitchen.

JULIETTE HAS MADE a feast. The outdoor table is cloaked in French linen and dotted with sparkling glasses, heavy silver cutlery, and posies of herbs and flowers cut from the garden:

fragrant stalks of lavender, dill fronds, sprigs of rosemary, puffs of Lightlime hydrangeas, silvery sage leaves. Platters are piled high with food to share: buckwheat galettes stuffed with langoustine and artichokes bound with a cream sauce; a huge leek tart freckled with fresh thyme leaves; two simple salads, panzanella and a green one with slices of duck and scattered with walnuts; and a massive, heaving dish of local seafood. Max grabs Juliette's hand as she walks by and thanks her, but she simply smiles and shrugs. Juliette is the best thing for this house, his *Frankenstein's monster.*

Max glances now at Soleil, who is talking to Sophie. Sophie whom he remembers as a five-year-old but who suddenly looks twenty, though he knows she is fifteen. It's her face and the way she holds her mouth—dissatisfied, disappointed, knowing so much and scared of more than she'll admit. The look of an adult.

Soleil looks like she is enjoying her food, though Max has not yet seen her smile. She's folding and pushing a galette into her mouth like she hasn't eaten for days. Helen, sitting next to her, has her hand resting on Soleil's shoulder. She grins at Max and he raises his glass in reply.

Hugo, sitting at the head of the table, of course, though it isn't his table, leans over to shake Max's hand. "Hi, Max."

"Hi, Hugo."

"Happy birthday."

"Thanks, mate."

It's formal and forced. Hugo the surgeon, the smart one, better than everyone, seems uncomfortable. Max is glad. Max is also glad Hugo's hair seems to be thinning; his face is more lined, his expression more sour. Max hopes Rosie doesn't screw him much, hopes she no longer gives him blow jobs. She has barely looked over at her husband the whole lunch, whispering instead with Nina as they always do, like they're planning something. When Hugo stands up and excuses himself, no one pays much notice.

Max looks back to Helen. The lyrics of Elbow songs say it better than he could. *Violets exploding . . . when I meet your eyes . . . clouds of starlings . . .*

He should be kinder. It is the noble thing to do.

He must remember to be nice.

Max reaches over to the seafood platter: an arrangement of oysters in their shells, spider crab, a gleaming red lobster. Juliette is showing Beth how to extract *un bigorneau* from its shell with a toothpick. Max gives Beth a benevolent smile and tips an oyster into his mouth. Here is a sign of him being grown-up: he eats oysters now. The Cancale oysters are small and clear, dressed simply. A good oyster tastes simply of rock and ocean—fresh, salty, delicious—like a woman laid back in his bed.

Eddie slaps Max's back. "Hey, mate, remember that Christmas party in Borough?"

Nina and Rosie look over, listening in.

"Tell me," Max encourages him.

Eddie clears his throat. "We were in that old pub near the market. They were bankers—"

"Lawyers," Nina says.

"Lawyers. You're right. Of course. Hot, smart chicks in little skirts and the men—all wankers."

Beth, Eddie's girl, laughs. She's wearing a headscarf, blue with white flowers, against her red hair. It actually looks pretty good on her. Of course Max remembers the Christmas party; he just wants to hear Eddie tell it.

"We all got so drunk. You girls were drinking that horrible stuff. Wine coolers? What was in that stuff?"

"Not much wine. Not good wine, that was for sure," Rosie murmurs.

"We were wasted. I was trying to get Rosie to come to bed with me—"

Max glances at Hugo's seat beside him, but it's empty. He notices Beth turn toward the garden.

"You were?" Nina frowns. "But—"

"Yeah, I know. It was over but . . . ah, you know me. I was all, 'I love her!' 'I need her to be mine!' " Eddie clasps his hands together for effect. Rosie laughs, pleased.

Max swallows down the concern that he's exactly like that about Helen. A bit pathetic. Needy. But it's different. Max needs Helen but she needs him too. He glances over at her but she's talking to Soleil. A shame. This is a good story. Next to them, Sophie has her camera out and is taking photos. It's one of those small ones made to look old. She points it at Max and clicks. He blinks and smiles, but she's pointing it toward Juliette now, busy clearing plates.

"She was having none of it," Eddie says, and sighs.

"Rosie was with that lawyer in the broom cupboard, wasn't she?" Max asks, smiling.

Rosie pinches and twists her fingers by her mouth, pretending to lock her lips.

"Was she? Glad I didn't know that at the time. I would have been heartbroken."

"Oh, please." Nina rolls her eyes.

"Anyway, all of us blind, including you and Lars, if I recall . . ."

"Surely not," Lars says with mock sincerity.

"No, surely not," Eddie scoffs. "Anyway, so *all* of us drunk, but most especially Max. Max dying to impress Helen—"

"As per usual," Nina says.

"Hey!" Max protests.

"As per usual," Eddie echoes. "And then he, God knows how, negotiates an arrangement with the party Santa to swap his own clothes for the Santa suit."

Max chuckles. Eddie winks at him.

"He's got girls sitting on his knee all night, telling them whether they've been naughty or nice."

"Genius," Lars says.

"Absolute genius, except that it doesn't interest Helen at all, who is stuck in some debate about aid in Africa or the reduction of funding for the arts or some bullshit. So off Max goes to have some quality time with one of those lovely, short-skirted women somewhere or other, maybe the broom cupboard?" Eddie shakes his head. "I cannot believe I have never had sex in a broom cupboard." He turns to Nina, as though Max is not sitting next to him. "Do you reckon Max has a broom cupboard here?"

"I don't reckon Max has swept a floor in a good many years. You might have to ask Juliette—"

"I'm still here!" Max objects.

"Good idea," Eddie says to Nina, like he isn't.

"Back to the story," Nina demands.

"Yes. So there's Max, rooting some bird in the—let's just call it the broom cupboard, pissed as a newt, and eventually the girl leaves, and the cupboard, or whatever it is, is all his and he's drunk and sleepy and the Santa costume is snug and cozy and he falls asleep. Which is great. Except that when he wakes up the whole bar is shut and locked up . . ." Eddie snorts and slaps his thigh.

"How'd he get out?" Nina asks, laughing, already knowing the answer.

"Had to squeeze himself out the toilet window and jump a fence! In a bloody Santa suit! Wandering down the high street in a Santa costume!"

They are all in hysterics now. Helen finally looks over.

Eddie adds, "Didn't you say some kid on the tube asked his mummy if Santa was ill?"

"Yes, there was a kid, and God, I was sick." Max laughs, shaking his head.

Nina sighs. "I'd love to see the surveillance footage. Drunk Santa, squeezing himself out the loo window . . ."

"Are you talking about that Christmas party in Borough?" Helen asks.

Soleil, sitting next to her, is looking on, watching her sister smile at Max.

"God, you were a fool." Helen laughs.

Remembering the Christmas party makes Max long for the whole lot of them as they were back then. It seems like a different lifetime that they were so young, so unburdened.

Juliette passes around small plates and cake forks. Max watches Beth rise and join Sophie sitting in the garden, two pink spots on her cheeks. When the others go back to their conversations and Hugo returns to his chair, Max notices Lars staring at him.

"You miss it."

Max nods.

"It's hard not to," Lars sympathizes.

"We had a laugh."

"Sometimes I want to delete every year since and be back there in that life. It was so easy."

"I know what you mean," Max agrees.

"But . . ." Lars glances at his daughter, sitting on the grass, with so much love it almost makes Max wince. "Then we wouldn't have Soph."

Sophie appears to be taking a photo of her dirty plate—remains of tart and dressing-soaked salad leaves and sticky, smeared cream sauce—while Beth is doing her hair.

"No," Max says, though he doesn't really understand. He catches Nina looking over at them. "You got a good one here, Nina," he says, tipping his head to Lars.

"Don't I know it." Her face is soft and sweet.

"Hey, hey," Lars mocks. "Technically I'm still single." He presents his naked ring finger.

Max nods. "When are you making an honest man out of him, Nina?"

"I prefer him dishonest," Nina replies, smiling.

Max's parents had been married. He knows this because of another one of the photographs he'd pilfered and studied, rubbed over with his thumb as though doing so would bring the woman in it to life, would reanimate her. But she is trapped in black and white, dark hair rising up from her forehead, two stiff curls on either side of her dark, staring eyes. Her hands are hidden behind a small bouquet and she appears footless because her dress makes a tent over her shoes. Her face is the biggest mystery. Max has stared and stared, looking for clues, but he never finds any. Was she happy? Was she scared? Was she real? Her face gives nothing away. Max didn't know if his mother had wanted to marry his father. He didn't know if she had loved him. In the photo she is a mannequin, waxy and unreadable.

Thinking of proposals and weddings makes Max's heart race, makes him wish for a stiff drink.

"How many times have you proposed?" Max asks.

"Oh, mate, too many to remember," Lars replies, blowing out air dramatically. "I've given up. If you're ever thinking about it, come to me, I'm a pro."

Max gives an anxious laugh.

Lars pours Muscadet into the glasses around him and then passes the bottle along. Max serves himself a big glass and brings it to his lips, relishing the slight prickle of it against his tongue and the chill against his teeth.

From the garden two figures walk into Max's line of sight. He blinks away his nerves and memories. Two women giggling: Beth and Sophie returning from the garden. Sophie is actually smiling. She has pretty teeth. Nina's teeth, to be exact. And her freckles, she gets those from Lars; they peek through her makeup. Blue eyes and slender fingers from her father, sturdy ankles like her mother's. It still astounds Max that Sophie is made up of Nina and Lars, that she is constructed of them. He finds it baffling and unnerving. Makes him wonder about the elements he is made up from, equal parts bully and ghost.

"Your hair," Rosie exclaims.

Max has to look again. Sophie's hair is fixed in a braid that weaves across the front of her head. The black tips, just the odd streak or two, hide among the twists. Little light strands, too short to be contained, stick out and catch the light. It gives her a kind of halo.

"Lovely, darling," Lars says.

"You look beautiful," Helen agrees. "Like a Greek goddess."

"Athena," Hugo specifies.

"Thanks," Sophie mumbles, looking at the ground and then back up at Nina. "Glad someone noticed."

"Beth did it?" Nina asks gently.

"She's a hairdresser," Sophie replies, nodding toward Beth.

"She has such a pretty neck," Beth says, her Kentucky accent slow and rolling.

"Yes," Nina agrees quietly.

They talk of other things. House prices in London. Insurance. Mulching. But Max is still thinking about marriage and family, looking at Nina as she continues to stare at her daughter, wearing her crown of hair. Nina's eyes slowly fill with tears. Max is about to reach out when Nina stands up too fast. The glass in her hand falls and smashes on the tabletop, and Nina wobbles and then braces herself, palms upon the broken glass. She winces. Looks at Max. Then slumps back into her chair with a noise like someone being punched, air fleeing her lungs, pain about to follow.

Chapter Seven

JULIETTE

There is blood on the tablecloth: two large blots and several constellations of crimson specks.

Juliette attends to Nina with Helen as helper. The cuts aren't bad, but they're bad enough. Sophie is pale and Lars looks like he's been struck. Helen fetches a bowl of warm water and a soft cloth without being told where to find them. She instructs Max to get the antiseptic solution that Juliette says is in the bathroom annex next to her room at the front of the house. Beth comforts Sophie, explaining that the blood will soon clot and it won't look so dreadful. Soleil leaves and returns with Bach Rescue Remedy, which she places next to Juliette's knee as she squats in front of Nina. Rosie is sobbing; she has to turn away. Nina is crying a little too, though through the tears she keeps saying her hands are fine and she's fine, trying to catch Rosie's attention, to reassure her. Hugo stands to one side, tall and frowning. As useful as a bowling pin.

Helen and Juliette take a hand each and inspect them for fragments of glass, wiping each palm carefully with a cloth.

"It's not as bad as it looks," Hugo says, sounding haughty.

He glances sternly at his wife, who is still visibly shaken, then back to Helen and Juliette. "Don't let the cuts get infected."

"Thanks, Hugo," Helen snaps.

Juliette glances at Helen's fingers as she runs her fingertips over Nina's palm. Hugo finally leads Rosie away, sniffing, with an arm around her shoulders.

"They're fine," Nina demurs again, trying to withdraw her hands. "It's just shock. I'm okay. Truly."

Juliette catches her wrists. "You need some bandages."

Max returns with the antiseptic wash as instructed. Juliette pours a capful into the bowl of water. She and Helen take turns dipping cloths into it and cleaning the wounds. Soleil snips medical tape into smaller sizes. Nina needs two bandages on her right hand and three on her left. She has stopped crying now.

"Are you okay, Mum?" Sophie whispers.

"Fine, love. Perfectly fine." She holds up her palms. "See?"

"You just—" Lars says.

"Got off-balance. It's nothing. The heat, the wine . . . It's nothing."

Lars and Sophie nod together.

"Maybe you need some ocean air," Soleil suggests.

Juliette glances at the newcomer. She keeps trying to see Helen in Soleil, but of course they are very different. Soleil has none of Helen's beauty, though Soleil is very striking. Helen's beauty comes from her warmth; Soleil, on the other hand, is cool and aloof. Soleil's beauty is exotic and unpredictable. She's blunt and detached and, now, oddly helpful.

"Good idea," Beth enthuses. "I think Hugo took Rosie that way."

Max looks at Nina. "A walk on the beach?"

"Thank you but I think I'll just sit here for a bit. All of you go. It'll make me feel like less of a dunce."

Sophie looks to her mum. "Do you want me to stay—"

"No, love, you go."

"I'll stay," Lars says, dragging over a chair to sit beside her, stroking the hair from her face.

Max looks to Helen. Juliette picks up the bowl and backing paper from the bandages. She stands to move back inside.

"Will you go, Juliette?" Helen asks.

Juliette looks quickly at Max. "Oh. No, I'd better clean up from lunch." Juliette doesn't want to mention the cloths or the bowl of water, now a disconcerting shade of pink.

"Are you sure?"

"Yes, thank you."

"I'll help," Helen says.

Max frowns and tugs on Helen's arm. "She's fine, Helen, she just said so."

"No, she didn't," Helen says. "I'll help."

"I'm fine," Juliette assures Helen, glancing at her boss. Max stares at Helen, imploring.

"I want to make sure Nina is okay. You go, Max."

"But you said . . ." Max looks petulant. He glances at Juliette.

"It's okay, Helen, truly, it's my job," Juliette says quickly.

"Oh, don't be stupid," Helen rebukes. "No one likes doing dishes, for God's sake, I'll help."

Eddie calls out to Max. "You coming, mate? Show us the local bird life?"

To which Max forces a smile and says, "On my way."

HELEN FOLLOWS JULIETTE to the kitchen with the bowl of bloodied water, tipping it down the sink. The kitchen benches are covered with dirty plates and platters. Helen starts stacking them into the dishwasher while Juliette transfers leftovers to smaller bowls and wraps them with cling film.

"Thank you," Juliette says.

"That's okay."

Helen is stacking the plates haphazardly and some of the glasses she's put in are the wrong way up. They'll fill with water when the dishwasher starts.

"I hear you used to own a restaurant? In Paris?" Helen asks.

"I did." Juliette covers a small bowl of panzanella.

"What was it called?"

"Delphine. It's a name but it also means 'dolphin.' It sounds better in French, I think."

"Max says you make something delicious . . . what's it—"

"Kouign-amann."

"Queen . . . a man . . . ?"

Juliette smiles. "Something like that." She likes the sound of Helen's voice. British and American both, the edges raspy, probably from smoking, as though sandpapered rough. "It means 'butter cake,'" she explains. "It's actually just pastry and butter—a lot of butter—and sugar, but the key is the caramelization. It tastes a bit like croissant, a bit like brioche, and it is sticky throughout."

"Yum."

"It's basically a heart attack," Juliette admits.

Helen laughs. "Sounds amazing."

"It originated here, in Douarnenez. I grew up making it. It's become popular elsewhere now. It's simple once you know how. There's a chocolatier in Paris who sells hundreds and hundreds of them, all in different flavors. But I can't make flavors. To me there is only one flavor."

Her restaurant manager, Louis, had informed her that

her competitor Leon had added *kouignn-amann* to his dessert menu, rum-soaked and accompanied by pineapple sorbet.

"You're a traditionalist."

Juliette pauses. "Well, with *kouign-amann* I am. It's . . . I don't know . . . perfect as it is."

"Apart from the health effects," Helen jokes.

"But we're French, we don't worry about that. It's not the point."

"Do you ever miss it? Paris? Or the restaurant?"

Juliette pauses. Of course she has been asked before, especially by people in the village. She has a repertoire of standard answers that all elude the truth. Because the truth is like a cut diamond; it has many sides: yes, no, always, and never— all of them partially true and none of them completely true. Sometimes she missed the racket of the Delphine kitchen, the sibling-hood with the other chefs, the rowdy, laughing drinks at the end of a long shift. Sometimes she missed the lights of Paris, even that sparkling Tour Eiffel, a gaudy, year-round Christmas tree, which so many others hated. She missed the peacefulness of Musée de l'Orangerie on a weekday, when she had a rare day off from the restaurant; the pastries fresh out of Henri's oven and the way he talked of his dog as though it were an infant. She missed friends. For fleeting moments, she missed being important, being special. And then, at other times, she missed nothing at all. She had expected to miss more. One of the last times she had visited Paris, before her dad had died, she sat at a café table across the road from Delphine's entrance. She watched staff arrive, deliveries in boxes and crates dropped off at the side door, and blinds lifted. She had planned to get things in order for when she would return, for when her father was well again. Instead she sat across from Delphine and let the coffee she'd ordered grow cold. Pedestrians, bikes, dogs, and conversations rushed past her, the city bustling, honking, and clattering as always, and Juliette had never felt so alone, so dislocated. She longed for her mother, her love and wisdom, and her father's quiet and steadying presence. She longed for the person who had broken her heart, whom she was supposed to be forgetting. It was almost cruel how much a person needed kindnesses, needed touch. Juliette's longing made her ache. Louis had been right about many things, but particularly about dating a politician. Especially a married one. That was the problem with the heart, it didn't take good advice and it never listened to reason. Sitting across from Delphine, watching her old life as though in the audience of a play, Juliette had known with a sad, chilling emptiness in her stomach that her heart no longer belonged in Paris. Her bond with the city had loosened, had become unstitched.

"I came back to Douarnenez when my mother died," Juliette answers, as truthful as she can be while avoiding the questions directly.

"I am so sorry."

"You weren't to know."

"Are your parents—"

"My father died not long after. We didn't know he was ill too. He had been looking after my mother."

"Oh." Helen's voice is soft.

They work in silence for a moment while Helen tries to wedge dishes within the strange pattern and mess she's made of the ones she's already stacked. Juliette watches her out of the corner of her eye while expertly rearranging the fridge to make room for the leftovers to go in.

"You said that you own a gallery?" Juliette asks Helen.

"I do."

"That must be fascinating."

"Yeah," Helen says. "Actually . . ." She looks to the ceiling. "It was. It's become much more commercial, more of a game than it was. I mean, I really love art. I loved making art once too, but I have no time for that these days."

"That's a shame."

"I guess so. I don't know if I still have it in me, to be honest."

"Of course you do."

Helen laughs. "I'm not so sure."

"Those kinds of things don't get lost."

"It feels a bit lost."

"I'm sure it's all still there," Juliette encourages.

After her mom's death, Juliette had cooked for her father. She had made difficult phone calls. Helped to arrange a funeral. And then another after that. Juliette learned that impossible things were possible, even dreadful, impossible things.

Helen straightens up. "Did Max tell you we all met at Camberwell? At art college?"

"Yes. I've been meaning to ask about that . . . Max was an artist too?"

Helen nods. "Max was a photographer. Actually, he was pretty good. Now it's all channeled into music and lyrics, but he used to take incredible photographs."

"What about the others?"

"Oh. Well, Rosie was amazing. *Is* amazing. Great at detail work and very neat—you can probably imagine. Nina wasn't at school with us; she studied journalism and was dating Lars, obviously. Lars majored in sculpture, like me, but was mostly interested in ceramics. Eddie studied graphic design." Helen smiles to herself.

"You were close," Juliette says.

"Very. It was, I don't know . . . a moment in time, you know? We partied. A lot. We drank too much. We played music and talked about art till the sun came up. We forgot to eat. We went without sleep. We wore each other's clothes. We smoked hundreds of cigarettes."

Juliette can picture it. Younger versions of Rosie and Nina whispering and giggling, just as they do now. Lars and Eddie choosing music. Max smoking and Helen sitting on his knee. The room dark and warm, smelling of take-out food—smoke, grease, and salt—of spilled red wine. Bright young faces. Lives ahead of them.

"We had nothing," says Helen. "No money, no responsibilities, no mortgages, no kids. We just had each other."

"Max speaks very fondly of you all."

Except for Hugo, Juliette doesn't add. Rosie, "bless her cotton socks"; Nina, "who keeps us all in check"; Lars, "most decent bloke you'll ever meet"; Eddie, "funny, *so* funny, more of a brother than a mate."

Helen.

"Does he? Bless him. What does he say?" Helen asks.

"You can tell he cares for you all. Very much."

Helen narrows her eyes. "Has he sworn you to secrecy?"

"No . . ."

Helen laughs. "It's okay, you don't have to say."

Lars sticks his head into the kitchen, blinking his long, pale lashes. Helen pauses, holding a plate.

"Hey," Helen says.

"Hey," Lars replies. "I'm just going to take Nina upstairs. For a quick lie-down."

"Is she okay?"

"She's fine. Just tired."

"She works too hard," Helen says.

Lars nods. "You okay here? Juliette? Need a hand?"

"I'm fine, thank you. Helen is helping."

Lars peers over to the dishwasher. "Yeah, I can see that. Looks like Helen's handiwork."

"What do you mean?" Helen asks.

"Trust fund baby," Lars whispers to Juliette. "Knows her way around a polo club, a scrubbing brush not so much."

Juliette tries not to smile while Helen rolls her eyes. "Fuck you, Lars."

"Fuck you too, Helen," Lars replies. He winks and leaves.

Helen and Juliette look down into the dishwasher together.

"It's bad, isn't it?" Helen murmurs.

"Well . . . ," Juliette says carefully. Then they both start laughing.

"I'm not very good at this kind of thing. Max and me— we're not very practical."

"You fixed up Nina's hands. You were great."

"Oh. Well. A crisis, you see. That's different."

"Then you are good in a crisis. That's something." Juliette thinks of how many crises there have been in the past year. One after the next, like dominoes.

"But not helpful when you need to get the dishes done. You know, like, every day."

"Give that to me." Juliette plucks the plate out of Helen's hand. "I'm good at getting dishes done."

"God, Max is lucky," Helen says with a sigh. She leans back against the counter, crosses one slender ankle over the other and blows back the dark hair that has fallen over her face.

"Yes, he is," Juliette agrees.

DOUARNENEZ, 2014

They sat on the seawall together, looking down at the harbor, dark green and briny, a couple of disinterested tourists walking over one of the moored boats, a display for the nearby maritime museum. Louis opened the brown paper bag and peered inside, nose wrinkling. Louis's first reaction was nearly always resistance. He was a cautious person by nature. He removed the pastry with his thumb and forefinger and took a bite. Juliette watched his face soften.

"Well."

"See?"

Louis glanced around them. "It is probably the best thing about this place."

"You've honestly never eaten kouign-amann *before? We had it on the dessert menu, Louis.*"

Louis took another bite and shook his head. "Truly. This *is the best thing about this place.*"

Juliette looked down at her shoes.

"Apart from you," *he added.* "Sorry."

"Thank you for coming. I know it's a long way."

"I'm being bitchy. I've missed you." *Louis hesitated.* "We've all missed you."

"Well, I appreciate it. I couldn't face Paris again. Not right now."

"Beautiful, dog-shitty Paris? No," *Louis mocked, nudging her.*

"You love it."

Louis sighed. "You're right, I really do."

The tourists' eyes slid over to them. They were speaking English. Juliette caught pieces of their conversation: "I thought it was going to be warmer . . . didn't you say it was going to be warmer?"

Juliette watched a gull, perched on a post in the water, stab at a small silver fish with its bright red beak.

"Is there anything else to do? Apart from the museum. Isn't there a market?"

"And what about you?" Louis asked.

"Sardines? God, no. I can't learn anything more about sardines. Please. Let's go back to the B&B."

"Juliette?"

Juliette cleared her throat. "I can't go back, Louis."

Louis laid down the paper bag. "Why not?"

"You know why not."

"The review? We can get over that."

Dusollier's visit had not gone as planned and her review had been worse than scathing; it had been lackluster. She'd suggested mediocrity and laziness, apathy. Juliette had hoped for a score of 14; Delphine had received a 10.5. Just enough to be listed in the guide but with such a low score it would plant doubt in customers' minds.

"It's Gault et Millau. You don't get over that."

"You can't be blamed. It was your mother, for God's sake."

"It's still my fault," Juliette replied firmly. "But it's not just that."

"Is it . . ." Louis paused, choosing his words. "Your father?"

Juliette's head hung. Things had gotten so bad so quickly. He was thin and quiet, the cancer in his pancreas now, his liver. Juliette should have known he was ill. The signs were there but they'd all ignored them, including her father. Now, with her mother gone, he was fading so fast. Dissolving. Some mornings Juliette woke up and imagined she'd find him evaporated, just his pajamas left in the bed in the shape of him.

"We could make it work. You could come back here for things. Appointments . . . ," Louis urged.

Louis's parents were fighting fit. His mother wore her hair in an immaculate coif; his father always had a silk handkerchief in his pocket. They sat ramrod straight, rode horses, and played tennis; they brought their wealthy friends to Delphine and laughed in the full but empty way that very wealthy people did—har, har, har.

Juliette shook her head. "It's not just Dad."

Louis flicked a crumb from his fingertip. The seagull raised its head, scales on its beak—blood.

"*The politician?*"

Juliette winced. She felt guilty. The state of her father should hurt her more. The loss of her mother. But the thought of losing her lover broke her heart. It was selfish, but she couldn't help it. Perhaps there was a strange comfort in that particular pain, perhaps it was simpler to process. It didn't feel simple. It felt like knives.

"*I told you—*"

"*Louis. It's too late for that,*" *she said, cutting him off. It really was too late. Juliette had given her heart away, she had trusted, and Louis's warnings had come to pass.*

"*Sorry.* Merde." *Louis sighed. His face was pained too.* "*I don't know what to do.*"

Juliette squeezed his hand. "*I know. It's okay.*"

They both watched the tourists helping one another off the boat, wobbling. No sea legs. They wouldn't last long in Douarnenez. You needed sea legs to thrive here. You had to be able to see the beauty in rolling gray clouds, in mists like wet lace, in the violent cries of seagulls. Be hardy enough to walk along the edge of the cliffs and not feel sick. Robust enough to handle lurching, salt spray in your wounds, able to form rusted scabs.

"*I've been thinking about Delphine. You should change the name.*"

"*What?*" *Louis balked.*

"*Rebranding. It's the best approach after the review. Start fresh.*"

"*Juliette—*"

"*Leon did that once, didn't he?*"

Louis frowned deeply at the mention of Leon's name. "*Leon? Leon of La Porte Blanche?*"

Juliette and Louis despised him equally. Louis once declared, "*The ugliness shines right out of his handsome face.*" *He was unused to hearing Juliette speak of anything Leon had done in a positive context. Juliette ignored his expression.*

"*And I think you should have it. Delphine.*"

"*Juliette!*"

"Not have." *Juliette shook her head slowly.* "Buy. I've got some debt you can take off my hands. Your parents perhaps . . . Anyway, I'd sell it for a good price."

"I can't."

"I've thought about it," *Juliette said emphatically.*

"But all your hard work. I couldn't . . ." *Louis's face paled, his eyes searched hers.* "Delphine is . . . it's yours, Juliette. She's yours."

Juliette gave a heavy smile. She looked to the seagull, taking flight now, half-devoured fish in its beak dripping innards into the oily water below.

"No. She is not mine," *she said sadly.*

Chapter Eight

MAX

Max presses his toes into the sand, pushing through the powdery blond layer to the cool, resistant sand beneath it. This is no tropical beach. Max has been to many of those in his travels. Fruity cocktails, the sound of crickets, seawater as warm as a bath. Frank, lead singer of the Jacks, actually owns an island in the Bahamas, like he thinks he is Richard Branson. Arrogant son of a bitch, Frank, but a charismatic front man. Looked the part in his stovepipe jeans too: long and thin, twitching over the stage like a spider.

Douarnenez is not the Bahamas, not an island Frank has given a name that in Sanskrit means "hope" or "freedom" or some bullshit. Here, the wind glances off the ocean with a bracing chill, the seagulls hover and flap like sheets on a line. The sky is flat and gray and impassive. Max loves it. It feels a bit like England but it isn't. Which is perfect for Max.

Max made Paris his permanent address almost a decade ago. He hadn't meant to, exactly, but the Jacks' accountant suggested they should spend less time in Britain if they didn't want to lose half their income to taxes. A couple of the guys based themselves in the United States; Frank had an address in Bangkok, as his wife is Thai; Max wound up in Paris. He considered New York, of course, but he hadn't come up with his Grand Plan then. He had been busy enacting the Plan Before the Grand Plan, which mostly involved cocaine and Frenchwomen.

Helen should be on this beach with him, cold in her thin dress so Max has to wrap his arm around her. Sharing a cigarette the way they shared joints in college—passing it between them without a word. Having her nestle into him, look up at him, that sweet, slightly crooked tooth, the hair that smells both lemony clean and smoky. Max tries not to sulk. Nothing worse than a man sulking—makes him look like a big baby. His father taught him that.

Max looks up from his feet in the sand and notices that the others, bar Rosie and Hugo, are far ahead of him. Sophie is staring at the sand as she steps; Soleil has let down her hair and is walking alone. Eddie is holding Beth's hand. Beth laughs and bumps against his side. She is about the same size as Rosie. Max still remembers when it was Rosie walking with Eddie. Rosie + Eddie, Lars + Nina—those were the equations of that time. They were the pillars. The 2 x 2 that had made things solid. They had made love seem possible, desirable even. Max glances at Rosie and Hugo, closer to him now. It is still disappointing to him that Rosie is with someone else, has had children with someone else. Particularly when that someone else is Hugo.

Rosie and Hugo dawdle and the wind blows their conversation toward Max. They're too engrossed to notice him. Rosie walks with her head down and arms crossed; Hugo's hands are jammed in his pockets.

"You keep leaving me with your friends."

"When?"

"At lunch, for starters."

"Weren't you talking to Eddie?"

"That was scintillating." Hugo's voice is clipped.

"What is that supposed to mean?"

"He didn't know where Madagascar was."

"Why were you talking about Madagascar?"

"That's not the point."

"I'm not sure I know where Madagascar is," Rosie admits.

Hugo cringes. "Don't say that, Rosie. You know where Madagascar is."

"Not really. Is it near Africa?"

Hugo gives a sigh. "Yes."

"You're too hard on everyone. Who cares if he doesn't know where Madagascar is?"

"It's basic geography."

Max resists the urge to interrupt, to defend Eddie and protect Rosie.

"I don't know what you two ever found to talk about . . . ," Hugo mutters.

"It's not the measure of a good person, Hugo, whether he adequately knows his geography," Rosie says curtly.

"It's *basic* geography."

Max glances up to see Rosie roll her eyes. She looks worn out. Poor Rosie. She really should have stuck with Eddie. Eddie might be a bit thick about some things but he isn't a twat.

"Not knowing where Madagascar is doesn't make Eddie a bad person. You're acting as though he's been convicted of something."

"Yes, well . . ."

"That's enough," Rosie cautions.

"I didn't realize there was a quota on marital discussion."

They stop and Max pauses too. He has heard too much but he can't stop listening now. And if Hugo lays a hand on Rosie he will have an excuse to punch his lights out. The thought is satisfying. Hugo pushes at a rock in the sand with the toe of his shoe.

"For God's sake, Hugo," Rosie says hotly, starting to walk again.

Hugo catches her arm. "Rosie—"

Max opens his mouth but Rosie gets a word in before he does. "What?" she shouts.

This is not the Rosie that Max knows. The Rosie that Max remembers hated confrontation. She was the good girl. This is Rosie after years of being married to a person like Hugo. Max stays close, watching and waiting.

"Don't speak to me like that."

"I'll speak however I want!" Rosie snaps. "Stop being such a prick to my friends."

"What has got into you?"

"You don't like my friends, Hugo? Fine. But don't ruin my time with them. I *want* to be here. I *want* to be here with *them*. I don't care if Eddie knows where Madagascar is—"

"Rosie . . ." Low, warning.

"I don't care if he knows where his fucking elbow is. He's my friend, Hugo. I *like* these people."

"Well, that's clear," Hugo spits. He drops her arm. "I've always come second to these people, right from the start."

Rosie stares. "You are being ridiculous!"

"You've always chosen them."

"Are you kidding?" Rosie jabs her finger at her husband's chest. "I chose *you* for the last two decades! It's all been about *you*. Hugo fucking Winstall. Orthopedic surgeon. King of the fucking jungle."

"I put bread on the table!" Hugo yells, his face pink.

"You put *nothing* on the table. You never set the table, never cook the food for the table, are barely ever home for dinner . . . One time I even bought a new table and you didn't notice for six months. Six months!"

A breeze lifts Rosie's hair and flicks it across her face. Max is frozen, watching.

"Don't you dare blame my job. My job provides for us. My job got us the house you wanted; it pays for our sons' educations. We wouldn't have been able to have Patrick without my job. Don't act like you didn't want any of it. You wanted it all. You wanted to stay at home, you wanted three kids . . ."

Rosie throws her arms up into the wind. "It *always* comes to this! *You wanted this, Rosie.* Like that makes it okay to be a total cunt—"

"Rosie!" Hugo's eyes narrow. He shakes his head as though she's an embarrassment. "I gave you everything. Everything you ever wanted. You treat me like some . . . some . . . *boil,* some virus, like you don't want to get close . . ."

"Oh, Hugo." Rosie looks up to the sky. "Is this the 'why don't we have sex?' conversation? Really? Again?"

"You ignore me!"

"I'm *exhausted,*" Rosie replies. "I give everything I have to the boys. I'm making dinner and cleaning the house, doing the school runs, worrying about whether Henry has his soccer cleats . . . I have nothing left, Hugo."

"You have enough for Fleet."

"Don't."

"Our marriage is less important than bloody jewelry. Can't you see that?"

Rosie cuts him off, raising her index finger. "It's the only thing. The *only* thing. That is mine. Don't—"

"So you'd rather give up—"

"Don't!" Rosie screams.

Hugo keeps shaking his head and then looks at the ocean, down at his feet, and back up again. "So where do I fit? Huh? Where do I fit, Rosie?"

Rosie rubs her forehead. "Hugo—"

"Where am I on the list? There's the boys, okay, there's Fleet . . ." He is checking them off on his long surgeon's fingers. "Where am I? Huh? Oh, and we can't forget to add Nina to the list . . ."

Rosie's expression is livid. Hugo carries on regardless.

"You talk to her, what, every day? That's a whole lot more than I get. I get told to remember to put the rubbish out and pay for school uniforms. The fucking rubbish . . . the fucking bills! Nina gets more of you than I do, your *husband*."

"You are not going to bring Nina into this, Hugo."

"Why not? She's on the priority list well ahead of me. You have lunch, what, at least once a week? That's more dates than you have with the person you said *vows* to."

Rosie shakes her head. Max has never seen her so mad. She stops and glances back toward the house, and when she does she sees Max. Her face is pale and brimming with rage. Max shouldn't be here; he shouldn't be listening. But Rosie looks past him and down the beach. She starts walking in the direction of the house.

"Rosie . . . ," Max murmurs.

Her gaze is flat.

"Are you okay?"

She glares and points at him. "You got it right, Max. Don't get married. Don't *ever* get married. It's a joke."

"I—"

"A fucking *con*."

"Rosie?"

But Rosie is walking fast now. Both Max and Hugo stare at her.

"Nina is my best friend, Hugo!" Rosie shouts over her shoulder, voice close to tears.

"Don't you walk away. Stop!" Hugo demands.

But she doesn't. And despite his posh, booming voice, his education and his arrogance, Hugo looks as though he wants to throw himself in front of her the way children do when they want something: milk, a piece of toast, a favorite toy. *Stop. Notice me. Stop.* Hugo looks pathetic.

Max walks past him, toward the others, and neither man says anything.

MAX TAKES IN a big mouthful of cold sea air, the mineral taste hitting the back of his throat. Rosie's words ricochet around his head. *Don't get married! Don't ever get married!* Max stares ahead, where Sophie is picking something out of the sand.

When Sophie looks up Max is reminded of the girl on her fifth birthday. Nina had sent him invitations to all of Sophie's birthday parties: her first one, held at Nina's parents' house; her second, a picnic in Hyde Park; her third, pirate themed; her fourth, a pink invite with a fairy stamped on the back of the envelope. He had finally made it to her fifth. He'd had a break in his touring schedule and it was July, the month for leaving Paris. He came direct from a tour in the States, buying a teddy bear at LAX. He felt stupid carrying it on the plane, but there was no room in his carry-on bag, as he'd jammed clothes and toiletries in there so he could send his other luggage on with the Jacks' manager. He had been hungover when he'd decided to shift his trip to London instead of Paris, but he slept the entire flight, and by the time he wolfed down a prawn sandwich from the Heathrow airport Boots store, he was feeling reinvigorated.

Sophie had liked the teddy bear. She was probably too old for teddy bears by then but didn't say so. Everyone was pleased to see him. Helen hadn't been there, but Nina and Lars and Rosie and Eddie were. They felt like family. They felt like home. Max hadn't realized he'd been needing that.

Sophie's expression now is equal parts hopeful and careful, wondering if she can trust him, unable to make up her mind. It's a disconcerting look for Max. He is used to adoration, even used to disdain; he could usually turn the latter around, but Sophie's girl-face, innocence and mistrust both, unstitches his confidence. He doesn't need any help with that after witnessing Rosie and Hugo's argument.

"What are you collecting?"

Sophie opens her hand to show him: shells, a crab pincer, desiccated seaweed.

"Cool," he says dumbly.

Max could turn around now and head back to the house, but Hugo is in that direction and Max does not want to talk to him. Eddie and Beth are sitting on a dune, kissing. Max is not about to interrupt that. Eddie is an ugly kisser, Max observes uneasily.

"Were they fighting?" Sophie asks. She nods toward Hugo. Rosie has already vanished down the path that leads back to the house.

Max wonders if he should lie. The rules of talking to children are never clear to him. He was told not to lie—at school, for example—but he got lied to all the time. *Your mum'll come back. Your old man loves you, ya know. You're gonna be all right.*

"Ah, yeah."

Sophie seems unmoved. She plucks a small white shell from the sand. It is a perfect, almost transparent spiral.

"Do they do that a lot?" Max asks.

Sophie shrugs. She's not looking at Max but down at the shell. "Seems like it."

Farther down the beach Soleil is looking out over the water. Her hair is flying back in those thick tendrils. She looks like something out of a fable, a Celtic myth. She glances over at them.

"I don't know why anyone gets married," Sophie mutters, as though she heard Rosie's warnings.

"Yeah? Why is that?"

"It's stupid. It never lasts." Sophie pinches the shell between her thumb and index finger, crushing it to a fine white powder.

"What about your parents?"

"They're not married."

He did keep forgetting that. "They practically are."

Sophie frowns, conceding. Max feels a little reassured. There are exceptions to every rule.

"It never lasts," Sophie repeats, under her breath, looking to Soleil approaching them.

Soleil's nipples are sticking up beneath her silky orange crop top. It has a paisley pattern embossed on it. Max tries not to look at her nipples directly.

"It's windy," she declares.

Sophie nods.

"Is everyone going back?"

The three of them turn toward the house and watch Hugo's figure receding in that direction. Max turns to Eddie and Beth, but they're against the sand and Eddie's shorts are tented in the crotch.

"Yeah, might be time to head back."

Sophie looks down at the collection in her hand. "I should check on Mum."

"Good idea," Max agrees.

They walk back together, Sophie trailing behind.

Helen should be on this beach, Max thinks again, allowing himself a small moment of sulking.

Then Soleil says, "I need a drink."

LONDON, 1995

They were smoking in bed. At the time there was that fire safety advertisement about not doing just that, but Max and Helen were wired for rebellion. Though from completely, utterly different worlds, they were compelled to behave the same way. Contrary. Angry. Disbelieving. It used to make Max laugh, especially when Helen spoke. Nothing she could do about that voice. It was like cut crystal, like facets of a diamond, like polo and dark carpets and wood paneling. It made Helen sound like she came from another planet. Max could have listened to her speak twenty-four hours a day.

Helen blew smoke toward the ceiling. The room was in a fug anyway. It was cold so they were under the duvet. Helen's flat was arctic cold in winter; the heating wasn't good. Because it was never supposed to be a flat, Max guessed; it was supposed to be an attic in a big, old house. Helen inched closer to him, put her cold, bare feet on top of his. Max shivered. Helen laughed.

"You are such a wimp, Max."

"Fuck you. It's cold."

"Surely you've lived in cold before. It's not that bad."

"Council flats are heated better than this."

"We'll just have to use body heat." Helen laughed. Max shot her a

look. "Kidding," she said, still giggling. "What are they like? Council flats, I mean."

"You doing a social experiment?"

"What do you mean?"

"Are you just an upper-class girl seeing what it's like to slum it with the common people?" Max asked.

Helen put her finger to her lips, pretending to consider. "Yes."

Max laughed. "They are shit. Council housing is shit."

"But warmer than this?"

"Everywhere is warmer than this. The North Pole is warmer than this."

Since Max met Helen they'd seen each other often. A lot. Almost every day. Max wasn't normally like that. Up until this point, Max made friends, but they came and went, like tides. He didn't get attached. Max got nervous when he saw someone too much, when they became too important to him or he to them. It was better to move along. Besides, he was better with new people. New people didn't know his stories, weren't angry that he was late or that he sometimes stunk, or was regularly drunk or stoned or both. New people thought he was "the craic" and "talented" and "funny" and "bohemian." They saw Max's unreliability as an inevitable part of his creative talent and not just Max being a wanker.

"You know, I saw your work the other day, Max. Ms. Bertrand had it hanging up. In her office."

Max nodded. He had seen that too. It was a photograph Max had taken by the Thames. It was one of his not-quite-right photographs, the person in the background in focus (a homeless guy napping on a bench—a guy with one shoe and blackened toenails and his open mouth full of dark holes where teeth should be) and foreground blurred (a pigeon taking flight, leaving feathers from the effort). There was *something about the man that had reminded Max of his father. So much so that Max had almost gone to wake him up—wake him and punch him in his toothless face. But it hadn't been Max's father. It wasn't his face. Just similar.*

"It's so good, Max," Helen said.

Max shrugged. He was better with compliments when he was drunk. "Got any whiskey?"

Helen leaned out of bed and lifted up a bottle. It was her father's. She had been stealing his good booze and the pair of them had been drinking it. She passed it to him. The bottle's glass was thick, the whiskey a good strong color. Max pulled out the stopper and Helen wriggled back down under the duvet, closer to him. The smell of the whiskey filled the space. Max poured some down his throat. It scalded pleasantly. Helen stubbed out her cigarette and reached out for the bottle. Max passed it over.

"Father saw me take it," she confessed, before taking a slug. She shuddered as it went down.

"Are you in trouble?"

Max's father would have beaten him to a pulp if Max had taken his liquor, which Max had still done on occasion, because, well, fuck him.

Helen shook her head. Her hair was long and tangled, most of it tucked behind her shoulders. "He didn't say anything. He just watched me."

"Lucky."

Helen laughed. "Not really. Would have been better if he'd been mad. That was him telling me I'm a failure. A disappointment."

"Yeah?"

Helen's people behaved oddly; Max was still figuring them out. They didn't make sense to him. Helen lit another cigarette. She smoked more than Max did.

"Yeah. But what's new?" Helen said. She smoked for a few

moments and then turned her head to face Max. She picked a bit of tobacco off the end of her tongue. The whiskey bottle was back in Max's hand now.

"I have a bit of a problem, Max. I don't have the talent you have," she said softly.

"That's not true."

"It is. I'm not without talent, but it's not like yours. Yours is special, yours is authentic. I can't help but copy what I've already seen before. I've been conditioned to please and mimic. I've seen too much . . ."

"I don't know what I'm doing. I don't care about it enough," Max said.

"But it works. I've seen it." Smoke rose in curls from her cigarette.

"I don't know if it's what I want to do," Max admitted.

Helen nodded. "I've got to make something work so I can live on my own. Without his help, his money."

Helen spoke of her father a lot but Max had never met him. He was like a ghost who haunted her, an invisible shadow always hanging around.

"And his whiskey," she added, taking the bottle and drinking.

It startled Max that someone so rich could be so wounded. He hadn't expected that. He couldn't believe someone from a world of whiskey and posh accents and big country houses could be so much like him. He stared at Helen lying back in her bed. Her duvet was pink, clearly one she had nabbed from home. It was lumpy, unwashed, stunk of smoke and open-mouthed sleep. Underneath it Helen was wearing a turtleneck the color of beer-bottle sea glass, the top rolled just under her chin. Her dark, fluffy hair seemed to be everywhere—underneath her, underneath Max, covering all the pillows. Maybe Helen wasn't the most beautiful girl Max had ever met. She was too strange and wild and unkempt and weirdly tortured for that. She laughed like a man and her legs were unshaven. But her eyes shined like no one else's; her *body near his made him yearn like he had never yearned before. She was a marvel, a broken marvel, like a bad pixie or a wild horse or some shit. Helen made Max feel odd—odd in a tingling and alive way.*

Max felt the whiskey working through his veins. That was better. That made him feel more like himself. He leaned against Helen and felt her breath on his cheek, warm and slightly wet. She was right there. Max rolled his face toward hers. His lips touched hers for the briefest moment. Even now Max can still remember: soft, a little dry, and relenting. Max's body sung. His head spun. He moved closer without a conscious thought. And Helen moved the other way. Her fingers were on his mouth.

"No, Max."

Max felt suddenly suspended.

"Please no. I can't." Helen's voice was instantly close to tears.

"I . . . ," Max started to explain, but there was no explanation.

"It's all I have. It's too good. If we do this it'll be a mess. You'll ruin it or I will. It's what we do."

Max opened his mouth to protest. They could do this. They could make it work. But, with the smells of smoke and whiskey and unwashed sheets all around, Max knew she was right.

"I'll wreck it," Helen begged. "I can't wreck it."

Max scrambled for a joke and wished for a way to not care, to not think, I am not good enough for her, *when that thought was now pulsing through him, flooding him like a poison. At least it was a familiar thought; his body seemed to soak it up.*

Max cleared his throat. "Whiskey?" he asked, and Helen handed it over.

"I can fuck you," Helen whispered. "But then I can't love you."

Max looked at her. He studied her face. Something in him got it, really got it, though he felt stupid and inadequate and scared. Fearful that now that he'd found Helen, no one else would ever do, would ever live up to her. Max thought for a moment about leaving, about never seeing Helen again. But then Helen said, in a tiny voice, more to herself than to him, "And if we don't wreck it now, then maybe it will be unbroken . . . for later."

Max lifted the whiskey bottle to his lips. The lips that had felt Helen's lips against them. The lips that wanted to kiss Helen's mouth and face and neck and skin all night until the sun came up and then sleep all day, like bats, wrapped around each other, so they could kiss again and again the whole next night. And on and on. Max would give up almost anything for that: school, booze, drugs, cigarettes, maybe even his music.

Max gathered up the word later like confetti in his palm. He drew up the hurt and confusion, which felt so normal anyway—he could live with that—and grinned back at her.

"Okay," he said, like it was no big deal.

Chapter Nine

ROSIE

When Rosie returns to the house the sky is beginning to darken, though it is only five o'clock. She steps along the path at the back of Max's house; it is made of broken shells bleached white as bones that crunch with each footfall. The sound satisfies her; she's still furious, her chest hot and taut at the top of her rib cage, her breathing fast. At the edge of the deck, Nina sits with her legs hanging over the side. She is wearing a loose dress hitched up to her knees, her head tipped back and eyes closed, as though there is still sunshine in the sky. Her cheeks are pink, her hair askew, and her feet, dangling down, are shoeless. There is a mostly full glass of champagne beside her.

"Rosie?"

"Hey." Rosie's voice comes out a little choked. Nina squints at her but Rosie looks away.

Juliette, bending over some bushes, colander and scissors in hand, straightens and waves.

"Hi, Juliette."

"Can I get you something to drink?" Juliette asks.

Rosie glances at Nina's champagne. Before she can answer, Nina passes it over. "Have mine."

Rosie lowers herself down next to her friend and takes the glass.

"Was the beach lovely?" Nina's voice is soft. "I've been listening to the gulls . . . Doesn't the air smell good?"

Rosie turns to her friend. Nina's expression is dreamy.

"I should go down. But I think a storm might be coming."

Usually Nina would be down on that beach in a flash, storm or no storm, too bold and curious to let raindrops hold her up. Nina is the type of person to be in the rock pools with Rosie's sons, sticking her fingers into sea anemones and unafraid to pick up crabs. Laughing and prodding at life, daring it to mess with her.

Nina gets more of you than I do.

Rosie feels the muscles in her face giving way, the tightness in her chest turning liquid, threatening to pour out. Tears are in her eyes and she knows it's useless to quell them.

"Rosie?" Nina murmurs.

Juliette turns away to clip some purple sage.

"Please . . ." Nina's voice is pleading. "Don't panic."

Rosie's rage disintegrates into sadness, into fear, into a dark and cold mercury inside her. Hugo is right. Nina does get more of her. Nina returns Rosie's e-mails within minutes and never ignores her phone calls. She knows the names of her sons' teachers, their favorite animals, probably even their shoe sizes. She had deliberated with her about "oat" versus "wheat" for the color of her couch cushions. When there was a cattle disease scare she didn't dwell on the impact on the pound sterling, as Hugo had done, frowning over his dinner of Beef Wellington; rather, she had immediately called and asked after Rosie's father, had worried with her about his butchery business. Rosie couldn't remember the last time

Nina asked, "Can I help?" She is simply there when needed, knowing exactly what is needed, without having to ask: a box of Rosie's favorite muffins, a chat, an embrace, cups of tea made in quick succession. Nina, her palm still covered in bandages, reaches for Rosie's hand. "It's okay . . ."

"I need you . . ."

Rosie's voice is thick as syrup with emotion, pain, and grief. It swells in her throat, making it difficult to breathe.

"Shh, shh . . . ," Nina whispers. "Not here, Rosie, please."

WHEN THE OTHERS return home, Rosie is watching them from the upstairs landing, a gin and tonic in hand. She's splashed cold water on her face, and the drink—the tonic part—seems to be delivering on its promises. Hugo arrives back first, fists jammed into pockets, expression as dark as the gathering rain clouds. He walks straight past Nina and Lars into the house, and Rosie knows he will soon be settled into the armchair he favors with the book he has selected from Max's collection: a large architectural tome with thick, glossy pages. She's watched him folding the corners of those pages, as though the book were his to mark as he wishes. Max and Soleil are next. Max first and then Soleil, just behind. Rosie assesses Soleil's lean frame and the self-assured way she moves, all strength and sinew and dauntless spirit. She's not sure what to make of the woman yet. Max pauses in front of Nina and inspects Nina's hands. Nina rolls her eyes and looks, for a moment, just like her daughter. Max kisses the top of her head as Soleil moves inside. Eddie and Beth are ambling up the path, hand in hand. Rosie takes a large drink of her gin. Beth tucks a piece of her red hair behind her ear and smiles shyly, leaning toward her boyfriend.

Rosie's hand moves to her own hair. It used to be thicker—thick enough to require smoothing down with gel, to request thinning at the hairdresser's. She doesn't have those problems these days, after her pregnancies. Rosie gave life to the boys and the boys took the life from her hair. It thinned around her forehead first; Rosie hadn't expected that. She still finds herself touching it there, feeling for new hairs that spring up grayer than she would like. As the couple approaches the house, Rosie watches as Eddie's hand slips away from Beth's; he uses it to swat Max's arse and laugh, head back. Max reaches out for Nina's drink, presumably to throw it at Eddie, but Nina bats him away. Beth, hands now slid into the back pockets of her shorts, shifts from one foot to the other. She watches the conversation like a tennis match, volleying from one friend to another: Eddie making a joke, Max teasing Lars, Lars passing a reply back to Eddie. Beth's smile sags. She whispers to Eddie before they both move into the house. Those who remain—Max, Nina, and Lars—wait for only a short beat before leaning toward one another. Rosie knows they are discussing the newcomers. Gossiping.

There is movement on the stairs.

"Hi, Rosie."

Rosie wills herself not to but she glances down at Beth's legs before meeting her eyes. It's the shorts. They are so short.

"Hi, Beth."

"Nice out there, isn't it? So wild."

"Hmm," Rosie replies. "Storm's coming."

"You're right, time to come in. I'm going to shower."

Eddie comes up the stairs behind her. He's puffing a little.

"I'm going to shower before supper," Beth tells him.

Eddie nods and then smiles at her. Rosie looks down into her glass as Beth heads to their room. The large ice cubes roll and bump into one another. Eddie stands beside her, gazing out the window.

"You weren't out there long."

Rosie thinks of Hugo, of the names she called him, of the vicious thoughts she'd had. "It was getting cold."

"It's not warm, that's for sure," Eddie agrees. "Bloody nice house though, don't you think?"

"Very nice."

"Max lands on his feet." Eddie shakes his head. "This place should be in a magazine."

"He's done a good job with it. I like Douarnenez too."

"How was the market?"

"Quaint. Sweet. Beth enjoyed it, I think."

"Hmm. She's into that kind of thing. She goes to Borough Market on the weekends, says there's nothing like it in the States. Buys Eccles cakes, can you believe it?"

Rosie screws up her face; she isn't keen on currants or raisins. "I don't really like Eccles cakes."

"I know," Eddie replies, chuckling. "I remember."

Outside the window Rosie spots Sophie by the beginning of the path, coming up off the beach. She's walking slowly, the swelling wind lifting her loose hair as she peers down at the ground. Rosie clears her throat. "You don't go with her? Beth? To the market?"

"I'm working a lot."

"The whiskey bar."

Eddie nods. They both watch as Sophie picks up something and puts it into her sweatshirt; she's got the hem lifted to make a kind of basket. She glances to one side and then straightens. Rosie follows her gaze to a teenage boy walking toward her from the neighbors' property. He's got his jersey sleeves pulled down over his hands.

"How is it?" Rosie asks

"The bar? Good." There is pride in Eddie's voice. "I've bought in actually."

Sophie and the boy are talking now, or so Rosie assumes. Sophie has one hand gripping her sweatshirt and the other one at her mouth, nibbling her pinkie nail, it looks like. The boy stares down at the sand.

Rosie turns to Eddie. "You own it?"

He's still watching the teenagers on the beach.

"A part of it. Thirty percent."

"Thirty? That's . . ." Rosie pauses, feeling strangely sad again. She takes a breath. "Great. Really great, Eddie."

Eddie smiles. "Thanks, Rosie."

They turn back to Sophie and the boy. The boy crouches and reaches for something, a shell perhaps or a stone. He holds it out to her, turning it in his fingers. Sophie shrugs. He drops it back into the sand. They both laugh.

"I was thinking about that time we went . . ." Rosie hesitates. She recalls the cold stones against her back, the smell of cigarettes and the mineral sea air, Eddie's lips warm and wet against hers, the heat of his body through his clothes. It seems like another life—a life without Hugo, without her sons. Another Rosie. One with thicker hair.

"Sorry?"

"Nothing. It doesn't matter."

Sophie has turned, slightly, toward the house. The boy scratches the back of his head and then reaches out and touches her sleeve.

"We should go downstairs . . . ," Rosie murmurs.

"What do you think is going on there?" Eddie asks, his voice low.

"With Sophie?"

Rosie watches the girl press the sweatshirt closer to her

chest, lick her lips and smile. There is color on her cheeks. Light rain speckles the windows.

"Young love," she says ruefully.

WHILE JULIETTE COOKS dinner they sit in the lounge and listen to music Max selects. Hugo is in his armchair, his brooding face intent on the architecture book in his lap, pretending to ignore the music Rosie knows he deplores and the company he dislikes. Rosie tries not to look at him: the gathered eyebrows, the pursed, sulking mouth.

"Nina! Remember this?" Lars calls out. Nina grins in reply.

"Know this song, Soleil?" Helen asks her sister, who shakes her head. Helen is on a couch with her finger in a novel she isn't reading, leaning against Max. Soleil is perched on the arm of the couch.

"You have to know this one. The Cure. You know the Cure," Max implores.

"Before my time."

Helen laughs. "She's too young."

"Yeah, but the Cure are classic. Everyone should know the Cure."

"Beth knows the Cure," Eddie says. Beth is curled up next to him, hair wet and face fresh. Her eyes are dewy and wide.

"See?" Max enthuses.

"I've been getting an education," Beth gushes, tipping her head toward Eddie. Rosie presses her lips together, trying not to find the affection irritating.

"Should I know them?" Soleil asks Helen.

"Yes!" Max replies for her.

"You don't have to know them," Rosie snaps, still looking at Beth. Nina shoots her a look; she has her feet in Lars's lap.

"They were pretty big when we were young. A long time ago . . . ," Helen replies.

"Steady on," Max grumbles.

"She's too young," Helen soothes.

"That's like saying someone is too young for Shakespeare," he replies.

Hugo looks up from his book at that, raising an eyebrow, unconvinced. Hugo loves Shakespeare. When he notices Rosie looking at him he drops his gaze, eyebrows gathering again.

"I'm not that young," Soleil mutters.

Lars clears his throat. He is rubbing the soles of Nina's feet. "What do you do, Soleil? Helen said you were at college."

"I was."

"What were you studying?" Rosie asks.

"Environmental science."

"Soleil is getting her PhD," Helen adds.

"Oh, wow," Eddie says.

"Was," Soleil corrects.

"You're not going to finish it?" Nina asks, lifting her head from the cushions.

Soleil shrugs. "Seems unlikely."

"You don't know that," Helen says.

"University isn't everything," Max says, gesturing around the group with his glass. "I didn't finish my studies. Those of us that did . . . Well, does anyone even use their qualifications?"

"I do," Nina replies.

"I guess I do too. Now," Rosie adds. She remembers Hugo's comments on the beach about Fleet. She watches him dog-earring a page in Max's book.

"It's mostly a waste of time," Max says, ignoring them both. "And the UK spends a ton of taxes on it."

Nina frowns. "I don't think it's a waste of time."

"Plus we rush into it. If it cost more we might consider our choices better."

"Society benefits from having an educated population," Soleil asserts.

"I agree," Nina says, and Helen nods.

Max looks to Helen and then back at Soleil. "Yeah, but educated in what?"

"Anything," Soleil responds crisply. "Keeping the costs low allows people to make choices based on their personal curiosities—"

"Well, that's ridiculous," Max scoffs. He lifts his glass to his mouth.

"Max . . . ," Helen murmurs, frowning.

"—which leads to a happier, more diverse society," Soleil concludes.

"Yeah. You wind up with an entire population educated in French art of the Middle Ages—"

"That wouldn't happen," Soleil interrupts.

"Or ceramics." Max waves his hand in Lars's direction.

"Ouch." Lars grins lazily. He's still gently kneading Nina's feet.

"Well, come on, it's a crazy idea. Where does it lead us? We have to be practical."

"When did you become so 'practical'?" Rosie asks. Hugo lowers the book and looks up. They have had this argument before, Hugo asserting that tertiary education should be less subsidized, Rosie disagreeing. If tertiary education had been costly she couldn't have afforded it, and Rosie doesn't believe less well-off families, like hers had been, should miss out.

Max's expression is disgruntled, though he is trying to mask it; he's trying to seem playful.

"Research clearly shows that the extent of education in a population, especially with regard to the women, effects all sorts of positive outcomes," Soleil says.

"Yeah? Like what?" Max counters.

"Health, particularly that of the children; happiness; gross domestic product. It's an encouragingly simple equation with few contrary results. Educate people, make things better."

Max laughs into his drink.

Helen looks at him, puzzled. "When did you become a Tory?"

Rosie had been thinking the same thing. Hugo too is staring at Max.

"I'm not."

"Who did you vote for in the last election?" Soleil asks.

"That's private. Besides, I live in France."

"But you still vote, right?"

Max doesn't say anything.

"Max!" Helen cries.

"He shouldn't get to vote," Soleil says.

"Oh yeah, why is that?" Max says tersely.

"I'm guessing you don't pay British taxes. That's part of the reason you live in France, right?"

"I pay taxes!"

"But not as much as you should," Soleil retorts.

Lars laughs. "I think you've found your match there, Max."

"I have to pay tax twice," Beth says with a sigh. "British and American."

Max ignores them both. "I pay my taxes. What I do and where I live is totally valid."

Soleil shrugs. "I wasn't suggesting you do anything illegal."

"You're right. I don't."

"But there is a difference between a legal obligation and a moral one. If you want to comment on British politics and complain about a political system, including funding for education, then you have to contribute to it."

Eddie claps. Max stiffens.

"So what, you'd make tertiary education free for everyone? You'd have a population schooled in . . . pottery and . . . Renaissance handbags and—"

"That's an unnecessary leap. But yes, I think tertiary education should be free," Soleil promptly replies.

"Do you know how many people would take advantage of that?"

"I hope everyone would."

"And who would pay for it?"

"Everyone."

Rosie watches Soleil's face. It hasn't changed a bit: smooth and unruffled and almost expressionless.

"Spoken like a rich girl," Max mutters.

Rosie glances at him sharply.

"Max. That's unfair," Helen quickly intervenes.

"Didn't you take advantage of low-cost tertiary education, Max?" Nina asks firmly. "You went to *arts* college. How would you have paid for it if it'd been more expensive? Don't you think it served you? Even if you didn't finish it?"

"That's my point. I have never used it. It was a waste of time." His tone is petulant.

It's too much for this hour of the day, with some light still in the sky and not enough alcohol in their systems to take the bitter edge off; with Max not completely in control, not being the steady, charming, happy center. This is not holiday conversation; it's disorienting.

"But it's how you met us," Rosie hears herself say, her voice more wounded than she expected.

Max doesn't reply.

Lars gives Soleil a steady look. "If you are a big advocate of education, why won't you be completing your PhD?"

"Exactly," Max mumbles.

Soleil glances at Max and Rosie notices the first flash of irritation flit across her face. "The university board wouldn't approve my research."

"Why?" Lars asks.

Soleil clears her throat. "The official line was that it didn't fit within the scope and remit of the department of environmental science and the subject was too broad and unwieldy."

"Soleil was looking into the effects of organically farmed food on the brains of developing children," Helen adds proudly.

"Sort of," Soleil replies.

"That sounds interesting," Rosie says encouragingly.

"More helpful than ceramics," Lars adds amiably.

"They said it would be too difficult to establish controls, the research period would be too long and too expensive, and the topic is more aligned with nutritional medicine," Soleil explains.

"That's a real shame," Beth says.

"I agree," says Helen, nodding.

"What was the unofficial reason?" Max asks.

"Pardon?"

"You said that was the official reason. What was the unofficial reason?"

Soleil lifts her chin and faces Max. "I fucked my professor."

Eddie chokes on his drink and starts coughing.

"And then I stopped fucking him."

There is a short silence. Hugo gives a brief, disgusted snort and looks back to his book.

"Where is Sophie?" Nina murmurs, glancing around.

Soleil continues: "He wasn't happy about that."

"Well," says Lars, with a trace of admiration in his voice. "That'll do it."

"I didn't know about that," Helen murmurs.

Max is silent but looks vaguely smug. The song changes. Max leans forward for the remote and turns up the volume. The conversation breaks up like rainwater, splitting into streams and puddles. Lars stands up to look for his daughter and Max gestures to Juliette with his glass.

"Can I get another drink?"

Rosie's glass is empty. She runs a fingertip around the rim and observes the group from her single chair. It is a modern specimen of light-colored wood and tan leather, too upright to be comfortable, more the shape of an examiner's chair in a school hall, but it's "on trend," as her PTA friends would say, reverence in their voices. It was probably a Someone—a Prouvé or a Perriand or an Eames. The design made it impossible to slouch. Feeling contrary, Rosie watches her glass make a wet ring on the leather armrest. She wishes the gin would work better and faster to dispel her rising edginess, but knows the opposite is often true. Perhaps her mother had been right about gin being "mothers' ruin." It had certainly discomposed Max. Rosie glances at him; he is now nodding in time with the music, Soleil glaring at him from her seat on the couch's armrest. Though Rosie wills herself not to look, her gaze slides toward Eddie and Beth, sitting so close together Beth is almost in his lap. Eddie has an arm around her so her shoulders are hunched; she peeks out as though the position is plainly uncomfortable but she's unwilling to move. She has her hand on Eddie's upper thigh.

Nina lifts her feet from Lars's lap and sits up. She stretches and looks over to Rosie. She tips her head toward Max before giving it a small, baffled, disapproving shake. Rosie raises her eyebrows in reply. Of course Nina is baffled and disapproves of his behavior; Nina doesn't comprehend what he is feeling. Nina has never been confused by the emotion, been knocked off-center by it. Not with Lars at her side—ever steady and ever loving. Constant.

Rosie turns her attention to the trio on the couch: Helen in the center, her leg pressed up against Max's, and Soleil on her other side, Helen's fingers resting upon Soleil's knee.

Jealousy.

Jealousy is the feeling Nina has not had to comprehend—humiliating, disorienting jealousy. The kind that makes you feel and act unlike yourself.

Chapter Ten

MAX

The least charming person he has ever met.

Max has met some really uncharming people before. Some champs. Some medal winners. But Soleil takes the cake. And what is truly irritating about her is that she looks perfectly nice, as though she *should* be charming. Small and pretty, exactly the sort of woman Max would usually sleep with. A tiny part of him wants to, which makes him feel antagonized.

He stands to join Nina, who is looking at the shelves, filled mainly with photography books.

"She's something," he mutters, as Nina runs her index finger down the spines.

"Who?"

"Soleil."

Nina frowns. "You didn't need to call her a rich girl."

Max scowls.

"I think that upset Helen," Nina adds.

"She's not exactly friendly herself," Max replies sullenly.

"She's young," Nina says. "Hey, you've got some beautiful books here."

"She's not that young," Max says. "She's not a teenager."

"Don't talk to me about teenagers," Nina says.

"She's rude," Max presses.

"Oh, Max."

Max shifts his weight. He hasn't had much experience with mothers. Nina might be as close as he is going to get. Something about the tone of her voice is the bittersweet blend of love and disappointment, the kind that makes you feel both good and terrible about yourself at once.

"Well, she is."

"She's Helen's sister."

"It's bloody hard to believe."

"You should probably try being nicer."

"I don't see why that's my job. She should try being nice to me."

Nina straightens and raises an eyebrow at him. "You sound like Hugo."

"Jesus Christ, Nina!"

Nina bursts into laughter.

"Take that back."

Nina voice softens. "Be nice, Max. It's your birthday. Have fun. Surely there are bigger things to worry about than Soleil. You seem wound up; it's not like you."

Max glances across the room at Helen. Her head is resting in the cup of her hand and she is smiling at something Rosie is saying. He takes a deep breath.

Next to Helen, Soleil remains perched on the arm of the couch, stiff and straight.

"Got to loosen up a bit, eh? Maybe you're right."

Nina pats his shoulder and smiles, returning to the books.

Max looks down at the drink Juliette has brought him—

clear with big chunks of ice. It is meant to be sipped. He tips his head back and takes a swig that burns all the way down his throat. It feels just right.

THE CURE.
The Smiths.
Jane's Addiction.
R.E.M.
These are the greats. These are the songs Max knows inside and out: every beat, every moment between beats, any imperfection.

Max falls into music the way a person falls into cool water; he swims in it. It is tangible to him and yet fluid, like the silk of water against skin. It fills him. It makes him whole.

Music saturates Max. It goes through to the bone. It changes his mood, moves his world, rearranges his cells. Makes him feel as though he can fly, makes him feel as though he cannot take another breath. It lifts and crushes him, soothes and lacerates him. It is better, worse, and wilder than any drug he has ever taken.

Music is Max's savior—that much is clear to him and probably everyone else. It hadn't mattered that his father teased him about it, had once broken a record over his head; music is in Max's blood and veins, there is no getting rid of it. Music has been the one constant. The thing he can count on. Music has kept Max alive.

As the song fades and Paul Simon, the master, starts to sing "Graceland," Sophie comes into the room with her father. Max notices, in a fuzzy, slightly drunk (on music and alcohol both) way, that Sophie's clothes and hair are wet.

"You're soaked," Nina says from the couch.

"I've been knocking on the door for about twenty minutes."

"Oh. Sorry, honey. The music—"

"Yeah, no shit." Sophie shoots Nina a look that could maim.

"Sophie . . ."

Sophie shakes her head, wet hair sticking to her face. "You all swear."

Lars laughs. "You've got to give her that. I'll get you a towel."

Sophie looks pointedly at Nina. "Thanks, Dad."

"Why didn't you just come around the back? We would have seen you." Nina gestures to the big glass doors.

Sophie crosses her arms.

"Are you hungry?" Nina asks, changing tack.

"All we do here is bloody eat. And drink," Sophie mutters.

Lars returns with a big towel, which he drapes around his daughter. Nina steps out of her seat and starts rubbing Sophie's arms.

"Mum!"

"You'll catch a cold."

Sophie backs herself into a chair so her mother cannot reach her.

"You should have a shower and get into some dry clothes," Nina says.

"I'm fine."

"Be nice to your mother," Lars instructs in a sharp tone. Sophie looks to the floor.

Song change.

"Aha!" Lars cries out. He raises both hands in the air, closes his eyes, nods his head.

Eddie looks over approvingly. "Oasis."

"Oh my God," Sophie mutters.

Everyone in the room sings the chorus at the same time. Max wants to laugh out loud but the liquor has made him dozy. Helen flashes him a smile that makes him feel like a boy with a present to unwrap. This is how it is supposed to be. This is how music saves people's lives. Lars winks at Sophie, who rolls her eyes. Nina returns to the couch and is now laughing at Lars, who is dancing, or his version of it. Helen shakes her hair over her eyes. It reminds Max of that woman, the musician, Feist, he met once—intense and sexy and cheekbone-y—or she had reminded him of Helen, Helen being the yardstick against which everyone else is measured.

Eddie plays air guitar, picking over imaginary strings, all the wrong notes. Max laughs and slaps his thigh. When he glances outside he sees the light has faded and the rain is easing up.

"Kate Bush!" Helen calls out.

"The Clash!" Eddie shouts over the top of her.

Helen, who has lit a cigarette even though Max doesn't normally let anyone smoke in the house—it makes the place smell like he's on tour—blows smoke in Eddie's face and he pretends to choke.

"Fleetwood Mac?" Rosie pleads.

Everyone groans, the standing joke.

Nina, who isn't requesting anything, stares around at her friends. She holds a full glass of wine delicately in her fingertips, her eyes glazed. The others start arguing about the music but Nina is set apart from all of that, watching them all, loving them all. Looking at them like they are the brightest, shiniest things she has ever seen. She reminds Max of one of those old photographs of Elizabeth Taylor, a candid shot, like the one he used to have in his bedroom at college. She is radiant and still and . . . something. Fragile? Max tips his head. He is drunk. Not very drunk but enough. He isn't seeing her right. *Fragile* is not a word for Nina. Nina is tough. Solid. Dependable. But something about her, about the light, makes her look like she might softly, silently dissolve.

She turns to him and her expression changes, the spell broken.

"You okay, Max?"

Her face has returned to the way Max thinks of it: sweet but stern. Relief floods through him.

"What do you want to listen to?" he asks her.

Nina glances at Hugo, who is in Max's favorite chair accepting a glass of wine from Juliette. He has one of Max's favorite architectural guides in his lap.

"Put on Fleetwood Mac," Nina says. "Hugo hates it."

"The Mac it is," Max replies, grinning.

GETTING OLDER HAD happened too suddenly for Max. He hadn't noticed it—the years flicking by; he had never given his age a thought. But now when he looks in the mirror, he sometimes feels a bit queasy. He isn't ugly; he has enough confidence to know that. Women still want to fuck him. That much is evident. But when he sees himself he suddenly sees someone else too. His father. He is the reason Max has started to sound like a Tory. Not because he is but because the "I'm owed" thing reminds him of his father. His father, who had fleeced every system he could lay his thick-knuckled hands on. Who, on paper, had been a cripple, was traumatized by a brutal childhood (while inflicting a worse one on his own son), had been in the army for five minutes and, thus, considered himself a war hero. His father, who despite paying practically no taxes in his life thought the world should give him something. Everything. His father: the cheat, the liar, the bully. Getting older and looking more and more like his father disgusted Max, made him feel like things were getting out of control, made him take more drugs. Max was now waking in the night, mouth dry, feeling his face, feeling his arms, checking his legs, checking his dick. As though he might have disappeared in his dreams, slipped away from this world without having done half the things he should have.

Helen lays a hand against Max, the one that isn't holding the cigarette to her lips. "This is nice, eh, Maxie?"

"Bloody perfect," he replies softly.

Helen is beaming. She loves these people as much as he does.

Helen's childhood was the polar opposite from his yet essentially exactly the same. Two parents who added up to less than one, who either completely ignored her or were on her case, reinforcing that she was never—would never be—good enough. Helen's father, appalled at her choice of college and career, told her that artists never made any money, that they were sponges on society, and she would be the laughingstock of the family. Though Camberwell College of Arts had changed its name years earlier and counted several famous artists among its alumni, Helen's father still referred to it as the "arts and crafts school." Worst of all, Helen's father told her that her art wasn't any good—planting the dark knot of doubt that led Helen to owning an art gallery rather than contributing to one. On the other hand, Helen's mother, indifferent toward her art, bemoaned how Helen looked. She constantly told her that her clothes were too gloomy, too boxy, not feminine enough; that some girls could get away with no makeup and Helen was not one of them. Helen wasn't the daughter she'd expected or hoped for, though God knows what kind of daughter would have made her happy. Together, Helen's parents were a narcissistic and inadequate sum. They

alternated between using Helen as a pawn in their own manip-
ulations and completely forgetting she existed. She was less of
a daughter and more of a pet or a fancy piece of furniture:
something to show off, something to shoo when the party was
over, something that fell out of favor and fashion, something
to send away to be looked after. That she had managed to
turn out kind, loyal, and generous was a bloody miracle.

"I got something for you," she says to him.

"I got something for you too."

Max is smiling. The gin—he's had a few glasses of it
now—has made his blood move slow and sweet.

"You did? It's *your* birthday."

Max shrugs.

"Well, I'm going first," she says.

"Okay."

Helen pats his leg before leaping up and heading upstairs.
Max watches her go. The swish of her skirt, the fine bones of
her ankles, the way her arse moves beneath the soft, dark fabric. He wants to press her against a wall and lift the dress up
above her waist, feel the warmth of her thighs under his palms.

When she is gone from view he glances at her side of the
couch. Soleil is still perched on the arm. *Be nice.* He gives her
a forced smile. She returns it.

It is baffling that the miracle of Helen came from the
same home as Soleil. It shouldn't surprise Max that Soleil is
such a pompous little shit, but he is surprised because of the
way Helen isn't. Soleil clearly does not take after her sister.
Max reminds himself they aren't really sisters at all; their
relationship is a result of circumstance, an accident. They
don't share anything other than history, a brief history that
hadn't even been their choosing.

Helen isn't Soleil's. Helen is his.

Max leans over. "So. What else are you into?"

"Other than?" Soleil asks.

Professors, he wants to say, and the thought almost makes him laugh out loud. "University?"

"Oh." Soleil hesitates. "I guess I am really into university. Um. Yoga. Environmental activism. Watercolors."

"Watercolors?" Max asks, laughing.

"Yeah, watercolors."

"Of what?"

"Flowers."

"Jesus, I thought I was old," he mutters.

"I find it calming," she explains icily.

"Okay."

"What are you into?" Soleil asks Max.

Your sister, he thinks. "My work takes up most of my time. I'm on tour a lot."

"Do you like it?"

"Work? Or touring?"

"Both."

Max looks at his gin. "I love my work. I like touring less than I used to."

"Is it lonely?"

"Yes, it's lonely," Max replies slowly. He loves performing. He loves being in and of the music. He just wishes there wasn't the getting there and sitting around and next-day hangovers that seem to be getting worse and worse. Plus, increasingly, he dislikes the people he meets on tour: the parade of aging PR women with makeup spread like wedding-cake frosting; doe-eyed, hopeful girls who won a contest to be there; the young guys, pretending to be apathetic, who want to give him songs they have written. Max longs for less touring. He yearns to be somewhere quiet and safe, wants to write more. Some of the music the Jacks have released lately feels like repeats of tunes they wrote before. Max has the sinking feeling that their winning formula has become formulaic. He hasn't told anyone that though. Least of all Frank.

"But it's fun, you know, seeing the world . . ."

This is something Max learned after dozens, hundreds, of interviews. Never complain too much. His life is more blessed than most. You have to be grateful. And he was. Is.

Soleil nods. "I listened to them, the Jacks. I mean, I looked them up."

"Yeah? And?"

"They're okay."

"Don't kill yourself with enthusiasm," Max mutters, shaking his head.

"I'm just not sure they're my kind of thing."

"Which is?"

"I don't know. I listen to a range of music," Soleil says.

"But not the Jacks and not the Cure."

"It's just a little . . . obvious? For me."

Max turns to face her fully.

"Especially the newer stuff," she adds.

"You know I wrote most of those songs?"

"Some of them were good."

"Which ones?"

"The one about the stars and the girl."

" 'It Takes a Tiny Light.' "

"Yeah."

It was one of Max's ballads. Frank hadn't wanted it on the album.

"And the turtle one."

Both songs were far from being the Jacks' top hits. They were too dark or blunt. They weren't commercial. They didn't follow the formula.

"Do you have favorites?"

"I'm proud of all our work," Max says guardedly.

"I just didn't like some of the newer tracks," Soleil says.

"You said that already."

Max empties the glass. He looks around for Juliette but she must be in the kitchen. He feels the familiar, internal itch for something stronger than alcohol. Max isn't unused to criticism. The Jacks have had plenty of bad reviews; that's just part of the job. But he is unused to criticism sitting in his lounge. He glances at the stairs, looking for Helen. When he doesn't see her, he turns back to Soleil. The booze gives Max's throat a pleasant, warming buzz.

"You can be pretty rude, you know."

Soleil blinks at him.

"This is my house. These are my friends. This is *my* birthday."

Her gaze hardens. "I was just being honest."

"I never asked you to be honest."

"Yes, you did. You asked me what I thought."

"I didn't expect you to be so bloody critical."

"Honest," she insists.

Max rubs his face. "Bloody hell."

"Maybe I was a bit harsh about your house."

"Yeah, you were." Max waits. "Is that it?"

"What else should there be?"

"Thank you for having me? Sorry I was rude about your music? Sorry I'm such a pain in the arse?"

"I was being *honest*," Soleil says again. "Why do people have such a problem with honesty?"

If Soleil were a guy Max probably would have punched her by now. He could have blamed it on the gin.

"There's honesty and then there's fucking rudeness," he repeats.

"You're saying I should never say what I really think? I should only say what suits you?"

Helen appears beside Max. "Hey, you two."

They both look up at her.

"Getting along?" she asks.

Max gives a dishonest smile and Soleil says nothing.

JULIETTE REFILLS HIS glass and Max grins at her gratefully.

"You spoil him, Juliette," Eddie says, shaking his head.

Juliette is a wonder. If Max mentions a cheese or a dish he likes, then it is served next time he comes. She sorts out all the bills, tells him not to worry about anything. And he doesn't. He should probably give her a pay rise. Come to think of it, Max isn't 100 percent sure what he does pay Juliette.

"Thanks, Juliette."

"*De rien.* It is your birthday, after all," she demurs. "I'll serve dinner in about half an hour. Does that suit?"

"Perfect," Max slurs, giving her a thumbs-up.

Helen giggles.

"What?"

"You're drunk."

"Is that so bad?"

Maybe he should ease up. Max always drinks more when he's not taking coke. He is dying to do some coke. He glances at Eddie. Eddie would do coke with him.

Helen passes him a box. "So."

"So. For me?"

It's about the size of a shoe box but upright.

"It's nothing you need."

Max puts down his drink. The box is wrapped in black paper with a pattern of staring milk-white calavera. He passes his thumb over one; it's raised and velvety. He peels off the red satin ribbon.

"Don't tip it," Helen warns.

He opens the lid.

Inside is a potted plant, except the pot is half a coconut and the stand is a colorful coil—a bedspring covered in different pieces of tightly wound wool.

"It's baby's tears. The plant, I mean."

Max lifts it out of the box carefully. Tiny leaves dot falling green tendrils hanging over the edge of the coconut shell. Max feels someone behind him.

"What is that?" Eddie leans on the back of the couch.

"Baby's tears," Max tells him.

"That'll definitely go with the decor," Eddie jokes.

Helen reaches out and gives him a shove. Max wishes Eddie wasn't there. He wishes it were just him and Helen somewhere dark and silent. Max runs his finger over a piece of mustard-yellow wool. Next to it soft mint green. Then red, then brown, then pink. The rainbow journeys up the coil and then runs around and back down again.

Helen pushes at him with her toe. "You remember?"

He looks over to her. "Of course I remember."

"Remember what?" Eddie asks.

Go away, Eddie.

"Max made me a potted plant holder just like that one when we were at college."

"Yeah? Didn't know you were such a crafter, mate."

"You know me. Multitalented."

"I'd failed an illustration paper . . . ," Helen says.

Max nods.

". . . and my father was being a shit." Helen turns to Eddie. "Max made me the holder and brought over a bottle of vodka. Made it all better."

"Aw," Eddie says, nudging Max's shoulder.

Fuck off, Eddie.

Helen leans toward Max. "'Cause that's what he always did. Made it all better. Eh, Max?" She reaches out and takes his hand, their fingers weaving together. He wishes Helen could read his mind.

I love you. I need you. It's you; you are it. It's always been you. Be mine.

Eddie hangs over the couch and stares at them both with a goofy, drunken smile on his face.

"I love it," Max replies.

Chapter Eleven

JULIETTE

It is eight o'clock when Juliette plates up Paol's catch. It fills three large platters piled with ice chips—small bright red crustaceans, new-shell spider crabs called *moussettes,* thin black *bigorneaux*—everything with claws and barnacles like little prehistoric monsters. A bounty. *Fruits de mer*—"fruits of the sea"; *trésors* ("treasures"), more like. From sweet fresh oysters to fat crab claws and everything in between—vermillion, black, and gray. Sophie comes into the kitchen as Juliette is preparing the garnishes: bouquets of garden herbs and juicy, fragrant lemon cheeks. Her hair is still wet. The music from the lounge can just be heard through the thick stone walls that cocoon the kitchen. Juliette smiles at her. "Do you like this music?"

Sophie rolls her eyes in reply.

"My parents liked Burt Bacharach," Juliette says.

"I don't know who that is."

"You are lucky."

Having plated up the seafood, Juliette moves on to finish preparing the other dishes. She deftly removes the outer leaves of an artichoke.

"Do your parents live here? In Douarnenez?" Sophie asks.

"They used to," Juliette replies, nodding and then pausing, fingers on the artichoke. "My parents passed away."

Sophie's cheeks redden at the comment. "So you were born here? In Douarnenez?" she says, as though that's what she meant all along.

Juliette places the prepared artichoke on a tray. "Yes. I grew up here and afterward I went to Paris. I moved back to take care of my father." She smiles. "I never thought I'd live here again."

"It's a small place."

"You live in London?" Juliette asks.

"Yes."

"Douarnenez is very small compared to London. Almost everywhere is though, no? Compared."

"I guess." Sophie shrugs. "So, do you . . . kind of . . . know everyone here?" she asks.

Juliette turns to her. Sophie quickly glances down at a platter. "Not everyone. But quite a few," she replies.

Sophie pushes some ice chips around with the tip of her finger. She clearly doesn't want to be in the lounge with her parents and her parents' friends. Juliette remembers that feeling. Fifteen is an uncomfortable age. Decade, even. Sometimes Juliette still feels uncomfortable in adult company—the burly, opinionated men lined up on the stools in the local bars; the women who gather in the hair salons, gossiping about neighbors who have left husbands and celebrities whose children have strange names. Though Douarnenez is Juliette's birthplace, the people often feel foreign to her.

Finished with the artichokes, Juliette places a huge piece of buttered and garlic-studded lamb atop a bed of celadon-colored beans. The pungent smell of raw garlic and softened, salted butter makes Juliette hungry.

"Who lives next door to here?" Sophie asks, waving casually across the garden.

Juliette's gaze follows her gesture.

"I mean, just generally," Sophie says as nonchalantly as possible, her voice catching and betraying her.

Juliette washes her hands. "Paol and Mari Reynaud and their children are in the house right next to this one. They have two boys and a girl. Paol is a fisherman—one of the few local fishermen left—and Mari is a schoolteacher. They're good people. I get all my seafood from Paol."

"Oh, okay," Sophie replies.

Juliette glances at the girl, wet and stalky. She remembers Etienne in the tree at the front of the house: the flash of his teeth, the muscles knotting under his skin. A boy outgrowing his boy-frame.

Juliette looks to the ceiling. "I think the eldest son helps Paol with the boats during school holidays. I can't remember his name . . . ," she lies, testing.

"Etienne," Sophie whispers.

Juliette smiles. "Right. Etienne."

Sophie's cheeks burn red.

So that is why the girl is drenched, Juliette muses, pretending to concentrate on putting the huge piece of lamb in the oven. She remembers the sensations: the quickened breath, the thumping heart, the feeling that you might float away. Those sensations are quite familiar to her at the moment. Juliette has a wave of affection for the thin, awkward girl standing in her kitchen, getting in her way.

"It's nice . . . Douarnenez. Even though it's small. The beach is cool."

Juliette nods. "It's rugged but it's pretty."

"Yeah. Rugged."

"Do your parents always take you on holiday with them?"

"We don't go on many holidays."

"You're close with your parents though?" Juliette asks gently.

"My dad, I suppose. Less my mum."

"Your mum works?"

"Yeah, but it's not that. It's . . . I don't know. Maybe I am more like my dad. Or maybe my dad kind of trusts me more. He knows what I can do. He knows I am not a kid . . .

"I'm not a kid," Sophie repeats, a little too assertively.

Juliette nods, understanding. She had been so hoped for that her parents had treated her with kid gloves. She knew they adored her, but it often made it worse, made it harder to grow up and make her own choices. Juliette knew, acutely, that her decisions might disappoint them. She had loved them and they loved her, but it had felt complicated. Now that they were both gone, it suddenly seemed very simple.

"Do you want help to set the table?" Sophie asks, her voice now soft.

"I'd love that," Juliette replies. She picks up a seafood platter and watches as Sophie picks up another. As they leave the kitchen, Sophie mumbles, "I'm really sorry about your parents, Juliette."

Juliette turns. "Me too."

MAX'S DINING ROOM, like most of the new rooms in the house, has a huge floor-to-ceiling window along one wall. The rain has left long satiny lines that reflect on the wineglasses that Juliette and Sophie place at each setting. It's warm enough, though the curtains aren't drawn. On the opposite wall is a massive black-and-white photograph of a woman. Her head is tipped forward, her long, curling hair blowing across her face and up above her as though she could be falling. Behind her the sky is charcoal, rain clouds gathering. She stands among tawny grasses wearing a thin white dress.

With the place settings complete and the seafood laid out ready for the birthday feast, Juliette lights candles in small brass bowls and places them down the center of the table and along the buffet. She watches Sophie skim her fingertips over the grain of the wood table and press down into the knots. She has watched Max do exactly the same thing, and Juliette too has imagined the dips and crevices as rivers, thought of finding tiny shells and stones she could press into the cracks. The silk of the wood has made her think of the silk of a river, her hand in the green water, the tendrils of a weeping willow overhead. Sunshine against her legs, the sound of the water running over stones. Someone beside her. Someone stroking her hair.

"Ready for us?"

Max is holding his glass and swaying a little. Helen is on his arm. She is still wearing the long dress but is now shoeless. She smiles at Juliette.

"Ready. Sit wherever you like."

Max takes a seat at the center of the table and draws out a chair for Helen. Sophie is still standing.

"Sit with us, Sophie?" Helen asks.

"Oh, thanks, but I should probably get changed," Sophie says, glancing down at her wet clothes.

As she leaves, the others start piling in: Eddie and Beth, Nina and Lars, Rosie, Soleil, and last of all Hugo. They settle into their seats as Juliette pours wine—more local Muscadet to complement the seafood.

Once the glasses are filled, Juliette places extra bottles

into ice buckets on the buffet and instructs everyone to help themselves. She has to shift a potted plant to make room for the wine buckets. The pot is made from half a coconut, and the base is some kind of wire covered in threads of different-colored wool. Juliette runs her finger along the fuzzy stripes, just as Sophie had done with the grain of the table. She senses someone standing beside her and turns to see Helen, arm across her front, left hand holding a wineglass.

"I know. It doesn't really go with anything."

"You made it?"

"Yes." Helen laughs, her mouth wide open.

"It's really beautiful."

"That's very generous of you. And completely untrue."

"No, really," Juliette insists. "There's not much . . . color . . ."

They both glance around the room: the huge photograph, the pale walls, the soft gray curtains, the large blackness of the window.

"I live in a pigsty," Helen mumbles.

Juliette wonders if she is drunk. Probably a little.

"Not *literally*," Helen adds. "I mean, my apartment is a complete mess. I'm not much of a housekeeper. I'm not tidy."

Juliette blinks. "I'm not that tidy either in my own house. It's actually my parents' . . . Clean, yes, but tidy, no."

"You're not one of those really organized people? You know, a place for everything and everything in its place."

"What gave you that idea?"

"I don't know. You seem like you have it all together."

Juliette laughs. It is so far from the truth. "Coming from the woman who looks like that." She gestures to the smooth bob, the elegant dress. Even Helen's toenails are painted, a light tea rose color. Juliette doesn't have the time or inclination to paint her toenails. Helen's feet are small, slender, and pale.

"Oh no," Helen replies. "This is all I manage and it took me long enough to sort this part of my life out. I get a good haircut and wear black. Dressing myself is about all I can do. I'm basically a five-year-old."

"Well, *I* don't have it all together," Juliette replies firmly.

Helen smiles. "That makes me feel better."

"I'm sure your place is not a pigsty."

"It is," Helen assures her. "But I quite like it that way. I think I might have gotten too old to change my ways."

"That does happen," Juliette agrees, thinking of the house, still cluttered with her parents' things. She should have moved on by now, from the things and from Douarnenez.

"I want to go with you next time you go into the village," Helen says. "I want to see it. Douarnenez reminds me so much of England."

"Yes, we call it Cornaille, like Cornwall. We have strong ties with that part."

"Hugo was saying something about that."

They both look over toward Hugo. He's slumped in his chair, tapping the edge of his glass.

"He's not really part of the . . . friends with you all?" Juliette asks delicately.

"You could say that."

"He's—"

"Pompous. Is that the word you were looking for?"

Juliette presses her lips together.

"It's okay, I've always been too blunt." Helen glances at Soleil, who is tackling a crab leg with a silver crab fork and serious resolve. "It seems to run in the family. Anyway, yes, Hugo is . . . different."

Juliette remains silent.

"We could be nicer," Helen says, her smile fading. "It's just that we love Rosie so much. Too much, probably. She's a grown woman; she can make her own choices. But she's the youngest of us all. Only by a bit, but it seems like more. She's sweet, you know? She had a good childhood." Helen hesitates. "She still believes in happily ever after."

Juliette takes a bottle from the ice bucket, opens it, and tops up Helen's glass.

"You don't?"

Helen shrugs. "I'd like to. I want to. I've just never seen it. Have you?"

Juliette sees her mother reaching out for her father, her father wrapping her mother's tiny hand in his. Both of them turning to her, eyes wide, hopeful, wanting only the best. Juliette feels the sharp, familiar stab of guilt.

"Once," Juliette answers. "Well, no, more than once probably, but once for sure."

"You're lucky."

"I guess so." Juliette nestles the bottle back into the ice. "Though sometimes I wonder if it makes it harder. I believe in happily ever after; I'm just not sure I believe it is possible . . ." She pauses. *For me,* she almost says. It rests at the front of her mouth the way a sad truth does, like a menthol pastille: slick and hard, the vapors filling your mouth and whooshing up your nose with spine-tingling clarity.

"I'd like to believe in it," Helen says again.

Juliette half expects to see Helen staring at Max. She has been watching them together and they are so close; there is no denying that. Helen lies against him on the couch, reaches for him when he is within reaching distance. Max stares at Helen the way a child stares at someone dressed in one of those animal costumes at a fair—entranced, baffled, enamored—trying to find the person inside.

Juliette remembers that feeling and the one that follows, the heady, dizzying awe succeeded by aching disappointment. There are only so many times a person can risk heartbreak. Juliette feels as though she may have reached her quota, that her heart might not withstand more shattering.

But when Juliette turns to her Helen is not looking at Max; she is gazing at the photograph on the wall. She gestures to it with her wineglass. "You can see that woman's nipples," she murmurs.

"Oui," Juliette replies, smiling.

"I just noticed." Helen grins. "It's brilliant."

"Oui," Juliette says again. They both laugh.

JULIETTE PLACES DOWN the birthday meal. Lamb. Artichokes. Beans. Lars helps her pass around plates. Chatter and the clattering of plates and tongs and cutlery syncopate one another.

"Sophie?" Juliette hears Nina ask.

The girl has returned dressed in another large sweater and narrow jeans. There is a piece of bread on her plate she has picked to pieces, pinching and rubbing it between thumb and forefinger into uniform-sized crumbs. Her eyes stare; her cheeks are pink. Juliette knows the name that is at her lips. *Etienne.*

"Sorry?"

"Lamb?" her mother asks.

"No."

"But you haven't eaten . . . ," Nina insists.

"I don't feel like it," Juliette hears Sophie say. She avoids looking at either of them.

Nina lowers her voice. "Darling, you've barely eaten all weekend—"

"I don't feel like it," Sophie says again, challenge in her voice.

Juliette wonders if Sophie is not eating for the reasons she didn't eat much last night or this morning or for new reasons—reasons that involve a boy who is crowding out all other thoughts, making her feel giddy, making her feel as if her stomach is full of bees. Nina glances over to Juliette, but Max calls out to her first.

"What is this lamb called again, Juliette?"

"*Pré-salé.* Salt-marsh lamb."

"That's right. What does it do? Drink salt water?"

Hugo raises his voice. "Feeds on marsh grass that grows in seawater."

"Marsh grass?" Rosie asks.

"Hugo is right," Juliette replies. "It's a special kind of lamb you can only get from this part of France. The regulations are very strict. The lamb has to feed on this grass for at least seventy days. Otherwise they cannot call it *pré-salé.*"

Sophie stares at Juliette and then reaches out for a small sliver for her plate.

"It's the best lamb I have ever tasted," Helen says.

Lars nods. "Hear, hear."

Juliette watches Max look at Helen and then back to her.

"Thanks, Juliette. Great job. As always."

"*Sans problème.*"

"What—" Beth whispers to Eddie.

"It means no problem," Hugo interrupts with a sigh, pushing a bean around his plate with his fork.

"Happy birthday, Max," Juliette says.

Max flashes her a smile. Then he shifts his gaze from Juliette to Beth. Tonight she has put on a silver necklace with a horseshoe-shaped pendant, and her shining red hair hangs in gentle waves. "So, Beth," Max says, his voice slightly slurred. "You're the new girl. You'll have to tell us more about you."

Beth smiles carefully. "What do you want to know?"

"What's a pretty girl like you doing with an ugly thug like Eddie?" Max tips his head back and laughs.

"Hey!" Eddie cries.

"Just ignore him," Nina advises Beth. "Max has no manners."

"It's true though. Look at her. She's bloody gorgeous."

"You're drunk," Rosie says wearily.

Max stares at Beth and takes a big gulp of wine. He gestures at her with his glass. "Batting above your average there, mate."

"Touché," Eddie says, still smiling. "Because she's so lovely or because I'm so unlovely?"

"Both," Max replies.

"Charming," Nina says, shaking her head. "Juliette, don't give him any more wine."

"It's my wine," Max contests.

"How did you two meet?" Rosie asks.

Beth looks down at the table. "It's not a very interesting story . . ."

"She felt sorry for him," Max says, giving another laugh.

"Give it a rest, Max," Nina mutters. "Tell us, Beth," she says encouragingly. "We know everyone else's stories. We're sick of them."

"We met at the hair salon," Eddie says, reaching his arm around Beth.

"Where I work," Beth adds.

"I bet you get hit on all the time," Helen says, but in a way that is sisterly.

Beth shrugs. "I don't pay much attention. People are different with hairdressers. They like being listened to; it makes 'em feel good."

"I love my hairdresser," Rosie confesses. "I'd follow him to the ends of the world. If he moved to Australia, I might have to move too."

"Well, that's nice," Hugo mutters.

"I don't have a hairdresser," Soleil says.

"No kidding," Max murmurs.

Nina nods at Rosie. "I feel the same. My hairdresser is a gay Japanese man. I would have his babies if he asked me."

"Aw, Mum, that is gross," Sophie groans. Juliette notices she has finished the lamb she put on her plate.

"Seriously!" Nina giggles. "Those head massages when he shampoos my hair . . . oh my God . . ."

"Mum!"

Nina and Lars laugh together.

"Do you give good head massages?" Max asks Beth, his voice a drunken purr.

Attention snaps back to him. Rosie shifts uncomfortably in her seat. Juliette watches Beth. She gives a polite smile, then turns to Eddie. "What do you think, babe?"

Eddie grins and mimics Nina. "Oh. My. God." He squeezes Beth closer to him. "I was getting my hair cut once a fortnight."

Beth admits, "It was pretty short."

"I finally worked up the courage to ask her out. To a movie. That one with . . ."

"George Clooney," Beth supplies.

"That's right. Spent the whole movie thinking what a fool

I was, taking her to watch George bloody Clooney and then hoping she would like the look of me after!"

Beth laughs. "I did." She kisses his cheek. "I do."

"That's sweet," Nina says softly.

Lars picks up her bandaged hand and holds it gently, like it is a stunned bird, in his palm. Then he reaches out and slowly rubs her back. Helen is watching them too. She glances over to Juliette. Juliette knows what she is thinking. She wants to revise her answer about happily ever after. She has seen it. Lars and Nina.

Max gets up from his chair. It topples over. "Whoops!"

"I'll get it," Juliette says, hurrying over.

"I'm off for a piss," he declares.

"MAX IS ON the juice tonight, eh, Helen?" Lars asks, once Max has left the room.

"I'm not his keeper."

"He was rude," Rosie says.

"I'm okay," Beth replies cheerfully, though to Juliette she looks a little fatigued.

Rosie ignores her. "Maybe he's worried about his birthday?"

"Maybe he's just rude," Hugo says, to which Helen shoots him a glare.

"Max drinks too much. So? That's not news," she says. "You don't know everything about him, about his life."

"His life's not too bad, Helen," Lars says.

"Maybe. Lonely though," she says softly.

"I think he makes sure he isn't lonely for long," Nina says wryly.

"Hey," Eddie says, chuckling. "Do you remember that time with his hat of change?"

Lars looks over to him. "What were we drinking?"

"God only knows. What was he *making* us drink?" Helen groans.

"Wasn't it whiskey and something? Something disgusting and creamy, like Kahlúa?" Rosie says.

Nina laughs. It really is a big, beautiful laugh, Juliette notices. A pink peony in full bloom.

"That's what it looked like coming back up, if I remember," Nina says, pointing at Rosie, who laughs too. Hugo glances disappointedly between the two of them.

Juliette begins gathering up empty plates. Soleil stands to help her.

"What did the hat change?" Juliette asks.

"It was a hat *full of* change. As in coins," Helen replies.

"Oh."

"He was working in a pub, collecting coins as tips. He put them into a woolen hat—" Eddie begins.

"Which he had to wear because Rosie and I had shaved off his gorgeous hair," Helen interrupts.

"Then when it was full," Eddie continues, "he invited us all to the pub, dropped the hat in the middle of the table, and told us we were going to spend it until we were—"

"Eddie." Nina tips her head at Sophie.

"Helen danced on the tables, do you remember that?" Lars says. "Had half the pub mesmerized."

"Oh, please," Helen replies, rolling her eyes.

"Especially you boys," Nina adds, looking pointedly at Eddie and Lars, clearly imagining Max with them.

"Max gave us horsey rides home, didn't he, Rosie?" Helen says.

"That's right. God. All that neighing and falling over on the grass. How did we ever drink that much? I can't drink that much anymore."

Eddie snorts. "Speak for yourself. I have the stamina of a racehorse."

Beth is rubbing her boyfriend's shoulder. "Oh, darlin' . . ." She says it so consolingly that everyone laughs except for Rosie.

Lars slaps the table. "Stamina of a what, Beth? Tell us the truth."

Helen and Nina join in. "Yeah, tell us, Beth, stamina of what?"

Rosie takes a big drink from her glass and glances away. Hugo stares at her.

"A lady doesn't like to say . . . ," Beth murmurs.

"Hey, hey!" Eddie interjects. "That's enough. You're badgering my girl."

"I can handle it," Beth replies, her voice teasing. Eddie scoops her into his lap and puts a hand over her laughing mouth. When Eddie pulls his hand away they are both giggling and Beth's lipstick is smudged.

"We're not giving up on you," Helen warns Beth.

The music starts up again. "Love Will Tear Us Apart" by Joy Division. Juliette hums along.

Nina leans back in her chair. "I think we can blame Max for the folly of our youth," she says wistfully. Everyone around the table nods.

"He always found money for booze," Eddie says admiringly.

"And nothing else," Helen says, shaking her head.

"Didn't you have to pay his rent once?" Rosie asks, a hint of disapproval in her voice.

"More than once." Helen turns to Juliette. "He's changed since then."

Hugo gives a small grunt. Helen swivels to face him.

"Did you want to say something, Hugo?"

"Hugo," Rosie hisses, warning him.

"No," he replies, clearing his throat, returning Rosie's glare.

"He wasn't great with money; he'd never had any before. He has it sorted now," Helen says to Juliette.

"He always spent it on us," Nina says.

Helen nods. "He'd use his last pound on us, buying us something to make us happy. Dinner. A book—"

"Beer." Eddie raises his glass.

Hugo stands up. "I'm going to bed."

"There's dessert ... the birthday cake—" Juliette says, thinking of the *kouign-amann* ready to be placed in the oven.

Hugo raises his palm. "Thank you, but I'm full. *C'était délicieux.*"

Juliette nods.

"Good night," Rosie says as Hugo bends to give her a kiss on the cheek. "I'll be up later."

"Yes," he replies briskly.

The music changes and everyone seems to drink at the same time. Juliette watches Sophie eat a few beans off her plate. Nina asks Helen, "What *were* you dancing to on the tables that night?"

"Pulp," Eddie answers for her.

"Oh, was I? I don't remember—" Helen starts to reply but dissolves into laughter.

"That's right," agrees Lars. " 'Common People.' "

"Don't judge me!" Helen pleads to Juliette, laughing so hard she is crying.

"I remember that song," Soleil says, giving a rare, diffident smile. She has a stack of plates in her hands. "You played it a lot when I was a kid." She glances at Lars. "She was on the tables?"

"Do not listen to any of them," Helen instructs with mock earnestness.

They all grin and look down at their drinks. Pause. Listen to the music; get lost in memories.

Suddenly there is a horrible retching noise. The smell reaches Juliette, sharp and acidic. Everyone turns at once to Beth, mess on the floor by her feet.

"Sorry," she says in a small voice.

Everyone is quickly out of their chairs.

"I'll get a cloth," Soleil says.

Juliette goes to Beth, her face pale, Eddie now rubbing her back. Nina passes her a glass of water. Lars and Helen attempt mopping up the mess with some cloth napkins. From down at the end of the table there is a disgusted sigh. Juliette glances across the detritus—wine and beer glasses, a candle shoved into an empty bottle, stained napkins screwed up into balls—to Sophie standing with her arms crossed.

"Grown-ups . . ."

Nina straightens. "Sophie?"

"Grown-ups are fucked up," she mutters, leaving the room.

Max passes Sophie on his way back into the room. His eyes are red-rimmed as he studies the vomit and the people gathered to clean it up. He claps his hands admiringly and guffaws. "Beth! Ha-ha!"

To which everyone looks over at him.

Soleil returns and passes Beth a cloth. As she presses it to her mouth, she looks up to Juliette, her gaze catching and holding, her mouth turning down. She looks so vulnerable. Her red hair frames her pallid face and her mouth opens and shuts, as though wanting to explain, and Juliette suddenly understands. The bag from the pharmacist. The vomit. The beseeching look in Beth's eyes that asks: *What do I do now?*

But she is not the right person to answer.

Because Juliette has never been pregnant.

Chapter Twelve

MAX

"Sorry about your floor," Eddie says.

Beth, having been tidied up, has decamped to the lounge, while Max and Eddie remain in the dining room.

Max shrugs. "It's just a floor."

"But it's such a classy house."

Max recalls Soleil's comments about the house and about the Jacks. He tips the glass in his hand from side to side and feels that itch bloom and deepen. More of a rash than an itch. It's making him restless. It's making him feel too much like his father.

Max isn't going to do drugs. He had promised himself. The stuff he'd taken in the car was to take the edge off. That was the last; he could go a weekend without it. He didn't want the others to think he had a problem. Besides, he didn't have a problem.

"Did you ever think you'd be here?" Eddie asks, leaning back in his chair.

"I never thought I'd leave Grahame Park, mate."

Max hasn't said the words *Grahame Park* for a long while.

He tries not to even think of them. It's easier that way. Because when he does the images of the place—the lines of bricks and lines of houses, everything in lines, and the sky like a wet rag and the faces of the people who have lived there too long, who would live there till they died though they were dying already it looked like—flash in his mind.

"Didn't think I'd get to forty either."

Eddie nods. "You make forty look pretty good, Max."

"Thanks." Max shifts in his chair. He hates this kind of talk. Eddie often wants to compliment Max and compliments don't sit well with Max. "I'll let you know if I change my mind about not being into blokes," he jokes.

Eddie laughs and that breaks it. The images of Grahame Park, the faces, scattering.

Max really wants some coke. He changes the subject. "You did well with her," he says, nodding toward Beth in the lounge.

"Yeah. You said that." Eddie smirks. "Batting above my average."

"I call it how I see it," Max replies.

"Yeah, I know," Eddie confesses. "She's gorgeous and she's not a nutcase. I mean, she's actually really nice."

"Not many of those."

"Sometimes she reminds me of Rosie a bit. You know, before . . ."

"Hugo?"

Eddie blinks. "Anyway, we have a laugh. She gets my humor."

"Ah. That's what's wrong with her," Max says.

Eddie grins. "Fuck you."

Max raises his glass.

Juliette comes into the dining room and nods at the two men. She is carrying a tray. They watch her pile it high with plates and glasses and dirty napkins.

"Cheers, Juliette," Max says as she leaves.

"No problem, Max," she replies.

Max is jiggling one leg. The itch-rash is still bugging him. He puts his hand against the leg. He turns to Eddie when Juliette is out of the room. "What do you think of Soleil?"

Eddie shrugs. "I don't know."

"She's a bitch, right? Nina wouldn't agree with me, but she's a bitch."

Eddie looks blank.

"She told me my house was a monstrosity." Max laughs bitterly.

"Well, that's not right . . ."

"And she hates the Jacks."

"Oh." Eddie considers and takes a drink. He has almost finished the glass. "But she's Helen's sister."

"Not really. Not technically."

"No, you're right. Not technically," Eddie agrees.

"She's . . ." Max tries to think of a way to explain what he means. *Caustic. Venomous.* ". . . nasty," he concludes inadequately. He wants to add that Soleil hasn't thanked him once and explain how rude she has been. Eddie is agreeing with him, but Max wants Eddie to agree with him more, to be on his side. Not even Hugo has bothered Max as much as Soleil has in just one day, which is pretty unusual considering how much Max dislikes Hugo.

"I don't know," Eddie says slowly. "I mean, she's kind of . . . hot?" He looks at Max, seeking agreement. "In her own way. Tough, kind of mean, doesn't care what anyone . . . She's not my type, but you know . . ."

Max nods, reluctantly conceding. "Yeah, I know. Not my type either, but there is something."

Eddie holds up his glass. "You want another drink? I'm going to get one."

Max stares at his friend, now getting to his feet. Reliable Eddie. Eddie had been getting Max drinks for years. Decades. They'd had some fun. At college. Traveling around Australia together. Eddie had driven Max a bit crazy then at times; there was such a thing as being too agreeable. But they always had a laugh. Not the deep and meaningful chats Max had with Helen, but then guys weren't like that. Max only ever had those kinds of conversations with her; she is something else, a different category.

Max knows that when Eddie is around he will have a good time. Eddie will drink with him till whatever hour, will agree to any misadventure, any high jinks. He is his wingman.

"How about something stronger?" Max says before Eddie leaves the room.

Eddie pivots to look at him. His face is doubtful. "I don't know . . . Beth, sick . . . It's not like her—"

Max laughs. "You do like her."

"Yeah. I like her."

"Come on, mate," Max urges.

"I've been laying off the—"

"Eddie? Seriously?"

"She is never sick," Eddie replies uncomfortably.

Max gestures toward the lounge. "She's being looked after by about a thousand people, including Nina and Rosie and Helen and Juliette. She's got a crew. She'll be fine."

"Yeah," Eddie replies slowly.

"Hey, mate . . . ," Max starts. He shouldn't say it. He promised himself. Eddie is saying no and Max should leave it at that. But damn if that itch isn't getting stronger and making him feel crazy, feel like his father, standing on the balcony at Grahame Park, his face pale and furious. Waiting for Max. Waiting to give Max a beating.

Max feels wrong before he says it. But he says it anyway. "Come on, it's my birthday."

STANDING ALONE ON the deck, before he lights up, Max smells *kouign-amann* baking. If the scent were a color it'd be honey, the yellow of summer afternoon sunshine; if it were a sound it'd be the National played loud. Fuck, he feels better. He had needed to loosen up. Have fun. See? That's what Nina had said. Nina was always right. Something to take the edge off. That's all it was.

Max hears a cough below him. Out on the grass Soleil is standing with a drink in one hand. She's looking out, even though it's dark, close to midnight now probably, and there's nothing to see. She is a shadow, a black paper cutout, of a woman with a glass in her hand. Max feels pretty buzzed. He feels tall, ten feet tall, like he is a magician. He walks down the steps toward her.

"Nice night for it," Max says, sounding old. It makes him laugh. The black paper cutout of her doesn't turn.

"Full moon," she says, lifting her glass to the sky.

Max nods and offers his cigarette. Soleil takes it. It reminds Max of when Helen was that age, when they were both that age, lying in bed sharing a smoke between them.

"Happy birthday."

"Thanks," Max replies.

She passes the cigarette back. "You can hear the sea."

Max nods. "Thought you hated the place."

"I never said that," Soleil disagrees. "I said I don't like what you've done with the house. There's a difference."

Max drags on the cigarette. He doesn't care much about

what Soleil thinks. Soleil could vanish and Max would barely bat an eyelid.

"Douarnenez is nice. The sea, the garden, Juliette, the birds . . . I like all of that."

Max doesn't reply. He is looking up at the moon and studying its shadows. He can see shapes; he can see a face. A woman's face, maybe. Soleil shifts; Max passes her the cigarette again.

"You're kind of prickly, you know?"

"Sorry?"

Max laughs. He didn't realize he'd said it out loud. Soleil glares at him. He can't really make out the glare in the darkness, but of course she is glaring.

"I was trying to be nice," Soleil mutters.

"What's not nice about being prickly?"

Max's body isn't complying now. It doesn't want to stand up straight. He falls from one leg to the other. He's just steady enough not to fall over completely.

"Cactuses are prickly . . ."

"Cacti. And you're wasted," Soleil accuses. Max laughs again.

Closer up and in the moonlight, Soleil's skin is something to behold. Shining and smooth. Unmarked. Taut. Firm and silk, both. The sequins on her dress wink and sparkle. They are little stars; they are little scales. She could be a sprite, a mermaid, a reptile. A wish, an illusion.

Max cannot see properly in this light, with drugs coursing through his blood. There's just a beautiful young woman, smoking. The memory of Helen floods his brain, bright and vivid. Helen in bed, Helen laughing, Helen passing him a bottle of whiskey . . .

"Has it been long enough?" Max slurs.

"What?"

"Is it later?" Max murmurs, reaching for her.

Max's lips find that pretty skin. It is as smooth as he thought and it tastes of something. Maybe sea salt. Maybe patchouli.

"Helen . . ."

"What are you doing?!"

Smoke, patchouli, sea salt.

"Get off me!"

Soleil's voice is like the muffled sounds of a party in another room, happening somewhere else but not here. Not that Max ever missed out on a party in another room. He feels a palm against his face, feels himself stumbling and falling now, his legs too jelly, his will too misplaced. His mouth is open when he falls onto the grass. That's what Max can smell now. Grass. Sweet, good grass, his face pressed into it, laughing. Then Soleil is close to him, above him. He cannot quite recall where she came from.

"You fuckwit. You fucking . . . *fuckwit.*" Soleil is so close to Max's face he can feel the spray of her words.

"Soleil?" Max asks, her name strange in his mouth. Soleil upends her glass all over Max's head. Max feels the wetness and then the bitter, quinine taste dripping down his lips. He wipes it away from his eyes. He cannot see properly. It's too dark. But there are stars coming closer.

"I'm not stupid, fuckwit. I see the way you look at my sister."

Max blinks, still unseeing.

"I know you think you love her. Everyone knows. But you are never, ever going to be good enough for her. Think you're some big-shot rock star? You are nothing. *Nothing.*"

Max feels his father's voice in his head like smashing saucepan lids together, hard and metal and mean. *Nothing. You are nothing.*

"You're all . . . *God.* I can't stand it here."

Max finds his voice. "Fuck you, arsehole," he growls.

There is movement against the grass. Footfalls. He opens one eye to see two figures on the deck. Someone made of stars and someone else reaching out for her as she rushes past.

Max's head falls against the grass, the velvet grass, and breathes in its damp greenness. All he needs is a nap—just a short nap—to gather the pieces, to get himself together.

"MAX?"

Someone is gently pressing his shoulder.

"Max?"

Max lifts his head. The person helps him roll over, then tries to sit him up.

"*Merde.*"

"Hey, Juliette."

"What are you doing out here? I've been looking for you. The others thought you had gone to bed."

"I came . . ." Max rubs his face, trying to remember. "I came for a smoke."

Juliette helps Max to his feet. "Let's get you inside."

Juliette slings Max's arm over her shoulder and they hobble together up the deck stairs. Juliette is strong and steady, despite her size.

They get up the stairs and into the house, Max now standing on his own while Juliette shuts the doors. It's much warmer inside. Max steadies himself. Juliette goes to the kitchen, and when she returns she is holding a cup of coffee and a piece of baguette stuffed with ham and cheese.

"Have this," she instructs. "It will sober you up."

Max nods and backs into a chair. Juliette places the coffee and food on a small side table.

"Food first," Juliette says. "The coffee is too hot."

Max does as he is told. He is still unsure of the day, of the time, but he's always found it best to let the details come to him. No need to kill a buzz too soon by looking for things to feel guilty about.

"Is it still my birthday?" Max asks, chewing on his sandwich. Juliette has spread it with mustard. It tingles his nostrils.

Juliette shakes her head.

"So I am officially forty."

"Officially," Juliette says.

She is watching him carefully. The sandwich is making Max feel better. They sit in silence for a few minutes while Max chews through it. Juliette passes him the coffee.

"Did you have a good birthday?"

Max sips. He can't remember some of the birthday, but that will come later. He'll sleep and remember things tomorrow. He gives Juliette a thumbs-up. "All to plan, my friend. Thank you."

Juliette blinks and frowns. "About that . . ."

Max feels a pinch of day-after guilt. It's too early, or late, for confessing.

"I was going to serve *kouign-amann*. As birthday cake. But I burned it."

"Oh."

"Sorry, Max. I'll make a new one tomorrow"

Max rests the coffee cup on his knee and shakes his head, relieved. "Is that all?"

Juliette is still frowning. "I got talking to Helen. I've never burned *kouign-amann* before."

Max waves his free hand. "Shit, Juliette, I thought it was going to be something serious, someone hurt or something. It's cool, mate. It's just cake, right?"

"*Oui,*" Juliette replies, still seeming disconcerted.

Max reaches out to pat her shoulder. He can feel the food in his belly, the caffeine in his bloodstream slowly taking effect.

"I know what Helen is like. The girl can talk."

Momentarily forgotten, she is now back on his mind. Helen laughing. Helen tipping an oyster into her mouth. Helen giving him something. A potted plant. *Helen. Helen. Helen.* Her name thumps in Max's head like a heartbeat. He stands quickly.

"Are you okay? To get to bed?" Juliette asks.

Helen's head against his shoulder. Helen smoking in bed with him. Helen the first time he saw her. Her lean frame, her dark hair like a cloud behind her. The thick eyebrows, the smile, the long, pale fingers wrapped with his.

Helen on the deck, reaching out for the glittering woman. Calling to her sister.

Running after her.

Max's heart plummets, his breath leaves him for a moment. Recalling things in pieces—like sea glass—broken, soft, and misted. Has he ruined everything?

"Max?" Juliette asks.

But he is already going.

WITH EVERY STEP Max sees Helen in all her incarnations: Helen in the park that day he first met her, at a bar buying beer, with her legs in the air that time she fell off a wall and into sand and the rich laughter that followed, her fingers around a wineglass, her lips around a cigarette. Helen in heels at an exhibition opening, the way everyone in a room turns when she enters it, the way she holds her shoulders, the roll of her walk. Helen reaching for one of her friends, the way she closes her eyes when she hugs someone, the way she rests her head on Max's shoulder; how when she laughs too hard she loses her laugh altogether and makes those funny wheezy noises, one hand pressed to her chest. Helen drunk on the bathroom floor, giggling. Helen on the trampoline Lars and Nina bought for Sophie when she was small, hair and blouse flying. Helen smiling. Helen sad. *Helen.*

Her room is black but Max finds the bed.

"Max?" It is the voice Max wants to wake up to every morning: soft, a little raspy, tipsy still, full of love.

"Helen . . . I'm so sorry . . ."

In the silence Max feels like his chest is in a vise. He holds his breath and prays—prays!—she'll forgive him. That he can rescue this. His fingers curl tightly around the box in his hand.

"I was drunk. I didn't know what I was doing . . ."

"Jesus, Max." Her voice is weary.

Max shuffles up on the bed, his head still spinning.

Please, please, please.

"I didn't think you even liked her." Helen's voice is strange. Wounded or confused, Max can't tell which. He wishes he was able to see her face, but that would involve turning on the light. He's not feeling bold enough for that, for her to be able to see him.

"I don't," Max mutters. "I mean . . . I know she's your sister, so . . ." He wants to say, *I've been trying to like her,* but the truth is he hasn't really. He's been despising her, despising her closeness to Helen, the fact she gets to call herself family. That she has what he wants.

"I don't understand."

"I'm so sorry." Max means it so much it pinches. He's squeezing the box so hard it's hurting his palm. He can save this. He has to.

Helen takes a deep breath. "Yeah."

Max waits. Breathes in and out, steadying himself.

"I tried talking to her, but she's angry."

"That's fair." Max swallows.

"But then she's angry about everything these days . . ." Helen's voice softens. "I don't know what to do."

"You're good to her."

Helen sighs. The sound allows Max to breathe properly again. "Not good enough."

"Please don't say that," Max begs.

"My family, we're all so fucked up. I thought with Soleil I could—"

"It isn't your fault. I messed up. I'm the idiot."

Helen is silent. She stretches. "I think I'm still drunk. Maybe we should sleep."

"I need to talk to you about something," Max pleads.

"Maybe in the morning." She is slurring, Max notices now. "It'll be okay. We'll be okay."

"Yes," Max says. "We will be okay."

Max hears Helen's hand patting the sheets by his face. He grasps it.

She turns to him. "Max?"

She brushes the side of his face with her free hand. Max takes a full breath.

This is it.

"Helen, I love you."

Her fingers on his face. "Oh, Max, I love you too."

Max's chest tightens. He must go on. No matter what.

He feels woozy. He's still a bit high. He squeezes his eyes

shut, though there is no light, and forces himself to continue. *This* is later. Later is now.

"Not like that, Helen. Like this."

He finds her hand, gently opens the fingers, and presses the ring box into her palm.

"Max?"

"I've loved you as long as I've known you, Helen. I love everything about you. Every good thing, every tiny flaw, *every-thing*. There is no one I love more."

"Oh, Max . . ." Her voice is thin and delicate.

"No one, Helen. You're it. You are my family. You're all I have. You're the only one I want."

Max finds her face in the dark and strokes her cheek with his finger. Beautiful Helen.

"I want to wake up with you, Helen. I want to go to sleep next to you. I want to share it all. Everything."

Max finds Helen's lips. He runs his fingertips over them. He leans toward her, to feel those lips against his.

"Max."

The weight of the word. It is solid. It is an anchor.

"Max."

It cleaves a space between them.

"I—"

"I'm sorry," she falters. "I can't."

Dimanche *(Sunday)*

Chapter Thirteen

MAX

The sunlight slaps Max's face. He squints. The beach rolls away from him like a page, makes him feel as though he is in the center of things and at risk of falling and being closed up all at once. He is dizzy. He squeezes his eyes shut and then opens them again, but the glare is worse. A long white beach, the air throbbing with heat, panting like its own kind of beast, and Max, half dressed, on his back and sweltering. He sits up and hugs his knees to him, feeling the grains of sand press into his skin like little diamond chips. This is not Douarnenez.

Down at the other end of the long expanse of beach there is something dark and wobbling, shimmering, coming into view.

Max's voice sticks in his throat. A person or a monster? Wobbling, focusing, wobbling. A mirage, he guesses, or perhaps he does need glasses as Frank, from the band, once suggested. Then there are legs. And a torso. And a dark head. Or is that hair?

Hair.

Dark hair.

The figure is in a swimsuit. She is carrying a towel and wearing sunglasses, round ones with black disks for lenses.

The black swimsuit is low on the thighs. She has a way of walking that reminds Max of Marilyn Monroe. What do you call that walk?

Sashay.

She *sashays*.

Max waits for her to say his name. His own voice is still stuck, his tongue like a thick and dry washcloth in his mouth. He blinks and stares at the woman and wants her to come closer. A hot breeze is scattering handfuls of sand across Max's legs.

This woman is an angel, Max decides, though there are no wings and no halo. She makes him feel warm inside. She is bringing something good, Max can tell. Not a thing, of course, but . . . something. A delivery of good fate, of luck. She is a bathing suit angel. A goddess. A messenger.

She's close now and smiling. She's close enough for Max to see her teeth and see that her lips are painted an almost-red orange. Her glasses have tortoiseshell frames. Her swimsuit has gathers or pin tucks or ruching, whatever those things are called, that look like river ripples down her sides. Her skin is pale—pale as full-cream milk, French milk, the good stuff—and she has pink-beige freckles on her kneecaps.

Max's heart pounds.

"Max?" She pulls off her sunglasses.

No.

Max wants to turn away. It cannot be her, because Max does not know what she looks like. Not like this. He knows her only in two dimensions, in photographs. The sun leans on him, bright and bullying. Max wants her to stop smiling. It's too kind.

Not you.

The woman looks into his face. It is her. Though she's not quite clear, not perfect, it is her.

"Max?"

It's the voice that doesn't belong, the voice Max knows from other dreams.

"Max? Are you okay?"

From another world.

Helen.

Max sits up too fast. It makes him feel ill, almost ill enough to throw up. The blinds in his room are wide open and sunlight pours in. Helen is perched on the edge of the bed. She lays her hand against him, calming him, encouraging him back down onto the pillows.

"Fuck," he mutters, blinking.

Helen's hair is wet and she's wearing a white shirt and navy shorts. She looks like she should be on a yacht. She looks like a magazine cover. High gloss. Max inhales through his nose and catches the smell of himself, sour and dirty.

"You were having a bad dream," Helen says, patting his leg.

He rubs his eyes; he's still half stuck on that beach. His eyes feel full of sand.

"Feeling rough?"

He nods. "I'll be all right after something to eat."

"Juliette is cooking breakfast," Helen replies.

"Breakfast?" He shakes his head, which seems stuffed with stones. Max has the nagging feeling there is something he should be feeling badly about but he's not awake enough to put his finger on it. Helen smiles gently. It makes Max think of the woman from the dream's smile, her teeth, her lipstick.

She turns to stare out the window. Max watches a drop of water from Helen's hair slide down her neck and into her shirt. He thinks about following it with his finger or the tip of his tongue. This thought is better, is more familiar. The feeling slinks over him like a clean shirt, settles his heartbeat, presses pause on the tightening of his head.

"I should have come here earlier. Before," Helen says wistfully.

"We have busy lives," Max replies. His head is starting to hurt, and it's still a little woolly from the night before. It pains him to think, to remember. He resolves to be kind in the meantime. He will be loving and kind. He can do that; he has it in him. He takes Helen's hand in his.

Helen looks at him. "Do you ever wonder what you're doing? I mean, why?" She glances down at Max's hand and whispers, "Sometimes it feels like my life is living me rather than the other way around."

Max wants to say, *I know exactly what you mean,* and for it to have poignancy, for it to resonate and amplify and clarify all that Helen is thinking, in that way that staring at fireworks bursting across a dark sky makes you feel alive and full of truth.

"You get this. Don't you? I know you do." Helen looks at him pointedly. Max's brain starts to function again.

Soleil. Last night. The ring box.

His stomach lurches.

"Sometimes it feels like I just woke up in my life," Helen says. "I'm just stumbling along. I can't figure out who made all the choices to get me to this point, you know? I know it was me but . . . what was I thinking? What did I want?"

Max's mind whirs. He gathers up the broken shards of memories. It takes him a few moments to put it back together—a few painful moments. Helen's cheek under his fingers, her lips. Her voice apologizing once, twice—each time driving a kind of dagger into Max. Staggering back to his room in the dark, throwing the box—that stupid box he'd placed all his hopes on—across the floor.

He really feels like he is going to be sick now.

Max searches for the right thing to say back. The perfect thing. The thing that lets Helen know he gets it, really gets it, that it's no big deal. But of course it is.

Instead he jokes, "This is pretty heavy for early in the morning, isn't it?"

Max, you are such a fool.

"I need to know you are okay." She looks so tortured.

The room sways and Max's head pounds. "I'm fine, I'm fine," he replies. "I'll be fine."

The moment shatters. *Fuck,* Max thinks. *Fuck, fuck, fuck.*

"I should find Soleil," Helen says.

"No. Stay," Max asks, his voice more desperate than he wants it to be. He clears his throat.

"Juliette is probably down there by herself too, cooking for all of us. I should find . . ." Helen is straightening now, ready to stand. She looks uncomfortable. She releases his hand. ". . . my sister."

"Stay here," Max begs, wobbling dangerously on that line between cool and wretched.

This isn't happening. This is not the plan.

Helen stands. "I'll see you downstairs." She turns to leave.

Max feels like he stood up too fast, like all the blood has rushed from his brain. "I'm sorry!"

Helen pauses, frowning, hand on the door handle. Max's fear, his shame, deepens like a wound to the chest.

"I need to think."

Max hesitates. "Okay."

Helen's nails tap against the handle. "Just let me . . . think."

Max nods.

A feeling like a single plucked string. Hope.

Chapter Fourteen

ROSIE

Rosie's hands are sunk in warm, soapy water. Though Juliette begged her not to, washing up gives her something to do, something familiar, something safe. She rubs a dishcloth over a plate and stares out the window into the garden. There is a breeze bossing the flowers and leaves. She watches the branches of the linden tree sway.

"Mornin'."

Beth is wearing a robin's-egg-blue short set and red lipstick. Her hair is in victory rolls on the top of her head. She lifts her palm to Juliette, who is preparing breakfast. Rosie shakes water from one hand and smoothes down her own hair.

"Bonjour," Juliette replies.

Beth picks up the dishcloth hanging over the tap.

"You don't have to—" Rosie says.

"I kind of made a mess last night."

"How are you feeling today?"

"Much better. So sorry about that."

Rosie shrugs. "I have three boys. You can't shock me with a little vomit."

Beth gives a tentative laugh.

"It's not an invitation to throw up again," Rosie warns.

"Got it," Beth replies.

The women stand shoulder to shoulder. Rosie glances again at Beth's clothes and hair, then down at her bare feet and back again. She had once been bold with the clothes she wore. It feels like a long time ago.

"I like your outfit."

"Thanks. I made this," Beth replies.

"You can sew?"

"A bit. My mama taught me."

"Taught you well, it looks like," Rosie says.

"Thank you."

"Where is Eddie?" Rosie asks.

"Sleeping off the hangover."

"That could take a while."

Heads down, they smile at the same time.

"He's not much help in the kitchen," Beth concedes.

"No," Rosie replies.

"When I moved in I had to pull out and wash every single cup and plate and pot in the cupboard. They were filthy."

Rosie nods.

"He's a lot of fun though," Beth adds quickly. "He makes me laugh." She reaches for one of the bigger pots, dunks it in the water, and sets to work scrubbing at it with the cloth. "Well, you know that about him."

Rosie watches Beth's cheeks color. "He's always made us laugh," she replies diplomatically. "Max too."

Juliette retrieves a bowl from a cupboard and returns to her chopping board.

"How did you and Hugo meet?" Beth asks, taking two plates and handing one to Rosie to wash.

Rosie looks down at the plate. "At a pub."

"You've been married for a long time?"

"Yes," Rosie replies, thinking, *So, so long.* Last night they had slept with their backs to each other, pretending the other didn't exist. Hugo hated it when Rosie drank too much; hated it when she had too much fun.

"Are you considering it? Marriage?" she asks, not looking directly at Beth.

"Oh, well. I don't know . . ." Beth pauses, pressing her lips together. "I don't know how I feel about marriage."

"Hmm."

"It seems—" Beth starts.

"Hard," Rosie finishes for her. "Yeah, it's hard."

Beth picks up a tea towel hanging on a rail and stands on the other side of Rosie, drying the dishes Rosie has washed. Rosie feels old and cynical. Beth is only young, Rosie reminds herself. Who knows how serious she and Eddie are? She glances over to Juliette.

"How about you, Juliette?"

"Pardon?"

"What do you think of marriage?"

"I don't have too many personal opinions about it," she says carefully.

"Have you been married?"

"Oh." Juliette looks to Beth first and then back to Rosie. "No, never been married."

The door opens. All three women turn to watch Eddie walk in.

"Ladies," he greets them, kissing Beth on the ear.

"Hey," she says, blushing.

Rosie clears her throat. "What are you doing up at this hour?" She passes Eddie a tea towel, which he drapes over his shoulder.

"I'm always up at this time. Aren't I, Beth?"

Beth smiles and shakes her head.

"I'm up, I go for a run, I return to do my yoga practice, I make a kale smoothie."

Eddie winks and runs a hand through his thick, boyish hair. The gesture makes Rosie jealous. The same number of years has passed for them both, and yet Rosie feels ancient while Eddie can still look and seem like a teenager.

"Always the joker. How do you live with it?" Rosie asks Beth.

Beth stares at Eddie lovingly. Eddie holds up his hands. "Hey, girls, please. Don't fight over me, it's embarrassing."

Beth cuddles into one side of him and Eddie reaches out to pull Rosie into his other side. Rosie squeals and Beth giggles.

"This is better. We should all just get along, don't you think?"

Juliette looks over and smiles; Rosie laughs.

The door opens again. Hugo looks directly to the trio by the sink. He stares at Rosie.

"Ah, my beautiful muses," Eddie says with a dramatic sigh. He hasn't noticed Hugo yet. "My past . . ." He kisses the top of Rosie's head. "And my present . . ." He kisses the top of Beth's head.

Rosie watches Beth's smile wane as she tips her head toward the flagstones on the floor. She knows Beth had expected him to say "future." When Rosie looks back to Hugo his expression is seething. His stare is so hard it could burn holes.

"Hugo?"

"For fuck's sake."

He turns, hand slapping against the door. All of them now look at the long, lean back of him exiting the kitchen.

"Hugo!" Rosie calls.

The door bangs.

"Shit." Rosie sighs, rushing after him. She pushes past

Helen and Max coming into the kitchen, Helen wearing a white shirt and navy shorts, Max with pillow creases on his cheek.

HAMPSTEAD HEATH, 1999

"Rosie?"

Rosie was lying back against a picnic blanket, a dark denim jacket tucked under her head. "Hmm?"

"I'm pregnant."

Rosie sat up. In front of them Lars and Eddie and Helen were kicking a soccer ball. Helen wore a long skirt and lots of bangles. She was hopeless but the boys weren't great either. They were all laughing and Helen's bangles jingled as she ran and Eddie was trying to trip Lars up with his foot. Rosie turned to face Nina.

"Are you sure?"

Nina laughed, broad and deep and clear, like she always did. She reached into her handbag and tossed Rosie the test stick. "Very sure."

Rosie stared at it. The stick was so light, so insignificant, not much bigger than a ballpoint pen. But there were the two blue stripes and the diagram beside them indicating just what that meant. Rosie turned it over as though there might be more information on the back, as though it might be a joke. Nina gently took it from her hands and put it back into her bag.

"How . . . ?"

"You need me to tell you how?" Nina replied.

Nina reached over to the container full of rice salad studded with fat raisins and ate a few forkfuls. They both watched Helen fall over, giggling, and Lars reaching out to lift her back up. Max was talking to some girl who had come racing over to get his autograph. He had been traveling a lot since the album had come out, most recently in the States, driving through deserts, buying cowboy boots and mirrored sunglasses, smoking pot, playing in bigger and bigger venues, sleeping with reedy, pretty girls with long, straight hair.

"What will you do?" Rosie asked.

"Win Lotto," Nina replied quickly.

"Nina—"

"Is Prince William too young to marry?"

"Yes."

"A shame."

Rosie wanted to say so many things all at once—you're not married, you don't have enough money, Lars doesn't have a proper job, you haven't got a house, you are only twenty-four—*but Nina interrupted her thoughts.*

"Everything is going to be fine, Rosie."

Rosie watched Nina eat more salad. She was too calm. Rosie glanced at Lars. He was a bit drunk. He lolloped across the grass, like he always did, with too much legginess, as though he might tumble over at any moment. Lars was likable, but he wasn't someone to bank your whole life on. The same was true about Eddie and that was exactly the reason Rosie had broken up with him. Lars wasn't going to look after Nina the way she should be looked after. Nina was so smart, so fearless and practical. She could be a publisher one day; she could run a business. Lars, on the other hand, had no ambition. He worked at a record store. He had worked at the same record store for years, part-time through college and now full-time; the pay and prospects were terrible. The manager, Bill, with the ZZ Top beard and the endless wardrobe of black T-shirts, was not going to quit until he died, probably on the shop floor. Rosie worked in retail too, for now, but she had other options. She had Hugo.

Max waved good-bye to the fangirl and hoisted Helen onto his back, piggybacking while he kicked the soccer ball to Eddie and Lars. His sunglasses were slipping down his nose. Max looked good these days. He kept his hair shaved short all the time now and his leather jackets were new instead of worn and faintly stinking. The rock-star thing suited him. Helen's bare feet stuck out from the bottom of her skirt, grass stained, with a silver ring on her second toe. She bounced up and down as Max raced after the ball. She laughed with her head back, barely holding on to him.

"Those two," Rosie said.

"Those two," Nina agreed.

"They should just get together."

Nina laughed. "Do you think so?"

"You don't?"

"They seem more like brother and sister to me."

"But Max wants to sleep with her so bad you can practically smell the . . ." Rosie searched for a word Hugo had once used. ". . . pheromones . . . coming off him."

"They're too much the same. They'd ruin it. They'd ruin what they have." Nina frowned.

Rosie watched as Helen finally fell back onto the grass. She laughed in big gulps and Max rolled on top of her. Helen slapped him away and he tumbled off the other side, onto his back. He squeezed his hand into his jeans pocket and wiggled out a packet of smokes.

"Helen knows. But she can't let him go."

Rosie looked at her friend. "You think so? Isn't that kind of mean?"

Nina shrugged. "She loves him. In her own way."

Eddie and Lars continued playing soccer as Max and Helen lay blowing smoke into the blue sky. Eddie was holding a beer bottle. Lars kicked the ball into a group of girls and the one who'd been talking to Max threw it back. Rosie tried to imagine Hugo with them, to imagine Eddie, Lars, and Hugo playing soccer together. Hugo did like soccer; he supported Chelsea. But somehow Rosie couldn't imagine Hugo among them. Hugo was supposed to come today but he was needed at the hospital. Rosie felt smug when Hugo was called away, when he was needed. He was important. He knew things. He could recite poetry. He was smart. He had his act together. Plus, he looked so good in a suit. *He would look so good on their wedding day. Hugo hadn't proposed, but he would. Rosie already knew the ring she wanted and the dress she wanted and the house she wanted with a nursery for the babies. It was all ahead of her.*

A song came on the stereo they'd brought with them and Rosie watched Lars flap his arms about. Lars's enthusiasm sparked through his whole body, sending his limbs flailing. He called out: "Yes! Turn it up, Nina!"

She nodded and reached over to the stereo. Rosie snuck a glance at her stomach. It looked exactly the same. And yet there was a baby in there. Rosie shook her head. No money. No house. No proper job. Rosie was the youngest but she sometimes felt like the eldest.

"You okay?" *Nina asked, peering at her.*

"Yeah . . ."

"Just say it, Rosie. You haven't stopped frowning."

Rosie wanted to know if Lars would get a proper job now. She wanted to know if they would get married. Instead the truth of it all came out in one "I just don't get it."

Nina sighed and leaned over, putting her head on Rosie's shoulder. "I'm scared too. I am. But we'll make it work. Somehow."

"But Lars . . ."

He was fist pumping to the music. He really did look like some kind of caricature.

"I love him, Rosie."

"But—"

"He's a good man."

Eddie was joining in now, hopping about on the grass, spilling his beer. Rosie stared at him. Helen sat up, nodding in time. Max passed Helen the cigarette and laughed at the two men dancing.

"But can he give you . . . what you want?"

Nina lifted her head and looked at her squarely. "What more do I want, Rosie?"

Chapter Fifteen

MAX

Max rubs his face. He sits on the edge of the deck, the clouds above him thin and streaky, the lawn below dark and thick. Juliette brings him a large mug of coffee dusted with chocolate powder and a plate of thick slices of hot bread with butter and sweet-smelling strawberry jam. Max lifts a piece of toast to his mouth, bites and chews. Max is used to avoiding thoughts and feelings that make him uncomfortable: the judgments of others, the unsettling sense he might be drinking too much; thoughts of his mother, his father, his childhood, Grahame Park. All of that. There is a place, like a black hole, that he tips it all into. It's deep and vast. It is a sinkhole. But right now last night's memories shower him in tiny, disjointed pieces. *Dress of stars, Helen's hand, grass against his face, his lips.* Embarrassment shivers through him.

He lifts his gaze to watch Sophie at the border of the garden. She has brushed her hair and put on a bit of makeup. She is wearing a dress. Max waves. "Hi," he calls out, but Sophie doesn't reply. Beth walks from the other side of the garden toward her carrying a small handful of flowers. They stand next to each other, talking, but Max can't hear what they are saying; Sophie looks down at her bare feet.

Women confuse Max. Whenever he finds a way to understand them, off they go being stranger and more baffling than before. The girls Max dated were always asking for things from Max's apartment. *Can I take that book? This T-shirt? Do you mind if I borrow this record?* They wanted promises and pieces of him, tokens to show Max was theirs. Then, after it was over between them, came the messy, unraveling stuff. Max doesn't get involved with *all that*. The tears and the questions. The conversations late in the night, in the dark, that go round and round. Max already thinking about the next gig, the next place, the next drink. He isn't cruel. At least he doesn't think he is. They both get something out of it. Sex. A T-shirt. A selfie. A blow job.

Juliette and the girls—Helen and Nina and Rosie—are setting up the outside table for brunch. Max glances over to them, trying not to look at Helen, who is apologizing to Juliette.

"She just called me. I'm so sorry. I didn't know."

Nina is holding a handful of cutlery. "She just left? Did she say why?"

Helen shakes her head but glances at Max. He turns away, shame pooling in his stomach.

"Was it us?" Rosie asks.

"No! No, I'm sure it wasn't . . . us . . . you . . ."

Max can hear the concern in her voice.

"She must have a lot on her mind," Nina says soothingly, "with university, what she is going to do next . . . Maybe she just needs some time, some space, to think."

"To think. Yes," Helen echoes. Max still does not meet her eyes. "I'm sorry, Juliette, she won't be here for brunch. She's already on a train to Paris."

"I'm sure she will be okay," Rosie says reassuringly.

"She did mention a friend living in Paris . . . ," Helen murmurs.

Max squeezes his eyes shut, urging the memories and rejection into that dark recess of his mind. *Breathe. Don't think.* The sea makes the air taste so clean and fresh he wants to drink it up all day, like a milkshake. It isn't the same in Paris; the air is full there—full of dust, car exhaust, hopes and worries. Max takes a few deep breaths before opening his eyes. Sophie and Beth have settled on the grass, Sophie cross-legged and slouching and Beth kneeling behind her. Beth is braiding Sophie's hair into a kind of crown, the black tips woven through, when Juliette lays a hand on Max's shoulder. "Brunch is ready."

A linen tablecloth is spread out on the outdoor table, the corners weighted by small silver drops on clips. The glasses sparkle in the late-morning light and the silverware glints like mirrors. Helen and Nina have placed full, open roses into short vases and Rosie has rolled a sprig of rosemary into each napkin. There is a breeze against the nape of Max's neck as he reaches for a piece of warm bread.

In France, Max has eaten food he could barely have imagined in England: oysters sweet and salty, periwinkles, licorice-like fennel, soft and creamy cheeses with ripe fruit. For brunch today Juliette brings out steaming pots of mussels cooked with cider and herbs, local sardines and violet artichokes marinated in garlic with thin slivers of mint. Max eats diligently, trying to avoid watching Helen, who is speaking with Juliette, their heads close together.

Today's mood is strange, electric and prickly. Perhaps Max's hangover is putting him on edge. The mood reminds Max of accelerando, the drumbeat slowly building, becoming faster and faster. The crowd growing anxious. Feverish. Desperate. Wanting, wanting, wanting. Like the music could go either way—explode into song or dissolve into nothing— everyone driven mad with the urgent hope it will go to song. Timing is everything.

Max glances around the table. Rosie is listening to Lars tell a long story, while down at the end of the table Hugo glares at her. Nina attempts to engage Hugo in conversation about his son Patrick.

"It's a challenging age," Max hears her say.

"They're all challenging ages," Hugo replies, still avoiding eye contact.

"They just want their mummies," Nina says. "Except Sophie, a daddy's girl from day one."

Max looks to Sophie, now seated at the table. She is staring out at the garden as though she is waiting for someone.

"*I* want their mummy," Hugo says.

Nina and Max look at each other. Hugo's expression is mutinous.

"You all think I am blind . . . ," he mutters without looking at anyone in particular. Then, loud enough for almost everyone to hear, "I'm not stupid. I can see what's going on."

"What are you talking about?" Nina's voice is steady.

"The flirting. Eddie hitting on my wife. *My* wife."

"What?" Max asks, half laughing. He looks around the table: sets of eyes blinking back at him. No one else laughing. Rosie and a few others not yet listening. Beth staring.

"I know how you all feel. You'd rather it was him with her. You think I'm a fucking twat."

"Hugo!" Nina hisses. She cocks her head at Sophie, who is looking at Hugo now too.

"I'm not an idiot. I've seen the way they carry on."

Nina leans toward Beth. "I'm so sorry, Beth." Then back

to Hugo, voice lowered, "Hugo, there is nothing going on that you don't know about."

Beth's cheeks have flushed as red as her hair. She's blinking fast and glancing around without saying anything, trying to work it all out.

"Eddie and Rosie ... they're not *anything*. Other than friends."

Hugo glares. "No? But they *were*."

"That was a thousand years ago, mate," Max protests.

Sophie looks among the three adults. "What?"

Nina shakes her head. "Nothing. Rosie and Eddie used to date. A long, loooong time ago." She tries to sound lighthearted.

"Oh, right," Sophie says, shrugging. "That."

Hugo seems enraged and terrified all at once. His face is both red and pale—it seems impossible, but there it is. He throws his head back. "Ha! Of course you know. Everyone knows, right? I wasn't supposed to interrupt the plan. I get it. They were supposed to stay together. That's what you all want."

Rosie is looking over now. "What's going on?" she asks Nina.

"Everyone knows *what*?" Helen asks, narrowing her eyes at Hugo.

"Eddie and Rosie," Hugo replies.

"Steady on ... ," Max says, holding up both his hands.

"We talked about this—" Rosie starts.

Eddie holds up his palms. "Whoa, Hugo. That was a long time ago." He blinks at Beth before adding, "There's my girl right there, man."

"Yeah, this week," Hugo mutters.

"Don't listen to him, Beth," Nina says firmly.

"Yeah, don't listen to me, Beth. No one else does. Join the club." Hugo snorts.

"Hugo, please . . . ," Rosie begs.

"Please what?" Hugo shouts.

Helen answers for her. "Stop being a despicable piece of shit."

Max's breath quickens. This is exactly it—accelerando.

Hugo sits up straighter in his chair. "Excuse me?" he says, his face blotchy, eyes wide.

"You heard. Stop bullying your wife. Stop making everything about you. We're sick of it." Helen is leaning forward in her chair now.

"You don't know anything about me," Hugo hisses.

"Yeah?" Helen asks, jabbing her index finger at him. "We know you're making Rosie feel bad. That's all we need to know." She looks at Max. "Right?"

"Right," Max replies. His heart is thumping. His hands are making fists under the table. Helen needs his support; they are back on the same team.

Please let me hit him, he thinks, feeling like he's back in the schoolyard in Grahame Park. *Please let me hit him.*

"Helen . . . ," Nina murmurs; she is rubbing Rosie's back.

"What?" Helen demands. "Helen what?"

"It's their marriage," Nina says softly.

"Oh, for God's sake!" Helen cries, shaking her dark head and pointing again. "Hugo is an arse. He's always been an arse."

Max is nodding. *Let me hit him, let me hit him.* He's almost twitching in anticipation.

"You know nothing about me, Helen!" Hugo roars. "Or marriage. Or any kind of commitment. *And* you." Hugo points at Max as he stands. "*Especially* fucking you!"

Max rises to standing and they eyeball each other.

"Actually, *I'm* not going anywhere," Hugo says. "You can fuck off, Helen."

"You can't speak to her like that," Max warns, jabbing at the table. "This is *my* fucking house. And my fucking birthday."

Helen stands now too. Max and Helen, standing together, pointing at Hugo.

"Don't you *dare* upset Rosie anymore, Hugo! You can't bully *me*. So they were a couple; it was a lifetime ago. You don't have a past? For fuck's sake. Get over it."

"Please!" Rosie suddenly cries out. "All of you . . . please!"

"You're going to lay into me too?" Hugo yells at her.

"Hugo, man, this isn't a big deal," Eddie implores him. "It was well before you were on the scene. Like Helen said, it's in the past."

Hugo shakes his head. "I'm not a fool, Eddie. I see the way you all look at me, like you wish I'd just fuck off. Rosie too . . ." Hugo's rage seems to melt, his voice saddening. ". . . doesn't want to look at me. Or touch me."

Nina pulls Rosie closer to her. She is sobbing hard now, Max can tell by the way her shoulders are trembling.

"Bloody hell." Max's fingers uncurl. Hugo's lips are quivering. He looks less threatening than he did a second ago. Max glances at Helen but she is still standing. Just in case.

"I don't think this is the place . . . ," Lars says, looking to Nina.

"I think this has got out of hand," Nina agrees. She looks a little pale. "Perhaps we all need to take a moment."

"Rosie?" Hugo asks for his wife but her head is hanging. "Rosie?" he tries again, now begging. "Talk to me. I'm your husband. Why can't you just talk to me?" His color is returning to normal, his expression more wretched than angry.

Rosie doesn't lift her head; she curls back into Nina.

Hugo stands up. "Goddamn, Rosie," he says sadly. "Why can't you choose me? *Us.* For once." He looks around the table. "It's always them. You always choose them."

Nina rubs Rosie's back in long, soothing strokes. She gives Hugo a funny look: a little like pity, a little like an apology. Everyone is staring at Hugo. He blinks and sways.

"Sorry," he mumbles, "sorry . . ." and then walks into the house.

"Shit," Sophie whispers.

Helen and Max look at each other and return to their chairs. There is silence. They all take a breath, like they are one person. Max looks at the table, at the used dishes, the empty mussel shells, salad dressing puddling around limp mounds of cucumber, bread cooling and hardening. Rosie finally lifts her head, her makeup smudged, her eyes wet. She sniffs.

"You okay?" Max whispers.

Rosie shrugs. She looks over at Beth. "Are you okay?" she asks.

Beth nods. "I knew already, about you guys dating. Eddie told me."

"Okay, good," Rosie says in a resolute but hollow voice. "Let's clear up," she instructs.

"Rosie . . . ," Helen starts to say, but Rosie raises her hand.

"Let's clear up," she says again.

They stand slowly from their chairs. Even Max stacks plates. Then he picks up napkins, some still tightly rolled around rosemary. The others carry in dishes and cutlery.

Max, Eddie, and Beth are the last ones at the table. Eddie takes napkins out of Beth's hands and places them on the table. Beth's back is to Max. Max watches Eddie wrap his arms around her waist.

"Hey," Eddie says.

"Hey."

"You sure you're okay?" He looks into her eyes.

"Yes," she whispers.

"You're not just my girl for this week. You know that, right?"

"Eddie, I have to tell you something—"

"I love you, you know that," Eddie interrupts.

Max looks down at the table, quietly gathering small vases onto a clean plate to carry inside.

"There's something—" Beth tries again.

"That is *exactly* why I'm glad we have what we have," Eddie says, stealing a quick glance over her shoulder at Max for reassurance. "Let's promise to never get married, never have kids, and never grow old and stupid together." He draws Beth close.

"Eddie—"

"Or let's just *keep* being stupid," Eddie corrects himself.

Beth has her hands on Eddie's arms now. "Eddie . . ." Her voice is begging.

"Are you all right?" Eddie asks, smile fading.

"No . . . yes . . ." Beth shakes her head. "I'm pregnant."

Eddie doesn't move. Max almost drops the plate in his hands.

Eddie looks at him.

"Eddie? Did you hear me? I'm pregnant."

Eddie is still staring at Max when there is a voice by the door. "Max?"

Beth twists around, suddenly realizing Max is there. But Max is staring at Helen, framed in the doorway.

"Max, you need to come. It's Nina. You need to come now."

Chapter Sixteen

JULIETTE

When Juliette recalls her mother's face, the many faces, none of them is the one she wore at the end. She remembers the concentrating face, her mother's head over knitting or a book, glasses at the end of her nose; the laughing-at-your-father face, head thrown right back, dark and gray curls bouncing like springs, eyes squeezed closed; even the bewildered face, asking what was wrong, wanting to know what Juliette was not ready to share. Juliette rarely, if ever, recalls the hospital face, the last one on the last day, the one wanting to fall from her skull, from her body; the one that was ready to go now, please. Pallid, loose, and unglued. Tired, so tired. Juliette doesn't allow herself to remember that face. And yet here it is. In Max's lounge.

"Nina? Oh my God. Nina?!"

The world, tipped for a moment, suddenly rights itself, snaps back into focus. It is Nina on the floor in a puddle of dark clothes.

In a moment almost everyone is there: Lars propping up Nina, murmuring, "It's okay. It's all right. She's all right."

Sophie with her hand over her mouth. Rosie running to the stairs and calling out, "Hugo!" Max rushing in, swearing, with Eddie and Beth close behind him. Eddie looking like he wants to keep going, out the front door and beyond. White, twitching, ready to run. Beth and Helen crouching down on either side of Nina; Helen looking up to Juliette and asking . . . asking, "Juliette?"

Helen is in front of her now.

"Who do we call? The ambulance? The doctor?" Juliette asks.

"I . . ."

Sophie is crying. Lars shushes and rocks Nina gently like she is a baby. Helen, radiant Helen, in front of her. Nina on the floor.

Juliette steadies herself. "I'll get my phone."

"She's coming around," Beth says. "Nina?" She turns to Sophie. "Go get your mom a glass of water."

Sophie obeys mutely as Rosie and Hugo appear at the bottom of the staircase. Rosie hurries to her friend, and Hugo, stern-faced and suddenly taller, more important, is close on her heels. He picks up Nina's wrist with his fingers.

Juliette leaves the room to grab her phone from the bedside table. By the time she returns Nina's eyes are open and her color is better. The muscles in her face are working again; she no longer looks like Juliette's mother.

"Who should I call? The doctor?" Juliette asks.

"I'm fine," Nina protests.

"She's much better," Lars agrees, though he looks like he is about to cry.

Sophie passes her mother the glass of water.

"I don't think she is fine," Helen says. Her voice is shaky.

"No," agrees Rosie.

Eddie sinks onto a couch as though he is the one who is unwell.

"Have you had episodes like this before?" Hugo asks Nina.

Nina waves her hand. "Episodes? Not episodes. I just stood up too fast . . ."

"She's much better," Lars repeats.

"Perhaps if we move you to the couch, you'll be more comfortable," Hugo says authoritatively.

Beth and Helen, as though under direct instruction, help Nina to her feet. She protests again, "I'm fine!"

"Mum. Stop it."

Juliette turns her head to Sophie. Her face is striped with the tracks of tears, mascara slipping, mouth twisted down.

Lars whispers, "Honey—"

"No," Sophie says, "she's *not* fine. She's sick. She needs to go to a doctor or a hospital. It's serious. Mum didn't want to tell anyone—"

"Sophie . . ." Nina's voice is a ghost of its former self.

Sophie continues: "She's been keeping it secret because she doesn't want to find out what it is. She doesn't want it to be bad."

Nina looks up to her daughter.

"How did you . . . ? Did someone . . . ?"

Sophie shakes her head. "I'm not stupid."

"No . . . ," Nina mumbles.

"You're sick?" Helen asks. Her lips are trembling. Juliette wants to reach out for her, but Max goes to her and they kneel in front of Nina together.

"The doctor said—" Lars starts to explain, but Nina interrupts.

"It's okay, love," she says. She reaches out to cup his face in her palm. "It's okay, love," she says again softly. Lars closes his eyes.

Nina turns back to her friends. "I need to get some tests." She looks to her daughter and gives a funny kind of smile. "But I am scared. Isn't that right, darling?" Her voice is a sweet whisper. Sophie nods and Juliette can almost see the love between them both, mother and daughter, as though it were a physical thing. A thread. Electricity. Light.

Silvery, binding, real.

THEY ALL GATHER in the driveway as Hugo reverses the car. Rosie is beside him, in the front passenger seat, looking suddenly older; Lars, Nina, and Sophie are in the back. Juliette lifts her hand and Rosie replies with a wan smile.

"How long will it take them?" Helen is beside her.

"To Rennes? A few hours, maybe three. It is the weekend, so the traffic shouldn't be too bad."

"I feel sick," Helen murmurs.

"They'll give us a call when they know more."

"Hugo is with them," Beth adds. "He's a doctor and he speaks French. He was speaking French at the market."

Juliette glances at Helen, who is still frowning.

The car turns onto the road and is quickly gone from sight.

"Let's go inside. We're not helping anyone out here," Max suggests.

When the others go to the lounge Juliette heads to the kitchen. She collects a pile of crumpled clean laundry—napkins, tablecloths, and tea towels—and takes them with her to fold, standing at the bench near the window. She works slowly. After seeing her mother's face on Nina's, a heavy sadness has settled on her. It's in the air, turned to syrup in the sudden quietness of the house. The kitchen is dim as the brightness of the midday light shifts away. Juliette concentrates on the pieces of cloth beneath her fingers. The simplicity and monotony of folding: halves and quarters, her palms spreading and pressing down.

Eddie is standing just outside with his back to Juliette, holding a glass in one hand and smoking a cigarette with the other. Beth approaches him, pulling the sides of a light cardigan across her front.

"Hey."

"Hey, babe."

"I couldn't find you anywhere," Beth says.

"Just getting some fresh air." Eddie blows smoke toward his feet.

Beth stands next to him. Even though the garden is a bit unkempt, most of the flowers are blooming, most of the trees have fresh, new green leaves. Juliette's father had loved spring. It was his one disappointment about their tiny village house, that there wasn't a garden. To compensate he had hung baskets by their red door and filled them with flowers, grown pots of mint and tarragon on the kitchen windowsill, ferns in the bathroom, rosemary—for remembrance—by the front step. "So you know which home to come back to," he'd always said, as though Juliette might forget.

"Nina, eh?" Eddie's voice is more strained than usual. "I didn't see that coming."

"I hope she's okay."

"Tough as nails, Nina," Eddie says, his voice betraying his uncertainty.

"She's been really nice to me."

"Don't know what we'd do without Nina."

"Sophie and Lars too. They're a good family," Beth murmurs.

Eddie clears his throat and stubs out his cigarette.

"Eddie?"

"Do you want something to drink, babe?"

"Eddie—"

"I might get a—"

"Eddie." Beth catches his sleeve. "Are you avoiding me?"

"What?"

"You don't smoke. Not usually."

"It's been such a crazy day. Helen and Max were having one—"

"We should talk."

"We should get inside—"

"Eddie, you haven't spoken to me since I told you." Beth's voice is unwavering. "I know you're worried about Nina, but this is important too."

"Yeah. Look, I know. It's just—"

"I don't know what to think either. Or how to feel. Could we do this? Should we?"

Eddie is silent, looking down at his drink.

"Don't you have questions?"

"Yeah, yeah, of course," Eddie mumbles.

"We weren't careful. We should have been more careful. But still I didn't think . . ." Beth bites her thumbnail. Eddie rubs her shoulder.

"It'll be okay."

Beth's face is hopeful. "Yeah?"

Juliette folds the last napkin and adds it to her stack.

"Whatever you decide . . . I love you. You know that," Eddie says.

Juliette's chest tightens at the intimacy. The wounds in her own heart still ache; they are still tender. So many losses, lined up, falling like dominoes. Her mother. Her father. Her lover.

Her ex had children—two shining, clever daughters. Juliette really only knew them from photographs, captured, frozen, in dark-haired, clear-skinned, smiling perfection. But they were real. They lived and breathed and took up space— space in the world, space in the heart.

"They take . . . so much of you," her lover had whispered one day, frowning, struggling to explain the love of a parent, the experience of it. Juliette had wanted to understand. She hadn't wanted to fracture a family, but she probably would have. The thought sends a bolt of shame through her. The heart is selfish.

Juliette watches Eddie fold Beth into an embrace.

"Whatever *we* decide," Beth murmurs sadly.

WHEN THEY RECEIVE the phone call later in the afternoon it is Hugo on the other end. Helen puts him on speakerphone and they gather around in the lounge to listen in.

"They think it might be a tumor on the cranial nerve."

They hear Rosie in the background. "In English, Hugo."

"It affects the ears. And balance."

"A tumor?" Max asks. He and Helen stare at each other.

Hugo continues, "She's been symptomatic: some ringing in the ears, the dizziness of course—"

"Can it be treated?" Beth asks.

"It depends. I'm not an oncologist."

"What does the oncologist say?" Helen asks.

"He wants her to go to Paris for further testing."

"Can she do it in London?"

"He wants her to do it soon. He can get her appointments tomorrow."

"That soon?" Eddie asks in a whisper.

"Rosie wants to speak with you."

They wait as the phone crackles and is passed from Hugo over to Rosie.

"Helen?"

"I'm here," Helen replies, holding the phone closer.

"We don't have all the details yet. They need to do more tests. We are going to Paris from here."

"You won't come back here first?"

"No . . . It's this exit, Hugo. Helen?"

"We're here," Max replies for her.

"We are on the road now. Nina is sleeping. We're going straight there."

"Where will you stay?" Juliette asks.

"We'll find somewhere. There's no point coming back to Douarnenez if the appointment is in the morning."

"No, it's in the wrong direction," Juliette agrees.

Helen reaches out for Max. "I want to go. How many can you fit in your apartment?"

Max glances around the group: Juliette, Eddie, Beth, and Helen all looking at him, eyes wide and waiting. In the silence there is the sound of a car motor and Hugo clearing his throat.

"Rosie?"

"Yes, Max?"

"You can stay at my place. I'll send you directions. I have a neighbor, Claudine . . . I should have her number. I'll get her to let you in."

"We are coming too," Helen says, speaking into the phone.

"So are we," Beth adds, though Eddie looks pale and unsure.

"It's a long way," Rosie warns.

Juliette turns to Max. "I can drive if you'd like me to."

Max looks at the glass in his hand. "Good idea."

"Ask Lars what he wants me to pack for Nina and we will bring it with us. Give me a call back," Helen adds.

"Okay."

Eddie kisses the top of Beth's head as she holds on to his arm. Max frowns, hands on hips, as Helen glances at Juliette. Neither party is hanging up, resistant to breaking the connection.

"But," Rosie says on the other end, "it's Max's birthday."

"Fuck that," Max replies. Juliette looks at him, wondering if he is a bit drunk. "The birthday was yesterday."

JULIETTE TAPS HER forehead. Phone charger. Underwear. Toothbrush. She bursts out of her room into the hall toward the bathroom and walks straight into Helen. They smack into each other, then fall apart, both of them reaching out for a wall.

"I'm so sorry!"

"*Merde,*" Juliette says, blinking hard. "It's my—"

"No, it's my fault . . . sorry," Helen says at the same time.

Perhaps in another moment they would have laughed. Instead Helen's eyes fill with tears.

"Helen?"

Her mouth turns down. "I'm so sorry . . . ," Helen murmurs, voice quivering.

"No. It's okay. I'm okay."

Juliette reaches out and Helen steps into her arms. Small frame in a soft dress. Helen's head against Juliette's shoulder. The fabric of Juliette's shirt becoming wet. Juliette shushes and moves her palm slowly over Helen's back. Helen's vertebrae are like the knucklebones Juliette used to play with in school, all lined up under the skin, making her seem so much more fragile. Juliette takes a deep breath.

"Are you all right?"

Helen nods, then shakes her head. She doesn't lift it from Juliette's shoulder. "Oh, Juliette."

Juliette keeps stroking her back. Keeps thinking: *It will be all right. It will be all right.* But not saying it. Because that's what people had said to Juliette about her parents, and they had made liars of themselves.

"I had no idea," Helen sobs.

"I think she wanted it that way."

"But . . . I'm her friend."

"I know. I know."

"It's not fair."

"No."

"It's not right."

"No."

"What if they can't make it better?"

Juliette doesn't answer that. Instead she recalls comforting memories. The sound of her mother singing softly. Her father collecting shells from the beach, the dogs ahead of him barking at something dead on the sand; him turning to smile at his daughter. The warm solidity of her lover in her arms. All that is left after a loss—sweet, wispy memories.

Helen pulls away a fraction, lifting her head. "I'm so sorry. Everything just feels so . . . different now."

Juliette's hands slide down Helen's arms. She takes Helen's hands in her own. "Don't be sorry."

Juliette studies Helen's face. Her skin is pale golden pink, like sunset cast upon sand, her cheekbones high and round and pinker still. Around her eyes the skin is soft and creased, showing how much she laughs and, now, revealing that she worries just as much. The whole of her is so vulnerable, and yet beyond the vulnerability is strength, loyalty, courage, a belief in love and beauty, which makes Juliette want to pull Helen back in toward her and keep her there forever. The feeling rips through Juliette like something lit and sparkling bright in her chest.

She wants to tell Helen everything. About ambition and lies. All the hurt and hiding of the past year. All the hurt and hiding before that. The losses, so many losses.

"Helen?" she murmurs.

Helen leans toward her and Juliette feels Helen's warm breath against her lips, Helen's lips against her lips, soft and tentative. Hopeful. Juliette feels Helen's hair brush against her cheek.

"Helen? Juliette?" It is Max's voice.

Closer now. Sounding hollow.

"I think we're all almost ready. I was just . . . Juliette, do you know where my coat is?"

Chapter Seventeen

MAX

What. The. Fuck.

Chapter Eighteen

JULIETTE

PARIS, 2014

Juliette chose a café they'd never been to before. It was small and hidden and empty. It was neutral ground, so as to preserve Juliette's memories of other places—places where they had felt brave enough to hold hands, impetuous enough to kiss, to press close to each other, close enough to feel the heat of their skins through their clothes, the beat of hearts beneath cages of bone.

"Bonjour, Juliette," she said, sitting carefully in the bentwood chair, like a hen might lower down onto new eggs. She was already treating Juliette like she couldn't cope, like she was fragile. Juliette felt herself simultaneously harden and crack.

"Bonjour, Celine," Juliette replied.

Celine was wearing a white suit jacket. She had pearls around her neck. Her dark hair was pushed back over her shoulders and Juliette wanted to reach out for it just one more time.

"How is Douarnenez?"

Juliette was about to answer when the waiter placed himself in the space between them.

"Bonjour, *ladies*."

Celine seemed to recede even further from Juliette. She smiled at the waiter. It was one of the smiles Celine always had on hand for staff, for strangers, for the press. Seemingly generous and genuine, but Juliette knew better. Juliette had seen Celine's true smile, had seen her laugh so hard she could see the amalgam fillings in her back teeth she hadn't yet had removed. The ones put in as a child in Shanghai. Juliette had seen Celine laugh till she wheezed, till she cried. Juliette had seen the smile she made after she'd been made love to, the smile that was gentle and sweet, capable of shattering Juliette's heart to pieces.

Celine placed her order: a tea, no milk, lemon, please, thank you, that would be perfect. Celine said that a lot—parfait, *"perfect"—in her delicate, Chinese-accented French, as though saying it often would make it all so. Juliette ordered a café au lait.*

"Douarnenez," Celine said again, when the waiter was gone.

"Yes . . . ," Juliette replied. On instruction, she hadn't called Celine while she had been home. It was too risky, Celine had said, with Leon, her husband, awaiting another Michelin star for La Porte Blanche, with her running for office. It wasn't Leon whom Celine had the loyalty to, per se, or the marriage, but the whole construction Celine had created and worked hard to perfect. The career, the profile, the children—the brilliant expatriate daughters who spoke four languages each—the apartment, the whole prettily painted picture. Each piece balanced upon another piece. It wasn't a good time, Celine had said.

"How is your father?" Celine asked briskly.

Juliette remembered when she had first learned of her mother's illness. Celine had sent the children to her mother-in-law's and booked a hotel room for two days, inventing a business trip. They had spent days and nights lying skin to skin. Celine's body next to Juliette's had felt so natural, so normal, she could barely stand the chill of being without it pressed next to her. Juliette resented even going to the bathroom or leaving for food. She had so wanted to introduce Celine to her mother, but she'd gone downhill too fast and there hadn't been a good time. There was never a good time.

"He is sicker than we thought," *Juliette replied, although there was no "we."*

The waiter delivered Celine's tea first. He stared at her a little longer than necessary, trying to place her. Juliette wanted to speak out and solve the problem for him—Yes, you've seen her before. She's a politician. You don't know her; you just think you do. Yes, she is pretty. But you don't know her. No one does. Not like I do.

But Juliette said nothing. Juliette had become so good, parfait *even, at saying nothing. The waiter stayed a beat longer before vanishing to retrieve Juliette's coffee.*

"That is no good," *Celine said with a frown. Juliette studied her face.* "What is the prognosis?"

Juliette paused for a moment. "Same as for all of us."

"Sorry?"

"Death, Celine."

The coffee arrived.

"Merci."

"De rien." *The waiter did not look at Juliette. She might as well have been wallpaper.*

"You don't need to make a scene," *Celine begged her.*

"How am I making a scene?" *Juliette asked, adding more sugar than usual.*

"I know you. When you say things like that . . ."

"My father is dying," *Juliette said, looking into her face, not adding that she would probably have to sell Delphine and move, not adding that her whole life seemed to be unraveling.*

"It's dreadful," *Celine conceded.*

After the weekend they'd spent together, wrapped in each other, Celine had urged Juliette back to the restaurant. "Throw yourself into it," she had encouraged.

Juliette stirred in the sugar as Celine prodded the lemon slice in her teacup. "I want you to meet him," Juliette said. "You never met Maman. I want you to meet my father."

"Oh, Juliette." Celine's frown deepened.

"Do me this one thing. Just meet him. If you still don't want me to say what you mean to me, what we mean to each other . . . well, that's fine." Juliette heard the pleading in her voice. She wished she could steady it, sound more businesslike; Celine always felt more comfortable when she used a stable, rational voice. "Just meet him. That Maman never knew you . . . it haunts me. I need to be honest with my father at least. I know you aren't the same way but . . ." Juliette took a breath. "Celine, I'm too old for this. I can't bear it."

"Anything else?" the waiter asked. It was unnecessary. It was so he could engage with Celine a moment longer, have the chance to put her image straight in his mind.

"Non, merci!" Celine called out cheerfully. Celine was cheerful with everyone. It was not out of kindness; it was part of her work. Everyone is a constituent. Everyone is a voter.

Juliette tried to engage her with eye contact.

"Celine?" she said hopefully. But Celine shook her head.

"I can't. I'm sorry, I can't. It's—"

"Not a good time," Juliette finished for her. "Christ, Celine."

"Juliette . . . ," Celine hissed. Not Juliette, please don't be upset *but* Juliette, please don't cause a disruption.

Juliette sipped her coffee. It wasn't good. She drank it anyway.

"So what is this then? Us meeting?"

"I think you know," Celine said, allowing sadness to creep into her voice.

"This is it? After all . . ." But Juliette couldn't bring herself to

finish, because it sounded too much like a cliché. Instead she cleared her throat.

"I'm sorry," Celine offered without looking at her, without reaching out her hand.

"Sorry for which part? For making me love you in the first place? For keeping us . . . me . . . a secret? For not meeting my mother? Refusing to meet my father? For breaking up with me over this . . . shit coffee?"

Celine looked down into her cup, looking for what Juliette could not determine.

"All of it," she said softly, so quietly Juliette could barely hear her. "All of it," she said again.

Juliette took a deep breath. They weren't wrong when they talked about your heart breaking. That is exactly what it felt like, a deep, painful chasm splitting open in her chest. Juliette pressed her fingers to the top of her nose to stop the tears.

"I just can't," Celine whispered. "You are braver than me. You have always been braver. This job, my parents, the children . . ."

Juliette had heard all the reasons before. They were reasonable. They made sense. But Juliette could no longer appreciate them. She hated them. She resented the reasons like they were their own beings.

"I need to ask you a favor," Celine said, her chin lifted and making eye contact. "I know I have no right to—"

"No," Juliette said quickly. "You don't."

She broke off the eye contact. Her heart felt like it had been taken to with an ax.

"Just listen for a moment," Celine asked, voice gathering strength. "Juliette?" And then, like drawing out a trick card, "Delphine? My dolphin?"

"Merde, Celine," Juliette muttered.

"I need what we had to be private. I know it's not fair. I know you've been carrying this a long time. But I have a reputation and

Leon has a profile, you know, and he can be unreasonable. The girls . . . Juliette . . . Delphine?"

Juliette pictured the photograph that featured on the website for *La Porte Blanche*. Leon with his thick, wind-ruffled silver hair, his linen shirt unbuttoned at the collar, sitting at a wooden table surrounded by his family: one dark-haired daughter on either side and his wife, Celine, behind him, her pale and slender fingers curled over his shoulder. The shine of her wedding band. The demure way she looked down to him—the way all of them looked to him while he looked out at the camera, his mouth open, smiling.

Juliette lifted her eyes just enough to stare at the rim of her coffee cup. She reached for the tiny handle and brought the cup to her lips. The grinds had been overheated; even the milk and sugar couldn't mask that. It was acrid; it went down her throat with a burn. She replaced the cup on its saucer with a thunk. A few loose grains sloshed in the milky remainder. She pushed the chair back and stood, put her handbag over her shoulder. She tried not to wince from the pain in her chest. She finally raised her eyes to meet Celine's. The eyes Juliette had stared at one thousand times, observing their shape, their color, and the love in them. But not now. It was as though a switch had been flicked off; Juliette could see that. She knew enough about Celine, about the many ways she had of looking at a person—the real versus the pretend—that it, whatever they had been or had, was extinguished. Celine had made her decision.

"You think you need to ask?" Juliette said, throat closing over from the tears trying to rise up. "If there is one thing I have learned, it is how to keep secrets."

Juliette turned and left the watching waiter and Celine behind her.

IN THE BACKSEAT: five bags, plus four coats.

In the middle seat: Helen, Beth, Eddie.

In the front seats: Max (cardboard box full of food at his feet), Juliette (driving).

The trip will take approximately six hours, depending on how fast Juliette drives and how many stops they make and what the traffic is like in Paris. Juliette has made this trip many times, but less and less often over the last few years. Nothing changes on a motorway. Features on repeat. The same gas stations and attached restaurants selling packaged food. The same roadside parks with old-fashioned toilets that dismay the tourists—no seats. The same on-and-on-ness that Juliette doesn't miss. She knows Max prefers the back roads, and so does she, but it is not the time for driving back roads. They have to get to Paris fast and safe. From the silence and grim faces, Juliette doesn't anticipate many requests to stop. The journey to Quimper is made without conversation. The light is already leaving the sky; it will be dark and late when they reach Paris. After Quimper, Juliette switches on the radio, on low volume.

When she turns her head to change lanes, she notices Max staring at her. She gestures toward the cardboard box. "Help yourself to anything. I packed some baguettes, fruit, cheeses . . . There is a knife and a board in there."

A woman's voice on the radio singing, raspy and sad. The thrum of the van's motor.

The silent, hard stare Max is giving fills her head.

Chapter Nineteen

MAX

On the street, Max inserts his key and pushes open the heavy door. Helen and then Juliette, Eddie, and Beth follow Max, single file, along the corridor and up the narrow stairs. Max never bought places with elevators; they remind him too much of hotels, of touring. He prefers the old apartment buildings, despite the inconveniences.

The wooden stairs are worn in the middle, where decades of residents have trudged up in the bitter cold of winter, in the sweaty heat of summer, during war, during peacetime. Max installed a coded security lock in his apartment door because he kept losing the key—the building's key was enough responsibility for him—so he punches in the code and lets the others walk in while he holds the door. Even on the top floor the noises of people talking and fighting and laughing, music, and car horns drift up from the streets below. Rosie embraces Helen. Max watches the two women. He is unused to the feeling he has, that nothing makes sense anymore. He tries to tell himself that there is still hope, that he, Max Dresner, knows Helen best of all. Better, perhaps, than she does. But the plan he had relied on, the one that was going to save him, seems to be slipping through his fingers like water. The women break apart.

In the lounge, behind Rosie, Sophie and Hugo are on the couch. Sophie waves, if not pleased then reassured somehow to see them. Though Max spends most of his time in this apartment alone, he has a similar feeling with them here, crowding the place: as though they all belong.

"Nina is having a rest. Lars is with her," Rosie whispers.

Juliette goes to the open kitchen, putting things in the fridge and opening cupboards, seeing where everything is. She hasn't spoken to Max since the drive.

"Claudine let you in?" Max asks Rosie. She nods. "You're okay with beds? Rooms?"

"Lars and Nina are in yours. I thought Eddie and Beth could go in the guest room with the twin singles; Hugo and I will take the couches, then you and Helen in the guest room sharing the big bed." Rosie takes a breath. "Is that everyone? I'm not thinking straight."

"I can sleep on a couch," Helen offers too quickly. Max looks at her sharply. "If it's easier."

"Helen—"

"I sent Soleil a message," Helen interrupts, "to say we are here in Paris. I haven't heard back from her yet."

"Didn't she have a friend to stay with?" Max asks, trying not to sound resistant.

"I think so. I'm not sure."

"There might not be enough room," Rosie says, "though we could work something out, right, Max?"

"Yeah," Max replies noncommittally. He watches Juliette unpack the box of food into the fridge and kitchen cupboards. Now she's placing tea bags and sugar and spoons and cups on a tray by the kettle. Max wants a proper drink, not a cup of tea. And he wants answers to the image he has seen over and over in his head during the hours they were driving. Who kissed whom? What do you want with her? How does she feel about you? What *is* this?

"Juliette?" Rosie asks. "Where are you sleeping?"

Juliette turns from the fridge. "I won't stay."

"You're not driving back to Douarnenez."

"No," she replies. "I'll stay with a friend."

"Who—" Helen starts to ask.

"That might be better. Like Rosie said, there's not much room," Max says tightly.

Juliette faces him and pauses. Max waits for embarrassment to wash over her face or for her to look away. But instead she holds his gaze and lifts her chin.

"Max . . . ," Helen murmurs.

"Yes," Juliette says slowly. She brushes her hands together. "You have everything you need. I will leave you alone."

"I'll see you out," Max offers.

Helen's head drops as Juliette walks past her. Rosie, confused, glances among the three of them.

Max walks Juliette to the front door. Her leather bag is held tight in her hand. Neither of them says anything until they are far from everyone else. She holds her slender frame upright and steady, her eyes meeting Max's.

"I haven't done anything wrong."

"Maybe. But she's all I've got."

"You've got more than that, Max," Juliette says softly.

"That's nothing," Max replies, glancing for a moment back into the apartment. "It's just stuff. I thought it meant something once. When I didn't have it, probably."

Juliette blinks. "I didn't mean the stuff."

As she turns Max reaches out, placing his hand on her shoulder.

"Hey, sorry," he says. "It's been a long day." He rubs his face. He is not handling this well. He needs a drink. "We'll see you tomorrow, eh?"

Juliette says nothing.

"To go to the hospital," Max adds levelly. He is Juliette's boss, after all. "What time?" he asks, switching to the details, the practicalities.

Juliette's expression is intractable. "There are seven of you, Max. I think you can figure it out for yourselves."

"But—"

"Good-bye, Max."

As Juliette descends, her leather sandals slap against each stair. Max is unsure whether he will see her again.

He wants to call out but doesn't know what to say.

THEY ORDER FOOD from King Falafel Palace for dinner. The restaurant is only a block away from the apartment on rue des Rosiers and is open late. Lars and Hugo go out to pick it up and return with plastic bags bulging with trays wrapped in silver foil: flatbread, salad, falafel, sliced onions, hummus, tabouleh, and hot, silky eggplant with garlic and mint. Max tries not to think of Juliette, the things she said, the strange look on her face as though he just didn't get it. Would *never* get it.

I can find another cook.

I can find another housekeeper.

It's not a big deal.

Nina comes out of the bedroom with her hair ruffled. She scolds them for coming but gives kisses and hugs all the same. She looks better. Rested. Helen, on the other hand, is quiet and pale and keeps glancing his way. Max distracts himself by finding enough plates. Sophie distributes paper napkins from one of the bags; Max places cold bottles of beer from the fridge in the middle of the table. Beth fetches glasses of water for those who want one. Nina reaches for a beer and twists open the top, then stands. Hands pause over the food.

"Take a beer," she demands. Max's is already open. Nina waits until all the bottles are popped open and all eyes are on her.

"First of all, thank you for coming here for me. I didn't expect that. I didn't expect any of this. And . . ." She pauses for a moment. "I'm sorry I kept it secret."

She looks to Rosie. Rosie is looking down at her plate, which has nothing on it yet. She raises her head and meets Nina's gaze.

"But this is not my party." Nina reaches over and rubs Max's head. "Bloody ruined it, didn't I, Max?"

"Nah, Nina, you didn't," Max replies uncomfortably.

Lars agrees: "You didn't."

"Well, maybe I did. But we're all together, right? In Paris? Eating falafel?"

Lars lifts his bottle. "Hear, hear!" Even Sophie gives a fleeting smile.

"We're all here and it's Max's weekend, so I want to say a toast." Nina takes a swig of beer. "That's better."

"You're supposed to speak first," Eddie heckles.

Nina turns to Max. "Max, darling Max, I remember when I first met you. It was at the Amersham Arms. You probably don't remember . . ."

They all laugh.

"You were wearing that horrible leather jacket. The black one. It stank. And you had hair then, of course. It was gorgeous hair. Truly it was pretty, wasn't it, Rosie? Helen?"

"Very pretty," Helen confirms. Max stares at her.

"Lars took me to see a band and Max was in it."

"The Cold Foxes," says Eddie.

"The Cold Foxes. That's it." Nina points her bottle at Eddie. "It wasn't a big gig—actually there was hardly anyone there—but Lars said I had to come, his friend was playing and his friend was good. And . . . he was. Weren't you, Max? You were really, really good. Much better than the rest of them. You were something special." Her voice drops. "You got us drinks on your band tab and made us laugh so hard—I can't even remember what we were talking about, but my sides hurt the next day, I remember that. And we got home when the sun was coming up. And soon enough we were seeing you all the time. Couldn't get rid of you. More gigs, more pubs, more laughs. So many laughs.

"And then there were Rosie and Helen, then there was Eddie, then there were all of Max's and Eddie's girlfriends . . ." Max watches Hugo glance down at his lap. Nina gestures to Beth. "Sorry, Beth. But believe me, Eddie's girlfriends were always better than Max's. For starters, they lasted longer. And they wore more clothes."

Max interrupts. "That's not true!"

"All right, Nina. We got the message," Eddie groans, reaching for Beth's hand.

"Anyway, that was that," Nina says. "We were a . . . what? Gang? Gaggle?" She looks to Helen. "Give me a collective noun, Helen."

"Skulk?" Helen offers. "Like foxes?"

"Yeah. We were a skulk. And together we all grew up. *Ish.*"

Nina gives Max a pointed look. It's supposed to be a joke but it makes Max feel a bit sick. The events of the last twenty-four hours want to flash in front of him like a horror movie you can only watch through your fingers: *the shimmer of Soleil's dress; the wet, warm grass on his face; Helen's refusal; Juliette's pitying, resolute expression before she turned down the stairs.* Helen is staring at him, he can feel it. But he doesn't dare look at her.

"Can we be done with the birthday stuff? The speeches?" he pleads.

"I can say what I want. I'm the sick one," Nina retorts.

Everyone is silent. Sophie laughs. Nina smiles at her.

"Okay, so the skulk sort of *almost* grew up," Nina says. "Got married. Moved away. Traveled. Made money. Found ourselves, I guess. Not seeing each other as much as we would like but . . . still friends. Still there for one another. And out of all of us, Max has done so, so well. He's still something special. We can all agree with that. I mean, look at him. He is doing what he loves—making music—for a job. He lives in this beautiful place, in this beautiful city, or Douarnenez when the mood takes him, with Juliette cooking! Bloody hell."

"Lucky bugger," Lars agrees.

Max wants Nina to stop, silently begs her to stop, but Nina continues: "He hasn't changed a bit. He's still Max. The Peter Pan. The life of the party. He doesn't judge us and we don't judge him. We're proud of him. His achievements feel like our achievements. And . . . we love him. Isn't that right?"

Max looks around the table. Everyone is looking at him. There is a weird prickling sensation in his chest. He glances at Helen.

"No matter how mental he is, how little we get to see of him these days, he's our mad, generous, famous mate. He's ours. He'll always be . . . *our* Max." Nina lifts her bottle again.

"I'll get the toast bit right this time ... To Max," she says deliberately, smiling at him. "Happy birthday."

"Happy birthday, Max!" echoes around the table.

Bottles clink against one another. Max reaches out his arm, on autopilot, and then withdraws it.

"Max?"

It's Eddie.

"You all right, mate?"

"Yup," he lies. "I'm fine."

EVERYONE ARRANGES THEMSELVES into rooms and into beds as Max watches from the couch and drinks too much. They get into pajamas, give each other good-night kisses, give Max good-night kisses, and he hears the whir of electric toothbrushes and water running and bare feet padding over floorboards. Behind him the window is open and springtime Paris nudges its way in: diners leaving cafés and calling out to one another, waitresses chatting after their shift, bike wheels on cobbled streets, high heels, whistles. Max just wants everyone to go to bed. To vanish. He puts on some music and lets it saturate him, just like the booze. Music, alcohol, taking him away, away, away like a tide, like sleep. In the morning everything will be different. In the morning he won't think about Soleil and Helen and Juliette. In the morning he'll be Max again. Everything will be fine. Max feels the bottle slip from his hand and doesn't reach out for it. Something thuds against his shoe.

"Where do you think you're going?" his father roars.

The backpack is light on Max's back. It has so little in it: a couple of pairs of shoes, some clothes; he doesn't even take his toothbrush.

"None of that is yours! I bought all that!"

His father is okay with screaming on the street now. He doesn't care. He's too drunk. Max watches a curtain in the opposite block being drawn across.

Max took only what he could grab. Other than the clothes he stuffed in some records and a couple of old photos. Truth is he could leave with nothing, could light a match and drop it, could watch the place become covered in flames, couldn't care less if his dad was inside, bloated, drunk, fists slack.

His father reaches for him but misses and stumbles. He's not so strong anymore. Can still land a lucky punch, but not like he used to.

"You look at me. You look at me!" His mouth is close enough for Max to feel the spray of spit on his cheek. "You think you are better than me, Max. But you're not."

Max keeps moving. Pigeons on rooftops in sentry lines, their feathers the same color as the sky, their eyes looking on.

"We're the same. Makes you sick, don't it?"

Max flinches but doesn't turn around. The buildings are square and unfeeling. They don't care that Max is going and will never be back. Everyone goes.

"We're the same, Max!"

Someone at Max's feet. Max can make out only a dark lump, a shadow.

"Christ, Max. There's beer everywhere."

"Rosie?"

He can hear her moving and breathing heavily, on hands and knees. Then he feels his shoes coming off. She lifts his legs and turns him so he is lying instead of sitting.

"I'm all right . . . ," he slurs.

He feels the socks being peeled from his feet, then hears the window lock squeaking closed. A blanket floats above him for a moment as if in slow motion, like a cloud, like something from his childhood he cannot place. Then it falls down onto him. Rosie pulls it over his bare feet, tucks it in around him.

"Rosie?"

She sighs. "Good night, Max."

He grabs her wrist before she goes. It's so small; his fingers go all the way around.

"Rosie?"

His music has been turned off. Paris is shut out. It's cool and dark and quiet now—quiet like a weight.

"Rosie? I did the wrong things."

Rosie doesn't move. Max lets go of her wrist and his arm flops like a doll's. Sadness fills him up like water in a glass. The dark, the quiet, the loneliness, and the mistakes, as real and cold as liquid.

"I know," Rosie murmurs.

Lundi *(Monday)*

Chapter Twenty

ROSIE

Rosie watches the city wake up, dusty-eyed and lumbering. Watches Parisians who seem not to have slept at all, in high-heel shoes that have become uncomfortable and short dresses, and those who may have slept but walk with one foot still in dreams, heads drooping and rubbing eyes. The garbage collectors, brightly clad, call to one another. Women bring out their small dogs for a morning piss as men smoking cigarettes stare at joggers. Rosie strokes the string of the window blind with her fingertips and watches. Everyone else is asleep: her husband, who moved quickly and unconsciously into the space she vacated when it was still dark; Beth and Eddie with the door left ajar, Beth's head on his chest, her red hair falling over his shoulder; Sophie curled neatly on a couch. Max on his back, head lolling, snoring lightly, blanket not reaching his feet. Sleeping like that, he reminds Rosie too much of one of her sons, and the thought makes her frown. He is a boy, when the world demands an adult.

Rosie unlatches one of the windows and pushes it open. She can hear traffic in the distance, though she cannot see any. It is more of a blur of noise, a thrum, than a proper sense—a rush that gives the impression of cars and taxis, the digestive-like rumbles of Métro trains, conversation, and industry. Soon the shutters on shop fronts and cafés will be rolled up. There is part of her that expects to see Juliette, part of her that hopes to see her. She has become a kind of ballast these last few days, steadying Rosie, all of them. A brunette woman in a red coat looks up and Rosie almost waves. It is no one she knows.

"How long have you known?"

Rosie turns to see Helen. She's in pajamas, her hair askew. She has a cigarette packet in her hand.

"About Nina?" Rosie asks.

Helen nods. She perches on the radiator under the window, taps out a smoke and lights it.

"A while," Rosie admits. "She made me promise I wouldn't tell anyone."

Helen inhales. She blows the smoke slowly out the open window. The scent wafts back toward Rosie. She realizes that no one in her everyday life smokes. Not a single person on her street, in her group of friends; not any of the members of the PTA. Rosie's father had smoked; the smell makes her nostalgic. It reminds her of summer evenings in the garden, with him leaning on a spade, smoking while surveying his dahlias.

Helen glances at the floor. "I wish she had told me."

"We see each other more, that's all."

"Maybe."

Rosie hesitates before taking the cigarette from Helen's fingers. She inhales cautiously. The sensation of it moving down her throat and filling her lungs is wild. She had forgotten how it felt. All of a sudden she is fourteen years old and huddled under a kitchen table with Mary Roberts, her high school friend, passing a stolen smoke between them, giggling and coughing and feeling like the rock stars they idolized so much—women who wore their eyeliner thick and played guitars.

"I should come back more," Helen says.

"You have a life in New York."

Helen frowns. She retrieves the cigarette and inhales deeply. They both look out the window, following the trail of smoke Helen puffs into the city.

Rosie and Hugo had come to Paris on their honeymoon. Rosie still remembers the thrill of packing her bag a few days before, folding her clothes into neat squares—the new underwear, the carefully chosen dresses and shoes. Nina had listened to her itemizing exactly what had gone into the case the night before the wedding. She had slept with Rosie at her parents' house, staying on a mattress on Rosie's bedroom floor. Sophie had been tiny then, but Nina left her to be bottle-fed by Lars. She had given Rosie all the quiet, devoted attention a bride deserved; helped her with her veil, fluffed her train, fetched water, and listened to last-minute worries and nerves; observed, patiently, the packed suitcase for Paris that Rosie couldn't help but proudly show her. She took big sunglasses that made her feel like Audrey Hepburn and books she didn't read but sat with, opened, looking out over tiny coffee cups in streetside cafés, Hugo next to her. Rosie fancied she looked like a local and had fantasized about the top-floor Parisian apartment she and Hugo would reside in, with their perfectly turned out children wearing navy coats and shiny patent leather shoes. In reality Rosie and Hugo had stayed in a room barely big enough for the bed, with a bathroom down the hall they had to share with other guests. The windows didn't open properly and it had been summer, claustrophobically hot. But back then, they had had fewer worries and a greater share of possibilities. There was no mortgage, no house, no children, no surgical practice to maintain or golf days to attend, no children's homework or secretarial duties for respective play centers, parent-teacher associations, and Scouts groups. Back then, despite the heat, Rosie had slept with her head on her husband's bare chest, just as Beth sleeps now upon Eddie's.

Helen passes Rosie the cigarette.

"Besides, you have Max. You've always been closest to him," Rosie says reassuringly.

Helen licks her lips. "We don't see each other often."

"But when you do . . ."

"Yes."

"You've always been so bonded with each other."

Max and Helen came from contrasting worlds but were so close. Rosie thinks of Hugo—the life he came from compared with hers. The noise, laughter, and chaos in her family home compared with his. His parents' home was always so quiet you could hear the clocks ticking. When they had come to Paris, Rosie had wanted to shop and to kiss in gardens, while Hugo had insisted on visiting museums, one after the other, striding quickly through the hot streets. He had read medical textbooks in those cafés where Rosie wore her Hepburn glasses and dreamed of other lives.

"We're not so different," Helen murmurs.

They both look toward Max then, still sprawled out on the couch, his clothes and shoes and socks in the neat pile Rosie made last night. It was his words that had Rosie sitting on the edge of the bed as her husband slept, his words that had kept her awake till the light changed and she'd left Hugo's side to stare out at the street and wait for the morning to come.

I did the wrong things.

I did the wrong things.

Max's drunken voice had been echoing around her head for hours now.

"Did you ever think about what it would be like, to be together?" Rosie asks Helen.

Helen sucks on the cigarette and nods. "Of course. I still do."

"And?"

"And I still don't know." Helen tips her head as she stares at Max's figure, one leg out of the covers, one leg dropped to the floor, mouth open. "This long and I still don't know. I thought I'd have it worked out by now."

Rosie gives a bitter laugh. "Join the club."

"How did you know?" Helen asks.

"With Hugo? I didn't."

"You must have thought you did."

"Oh yeah, I thought I did," Rosie replies. Her wedding day had been beautiful, not a drop of rain, just endless blue, blue sky. Her mother had tears in her eyes that she dabbed at with a lace-edged hankie. Even her brothers had suddenly been awkward with her, as though she were a perfect china doll, not the little sister they had pushed and shoved around her entire childhood. Rosie's father, walking her down the aisle so seriously, worried he might get it wrong, might trip. Everything sweet and perfect, like a film.

"Your wedding was gorgeous," Helen says, as though reading her mind. "Remember us all at the reception? You and me and Nina, all the boys, dancing? What a riot. I remember thinking we should have more weddings if they were all going to be like that."

Rosie remembers. They'd been dancing in a big group and then suddenly it was just them—Rosie, Eddie, Helen, Max, Lars, and Nina—like the old days, shutting everyone else out, jumping up and down and laughing so hard their stomachs hurt, and Max still trying to hold a beer but spilling it all over Eddie instead and the floor getting sticky, and Rosie worrying that her white shoes were getting dirty and then not caring and wanting to kick them off because they hurt. All of them singing—yelling, more like—and Helen bringing her in close and giggling and kissing her cheek hard and singing and getting the words wrong. Rosie had felt so radiant then, so full to the brim with love and possibility. Hugo had come up and gently extracted her from that circle, reminding her that the car was coming soon and that they had to leave; they were bound for Paris in the morning.

"But there weren't any more," Rosie says. "Weddings."

"That's true. First and last, so far."

"So far," Rosie agrees.

Rosie stares at Helen a moment. She looks invincible but Rosie knows she is fragile. She had always envied the money that seemed so easily available to Helen, the exotic vacations she took with her father and his wife du jour in places Rosie could only imagine. The gifts of expensive clothes and dinners at the Ivy, none of which Helen had seemed to count as special. Rosie had once thought that Helen was ungrateful and spoiled. She had been jealous. Now she understands that without love it all means nothing: smoke and mirrors, pretty lies.

"Did you hear from Soleil?"

"I spoke to her last night and told her about Nina." Helen pauses. "She was shocked. Quiet for a change. She's been so fiery lately. I don't know what she thought . . . that we were a bunch of bourgeois assholes probably."

"Yes."

Helen sighs. "She's still young. She thinks you can have . . .

an ideal life, I guess. Not compromise. Or turn into a cliché. Become something you didn't expect."

Rosie nods. She remembers feeling exactly like that.

Helen finishes her cigarette and stands. "I'm tired. I'm going to go back to bed for a while. Are you okay here? By yourself?"

"I'm okay," Rosie replies.

Helen bends over to kiss her cheek. "Wake me when you're going for breakfast?"

"I will," Rosie promises.

Thinking of the day breaking, of breakfast, makes Rosie envision the day ahead, the smell of hospitals and waiting on hard chairs and trying not to think the worst. It makes her want to cry, makes her feel small and unprotected.

Helen takes a few steps before turning. "It feels strange, doesn't it? Without Juliette?"

Rosie nods. "I looked for her on the street. I don't know why. Did Max say something to her? Is she gone for good?"

"I don't know," Helen murmurs. "Perhaps she is."

"I really liked her," Rosie replies.

Helen nods, turning back, mumbling, "Good night," though it is morning.

Rosie waits by the window a few more minutes, watching, listening, thoughts turning to soup, eyelids suddenly weighed down by fatigue. She runs a hand over her face and then rubs her eyes. Sleep pulls at her now, like one of her boys on the hem of her shirt. She stands and moves toward the room where Hugo sleeps but pauses before she gets there, at the room where the door is ajar. One of Lars's arms is flung over Nina as she lies on her side with her hands in a prayer position, tucked under one cheek. She looks so much younger when she sleeps. They have kept the door open for Sophie,

Rosie knows; it is a habit she has never gotten out of either. Hugo always wants the door closed and Rosie craves it open, just in case, so she can hear cries or odd sounds even when she is supposed to be sleeping. But Sophie is no child. She is growing up faster than any of them can bear to notice too acutely. She had been poring over her phone last night; Rosie recognized the widened eyes and pink cheeks, the expression of new, giddy love. The boy on the beach.

Rosie tiptoes inside Nina and Lars's room and sits on the edge of the mattress. Her breath slows, matching theirs. There is something about the two of them that reminds Rosie of her parents, or the feeling she has being around her parents: like nothing can go wrong with them about; like routines would be followed, bad guys vanquished, life safe. Rosie feels her whole body growing heavy, her skin, her eyelids. Nina stirs.

"Rosie?" she asks, opening her eyes to slits.

Rosie nods mutely. Nina lifts up the duvet and Rosie slides in beside her. Lars yawns and smacks his lips together.

"Who is it?"

"Rosie," Nina replies drowsily.

Rosie is already slipping into sleep, reality becoming soft and fuzzy.

"Hey, Rosie girl," Lars mumbles, reaching over Nina to pat her arm.

Chapter Twenty-One

JULIETTE

Juliette had forgotten how cold the kitchen is in the morning, that it takes a while for the ovens to heat the space and that the small window above the sink looking out to a tiny car park receives no sunlight until the afternoon. Which doesn't matter when your shift starts at two p.m., but it is only six a.m. and it is cold. Juliette reaches under the counter and pulls out the thin sweater she brought with her. Once on, she shakes out her shoulders and gets back to work. She rubs flour into the counter, not even glancing at the stand mixer with the dough hook already attached. Doing it by hand is the very point of it.

Juliette had sent Louis a text message last night. Did he mind? She still had a key. He had replied quickly: *"Bien sûr."* Of course. He hadn't changed the locks. He did owe her at least this favor, if not a few more, given how cheaply Juliette had sold him the restaurant. It was doing well too; Juliette got messages from her Parisian friends and read reviews every now and then. It had a shiny new name and some new tables and chairs, but otherwise it felt familiar and safe.

She had passed Leon's new bistro on her walk here; it had a sign across the window that read CHEZ LEON—OPENING SOON! with a black-and-white photograph of Leon in his chef whites, arms folded across his chest. She had slowed a little and stared at his face, cast in grays. She had thought of Celine and of the strange nature of love: How it was so rarely without a cost, so rarely free. How some people belonged to others. And how easily she could have been a thief; how happily she would have robbed him of her.

Juliette pushes the sleeves of her sweater up to her elbows, more flour (and yeast and water), shaggy little bits of it, now sticking to the knit. She feels the dough under her hands and pushes and pulls at it as she has done a thousand times before. This she knows. Other things—her life, what to do now—she has no idea. But making dough is always the best way for Juliette to feel her way into the future, to hold the possibilities lightly in her mind, while her hands stretch the flour and yeast, sugar and butter and water. Push, pull, this way, that way—dough and ideas becoming more elastic.

She had been rude to Max. Not rude exactly, but she had walked away. Juliette isn't the boss, not like she'd been here at the restaurant. Juliette had overstepped the mark and in one fell swoop upturned her whole life. Good work was hard to find in Douarnenez.

Plus, Max was right. Helen is not Juliette's, will never be Juliette's. If she does not belong with Max, then Helen belongs with someone else—someone vibrant, someone who has their act together, someone with more money, someone from her world. A world of rock stars and artists and gallery openings with trays of glasses filled with champagne that someone else has poured, that someone else passes around. A world of trips to Mexico with the sun shining bright, cocktails by a pool, the wet, sharp smell of chlorine on bikini fabric. Perhaps, later, Juliette will read about Max and Helen, see their picture in one of those big glossy magazines. A bohemian wedding, someplace where summer lasts all year, where the groom goes barefoot and the bride wears sunglasses and a short dress. Helen belonging with Max, just like Max said.

That is the way of things, the way things work. Juliette knows this. Theirs is the love story of all the love stories: a beautiful woman, a handsome man, waiting for each other, joining together. It is the way of things.

Juliette pauses, hands in dough. She can feel it pressing back, a little, against her fingers as she rests them. Resistance. Not much. But enough.

Juliette had learned to make *kouign-amann* in Stephanie Jeunet's bakery kitchen. Her mother had charmed Stephanie into it, like she often did. Plus, her mother liked to be busy, playing bridge, walking with her father, teaching; her mother busied, she collected and made things, as if her hands couldn't be trusted to sit idle. Stephanie had laughed at her mother's hopelessness with the dough, but Juliette, she observed, had an instinct for it. Juliette's mother had been so proud. They tried several more times for her mother to master it, each lesson Juliette and her mother bringing two big bottles of wine. The women got tipsy while Juliette, the girl between them, watched and learned and grew in confidence. She was always steps ahead of her mother, washing her hands while her mother's were still in dough.

"Isn't she a wonder?" Juliette's mother had said once, looking down disappointedly at her own sticky fingers.

"I could use a daughter like her," Stephanie confessed. "I don't know who will take over when I have to give it up."

Juliette remembered how she had turned away at that,

pretending not to listen, feeling the heat of the oven on her face as she dried her hands on a tea towel that hung near the oven door.

Juliette sees that she has been hiding. Feeling the weight of failure. Making herself smaller, reducing herself into halves, into quarters—pieces that can be secreted away. She has surrendered herself to it—the exile, guilt, and grief. To simply waking each day and doing only what she needs to do and nothing more, to not thinking too much, not wanting too much. Reasoning that she doesn't deserve to want for much more. It is safer. Safer to be in Douarnenez in her parents' cottage with mementos cluttered around her. Safer to have a basic job, a simple, small life. To serve others and bury her own desires, her own truth.

Juliette pushes against the dough one more time. It is ready. She forms it, gently, into a large, misshapen ball and lifts it back into the bowl, covering it with plastic wrap. She stands back, arms at her sides. She remembers how she had managed to be capable after her father died, how she had coped despite it all, arranging a funeral, clearing debts, finding work. She doesn't have all the answers. There is no plan. But there is one thing to do and she will do it and somehow it will lead to something else. She can feel it. The same way she can feel the dough, making the *kouign-amann* by hand, from scratch, with no recipe, no steps, and no guidance. It is embedded in her sensory memory—the smells of the market as a child, the taste of hot pastry and rich butter on her tongue, the laughter between her mother and Stephanie, the smiles on the faces of those she has made it for since—the women she has loved, those who loved her and those who didn't, the patrons at her restaurant, Celine, *bien sûr*, and Max. It is a knowing in Juliette's fingers and muscles and bones, a know-

ing that reaches back into the past but out into the future too.
The times she will make it, the people she will love, the possibilities she will grasp, the heartaches; the stepping forward
of time punctuated with love and loss and laughter.

Juliette will do what she knows she must do.

She will tell Helen how she feels, about who she is.

Because she knows the price of an untold truth.

Though telling is a kind of madness. Though Helen is not
hers to love.

Chapter Twenty-Two

MAX

Hospitals make Max feel carved out, empty. He stands in the hallway outside the consultation room. Nina, Lars, and Hugo are inside with the French doctor, the doctor who had seemed so much younger than Max expected, with a full head of hair, sneakers on his feet, and lithe beneath the white coat. The consultation room has a frosted-glass window in the closed door that reflects Max's face. He stares at it. The face reflected back at Max is so old. It's the face of a stranger. Beside it, Eddie's face tips down toward the linoleum floor, eyebrows drawn together.

Max glances down the hallway. Beth and Sophie sit in seats much farther away; there weren't enough for them all. Beth has her hands in her lap, staring straight ahead, while Sophie frowns at her phone. Beside them is a man in a tweed jacket with a walking cane between his knees. Max gazes at Beth in her bright floral dress and remembers that, somehow, like one of those Russian nesting dolls, there is a baby within. Max still cannot bend his head around it.

He peers farther down the hallway, looking for Helen. It remains empty, barring the intermittent interruption of an orderly or nurse in mint green or navy, rubber-soled shoes squeaking with each footstep, face set with purpose. Rosie had taken Helen with her to find coffee and Max feels dislocated without her, unsure what to do with himself and unsure what to think. He leans back into the wall behind him.

"Of all of us, you'd never think . . . ," Eddie murmurs. "Nina, I mean."

Max nods, though he wants to close his eyes and disappear.

"She's always been so tough."

"She'll be okay," Max mumbles, though he is much less sure than he was. The whole world is unsure this morning. Even the fluorescent lighting in the hallway shivers unsteadily.

Eddie's voice drops to a whisper. "Hey, look, I'm sorry about . . . what you heard. Beth didn't know you were there."

Max glances at Beth, but her expression does not shift.

"We're still working it out," Eddie admits.

"Oh yeah, sure, mate," Max says.

"Trying to decide what's best for both . . . well, all of us."

Max turns to his friend. Eddie's face looks older too. That makes Max feel a little better for a split second. "Sure, sure. No need to apologize. You'll work it out."

Eddie nods. "We haven't been together for very long. It's sudden. She's young. I'm not. I'm pretty terrible with kids, not that I've had much experience."

Max nods. He wills himself to do this, to talk and think about something other than Helen. "What does Beth want?"

Eddie looks at her and then back down to the floor. "She wants to know what I want."

"Do you know what you want?"

Eddie shakes his head. "That's always been my problem. I'm not good with decisions. Remember Australia?"

The Australian trip had been Max's itinerary the whole way, excepting a few pubs Eddie had wanted to go to, hostels he'd wanted to stay a little longer in, mainly because of girls he'd wanted to sleep with. Eddie is never in a rush. Max is more impatient. Eddie is easygoing; Eddie never minds that Max makes all the plans.

"Rosie couldn't stand it, see? I wasn't ambitious enough. She was always deciding where we would go, what we would do; she wanted to be with someone . . . well, someone stronger, I guess. Someone like Nina, like Hugo. She got sick of me." Eddie shrugs. "It was fine. I got it. I get sick of me too."

"Eddie, you're a good guy."

"Maybe. But I've just drifted along. You can't deny that."

"You go with the flow," Max counters.

Eddie gives a wry laugh. "You know who I always wanted to be?"

Max knows the answer before he says it.

"You," Eddie finishes. "I just wanted to be you. I did whatever you did. With women. With life. You know that already, don't you?"

"We're mates. We like the same things," Max replies hopefully. He feels squeamish, as though he might be partially responsible.

Eddie shakes his head. "That could be true. But I wouldn't know, would I? We might be the same or we might not be, Max. I never really tried to find out. Problem is that I don't, for sure, have your talent. So I'm fucked on the rockstar front."

"It's not all it's cracked up to be," Max mumbles.

Eddie continues: "I can't do it anymore. I can't live your life. I've got to make this huge decision . . ." Eddie looks to the floor, his hands gripped into fists. "And I've had no fucking practice. I'm about to go into my forties with no experience at living my own life."

"Eddie . . ."

"It's fucked up, Max. You have no idea."

"I have a bit of an idea."

"You've got it all sorted out, mate. The money. The girls. You're literally living the dream, Max. You're living it."

"I'm not, Eddie."

"Who am I supposed to be? How do I work this out?" Eddie's voice is rising. "Do we have this baby, Max? Do we try?" Eddie looks as though he might cry. Max glances again at Beth, who is still staring into space, hands neatly cupped like a little girl's in church. Eddie whispers, "I'm scared, Max."

Max blinks fast and nods. *I know. So am I, mate. So am I.*

"Who am I supposed to be?" Eddie asks again.

Sophie looks up from her phone at Max. For a moment he sees the child in her, the girl she once was, in the innocence in her eyes. He remembers the first photographs of her, sent from Lars: Her tiny face, pink and angry, peering out from between a knit hat and tightly wrapped muslin. Her impossibly small hand, the digits curled around one of her father's fingers. All of her contained, bundled, cradled in Lars's arms. Lars's broad grin, his eyes shining with tears, his cheeks flushed with pride.

"Be Lars," Max replies weakly.

A YOUNG WOMAN walks toward them. She wears a loose cardigan slung over the top of a long, patterned dress, the skirt flicking out with every purposeful step, revealing small feet in mustard-yellow sandals. Max straightens.

"Soleil."

She faces Eddie and lifts her chin. "Hi."

Eddie glances between her and Max.

"Do you know where my sister is?"

"She's gone to get coffees," Max answers.

Soleil's expression is cold.

"Soleil, I—"

"I'm not here for any of you."

Eddie pushes off the wall and coughs. "I'd better . . . I'm going to see Beth."

He picks up his jacket and wallet from the floor and moves toward his girlfriend. Max watches as he reaches out and Beth stares for a moment at his palm before placing her hand in his. Eddie crouches in front of her.

Max turns to Soleil. "I'm sorry."

She crosses her arms. "You are a creep."

Max nods. "Yes."

"Not everyone wants to fuck you, you know. Just because you play guitar in a band, just because people know your face . . ."

"No."

"Doesn't mean people want you."

"I know."

Soleil pauses, frowning at him.

"I was messed up that night. On drink and drugs. I wasn't thinking right."

"Just that night?" Her stare is hard. "You being messed up isn't my fault."

"No, it's not your fault."

Soleil studies him. "You need to sort yourself out."

"I really am sorry," he says again, feeling a bit ill and meaning it. The expression on Soleil's face is one of disgust.

"I'm only here for Helen," Soleil snaps. She turns toward

the tiny window in the consultation room door. "Nina's in there?"

"With Lars and Hugo. And the doctor."

Soleil unfolds her arms and pushes her hands into the pockets of her cardigan. Max glances over to Sophie, who blinks up at him and then back to the window herself. Max turns too. Soleil, Max, Sophie, all of them, staring at a window that gives nothing, shares nothing. Waiting. Directing their thoughts and wishes at it, as though they might somehow get through the glass. *Please be okay. Please make her okay.*

"She seems like a good mother," Soleil says, voice still starchy. "The three of them . . ."

"Yes," Max replies. "The three of them are something."

She sniffs. "Yeah, well, despise my parents."

Max looks at her. "So do I," he murmurs.

The truth of it knocks him. He always hated his father. The violence and name-calling, the brutality and selfishness of him. His father was unredeemable. But his mother . . .

Max takes a deep breath. He has been holding out hope for his mother. Just a tiny fraction. A match flicker. *Something.* Hoping that one of the two people who had created him wasn't abhorrent. Because otherwise, what chance was there for him? A whole, made from two rotten halves.

Soleil is looking down at her toes that peek out from the bottom of her dress. The pattern on the fabric is made up of thousands of dots in concentric swirls—gold, bronze, and brown dots. It makes her look like she is covered in hundreds of tiny suns.

"You can't take Helen away from me," Soleil says forcefully. "She may not be blood"—she seems to wince at that, as though the thought troubles her—"but it doesn't matter. You can't take her from me."

Max nods slowly.

"She's the only family I have."

Eddie rises from crouching and turns down the hallway. Max follows his gaze to the two women approaching, one dark, one blond, carrying coffee cups in a cardboard tray. Rosie leads, her face makeup-free and resolute. Beth stands when Rosie passes her a cup, their fingertips touching. Eddie reaches out to Helen, squeezing her shoulder. She seems so delicate today, her skin pale against her hair, her sweater a size too large. Max senses Soleil straightening. Helen moves to Sophie first, removing another cup from the tray and offering it to her. The girl nods in thanks.

Max watches the way Helen's lips curve and how the sheet of her hair slides across one cheek. He studies her fingers as they tuck the dark hair behind her ear—the pink beige of her nail polish, the delicate lines on the back of her hand, the way the colored stone in her ring catches the light. He stares at her face as she lifts herself back up, her eyes, pink-rimmed from tiredness, as they roam along the linoleum-tiled corridor. They find his and catch, then slide to find Soleil's. Max notices how they widen, notices as her shoulders drop and her face forms an expression that can only be described as relief. Though Max has never really known family, not personally, Max is sure this is how it feels. Helen and Max are family.

She's the only family I have.

But Helen is not Max's.

And she is not Soleil's.

It takes a succession of tiny sounds to pierce through Max's thoughts: the metal click and friction of a handle rotating, the protest of old hinges. A murmured conversation spills out from the widening gap and all eyes shift to the door with the small window, opening.

Un an plus tard *(one year later)*

Chapter Twenty-Three

JULIETTE

Juliette pushes the key into the lock. Outside, the potted plants are gone, replaced by planter boxes full of herbs and edible flowers and a long stone bench for waiting customers. The paint around the window frames is now glossy black; the sign hanging is black too, with brass letters. The ivy is still there, cut right back, determinedly regrowing in bright green shoots and quivering heart-shaped leaves. Juliette opens the door to the smell of baking and the sounds of rap, her assistant Xuan shouting along from the kitchen. Chairs are on tabletops, the newly tiled floor clean and shining.

Xuan turns down the stereo when she comes into the kitchen and wipes the sweat from his forehead with a corner of his apron. His thick black hair sticks up like exclamation marks. "I didn't know you were coming in."

"I woke early and couldn't get back to sleep."

Xuan nods, understanding. It is a baker's curse, the habit of waking before the sun does, a habit that is hard to break even on days off. Juliette has been awake since dawn, watching the light changing color against her skin, from mauve to gold to ivory, as her thoughts went through memories, dipped into wishes, and then turned to pragmatic things: special orders for the boulangerie-patisserie that bore her name, the supplies she needed to get more of, the e-mails that had been piling up requiring replies.

"How are you doing?" Juliette asks. "Do you need a hand with the orders?"

Xuan gestures toward a bench with four white boxes on top, their lids open and contents cooling. "Done. When is pickup?"

"This morning for the *kouign-amann*," she replies, making her voice steady, "for the wedding." This is the real reason she did not sleep, the reason she is in early, though she has tried not to think of it. She lifts her chin. "Lunchtime for the others."

Leaning over the boxes, Juliette surveys the caramelization of the two *kouign-amann*, the regularity and depth of the score marks. Xuan has learned so much in such a short time; he has the knack for pastry. Every now and then Juliette becomes fearful he will leave Douarnenez and her boulangerie-patisserie, but he doesn't seem to want to, not yet anyway. Juliette reviews the other orders—a *gâteau* Breton and a large quiche.

"These look great, Xuan. *Parfait.*"

"Thanks, Juliette."

"Anything else I can do?" she offers.

"Nope. I'm going to do some glazing and then I'll fill the cabinets."

"I'll help with that. If you need me, I'll be out front."

Xuan reaches for the stereo as Juliette scans the kitchen before leaving, balling up a piece of parchment paper and putting it in the trash on her way out.

———

Juliette takes the chairs down off tables, restocks napkins, and folds *gâteau* boxes. She wipes down the cabinets, though they appear spotless, and polishes the exterior of the glass so it reflects the light coming in from the window. She stands back and pauses, remembering the way it used to look, all the times she was here as a child, a teen, and an adult. She imagines Stephanie Jeunet behind the counter in her bright red turtleneck, the decorative wicker baskets behind her, calling out to Juliette as she entered. Juliette was lucky the store was still for sale when she inquired, though it was in such a state of disrepair it couldn't have attracted many buyers. Dust covered everything, and underneath the dust, grease, especially in the kitchen, which Juliette practically had to rebuild from scratch. The real estate agent impressed upon her that it would be easy to restore it to its former purpose, but Juliette knew most of the fixtures—ovens, tables, cash register—would need to be updated and replaced. Still, Juliette felt the presence of Stephanie Jeunet here, which she wouldn't have felt elsewhere, and that was worth something. Worth something to Juliette at least.

Stephanie's presence gave Juliette courage when she needed to replace the electrical wiring and when she discovered the ivy had grown into the water supply. It gave her reassurance when bills came in, when there had not yet been Xuan for support. It gave her comfort when she felt the loneliness that every business owner feels, the weight and burden of making it all work, of holding it together when things didn't go according to plan, when nothing went to plan.

Juliette often summons the memory of Stephanie in her usual spot, content in her place in the world, selling brioche and *gâteau* and bread made in the way she always made them, smiling, chatting, never rushing. Juliette rushes less these days too. Her Paris self would be appalled at her languid pace, the way she pauses before making decisions, the simple, traditional way she now approaches all her cooking.

Juliette looks up when the front door opens.

"Hi, Juliette."

Max is wearing a suit—a nice suit, charcoal gray, and either new or freshly pressed. No tie. Dark sunglasses. A bright white shirt, the top two buttons open. He is a little thinner than usual; otherwise he looks the same. He lifts the sunglasses onto his head.

She hadn't expected Max to come. She thought maybe one of the others instead. Or Helen. Of course she had wanted it to be Helen.

"Hi, Max," she replies. "You look good."

"I scrub up okay."

Juliette puts down her cloth as he gives her a kiss on each cheek.

"Helen is picking up flowers," he says, as though reading her mind. "Are you well?"

"Very."

Max glances around the room. "This is all yours?"

"*Oui.* All mine . . . and the bank's."

"It's magnificent."

"Thank you."

"Business good?"

"*Oui.*"

They pause and stare at each other; Juliette lets the silence bloom. She can hear Xuan's music in the kitchen and the metallic sound of baking trays being shifted on the counter.

"Beautiful day for a wedding," Juliette says finally.

"Yes," Max replies, clearing his throat. "I'm not used to being so sober on these occasions."

"How is that going?"

Max meets Juliette's gaze. "Getting better. Surviving it, so far. I have been meaning to call you . . ."

Juliette remembers the moment in the stairwell. Feeling ejected. She was not a part of them but they were now a part of her. Needing to leave but not wanting to go. The sound of her sandals striking each step on the way down.

"I wanted to—"

"Apologize," Juliette finishes for him. She knows it is part of therapy, to apologize to those you have wronged. She assesses him; his face is earnest.

"Yeah."

"You don't have to, Max. Things worked out well for me. I'm happy here." Juliette pauses. "Happier than I thought I might ever be in Douarnenez."

"Well . . ." Max glances around again. "It certainly suits you. You know, I went to the old restaurant last week, in Paris." He leans toward her. "The *kouign-amann* was nowhere near as good."

Juliette laughs. "You are a charmer, Max."

"It's the truth," he protests.

"Speaking of which, you've come for your order, right?" Juliette says. Max nods. Juliette goes to the kitchen and closes two of the white boxes, stacking them on top of each other in order to carry them easily.

"*Kouign-amann* for a wedding cake," she says, coming back out of the kitchen. "That's a first for me."

"Can you think of anything better?" Max asks, smiling.

"Not really."

Max pushes a set of keys into his trouser pocket and reaches out to accept the boxes.

"What do I owe you?"

Juliette shakes her head. "It's a wedding gift."

"I want to pay."

"I said it would be a gift, so it's a gift. I promised. Don't argue with me or I'll get angry," she jokes.

Max tips his head and grins. "That I'd like to see. Are you sure?"

"Take them."

Juliette waits for him to leave but instead he hesitates.

"Are you coming today, Juliette? You're invited."

Juliette takes a breath. Carrou, Stephanie Jeunet's niece, is Max's housekeeper now. She has been telling Juliette all about the wedding arrangements at the house. How the garden had been tidied, all the flowers in bloom; the boxes of fine champagne that had been delivered. Carrou, never married herself, was giddy with the details. A celebrant from Rennes, a jazz singer from Paris! Chairs rented, lanterns and candles for the evening, a caterer—Carrou would hardly have to do a thing, just tidy up here and there, the bathrooms and bedrooms for the guests, fresh towels, pass around a few canapés. She had even bought a new dress from one of the expensive tourist shops in Locronan, coral pink with a lace collar. Juliette saw them all there in her mind. She had been imagining them all morning, as dawn broke and sleep evaded her: Eddie and Beth and the new baby. Sophie, older now, probably standing next to Etienne. Rosie too, wearing jewelry she had made herself, looking strong, looking elegant. Carrou to one side, in the dress the color of flamingo feathers. Helen.

Juliette frowns.

"Maybe," she replies.

"Come," Max urges.

"We'll see."

Max nods, understanding, and half turns to leave. "Hey. I'm sorry all the same, you know, whether you need me to be or not. I was selfish."

"Thank you, Max," Juliette replies.

Juliette thinks about her own selfishness, about how much she wishes Helen had come instead of him, even knowing it would be a kind of torture to see her in person rather than in the sleepy daydreams of her mornings, the half-formed imaginings she had when business was slow. She half hoped and half dreaded that if she saw Helen, in person, the thoughts and fantasies would evaporate.

Juliette last saw her in l'Orangerie, Juliette's favorite museum, in Paris. Inside, the haziness and colors of Monet's huge works were soothing, the space light and quiet and unknown to many of the tourists who flooded the other galleries and museums. It was serene. Juliette had stood with Helen in front of one of the massive, concave paintings, studying the pale greens, soft blues, and violets, wishing she could reach for Helen's hand.

"I'm not asking for anything," Juliette had said, calmer than she imagined she might be. "I just want to be honest. I need to be honest."

Being with Helen in that space, confessing, had felt like the times she had written messages and stuffed them into bottles, casting them out to sea with her father on one of their Sunday beach walks. Her father by her side, their hands above their eyes, squinting at the bottles bobbing on the waves, watching till they disappeared, knowing they were unlikely to reach anyone but willing to try all the same. Hoping simply because there was joy in it, because there was really nothing to be lost.

Juliette and Helen had walked slowly around the same gallery once, twice—Juliette lost count—with those magnificent, blurred water lilies in the background, as Juliette explained it all, just as she had promised herself that she would. She confessed her past and her secrets. She told Helen all of it. About Celine. Maman and Dad. Regrets. Sadnesses. Hopes. Desires. Helen had listened, and when Juliette was finished, when all Juliette wanted was to pull Helen toward her and hold her, Helen had stood at arm's length and whispered, "I can't." Her voice had been shaking with tears.

As Max leaves the patisserie, Juliette watches him through the windows, wedding cakes in his arms, sunglasses returned to his face. She follows him until he is out of sight and then returns to the kitchen to help Xuan bring the trays of food to the counters. She distracts herself with the work, making rows of buns and tarts, elevating cakes onto stands, stacking baguettes into the bread bins. When all the food is laid out, Juliette stands back and assesses the display before heading out to snip herbs from the planter boxes for garnishing.

The light outside is brightening as the morning stretches and becomes comfortable. Juliette notices a woman with dark hair sitting on the stone bench by her door. She wears a plain white silk top and narrow light gray trousers the same color as Max's suit. Her hair, loose, is longer than it was before and wavy. She is as beautiful as Juliette remembers. It sends a shiver through her, and she is rooted to the spot, brass herb scissors in hand.

Helen gestures toward the inside of the boulangerie. "I didn't want to bother you. You looked busy."

"We're not open yet. Just getting ready."

"It's really lovely. The tiles, paint . . . You've done such a good job."

"Oh, well . . . ," Juliette replies. Her throat has dried up, the words sticking. "Max came in," she says, changing the subject. "He seems well."

"He's doing much better," Helen agrees. She's speaking quickly, nervously. "He has taken a break from the band. Did he tell you? He is writing new songs."

"That's great."

"His neighbor, Claudine, is here. She's singing. Jazz."

Juliette nods, recalling Carrou's descriptions.

"She's helped him to get sober, stay sober . . . Hey, did you know Eddie and Beth had their baby?"

"Sonny. Yes, I heard."

"And Rosie?" Helen pauses briefly. "Her and Hugo? No longer . . ."

"Yes. I'm sorry. I heard that too."

Helen glances at her feet. "The split has been tough on her. But she has the boys. And Fleet."

"Of course," Juliette says reassuringly. She looks down at the little scissors in her hand, held with thumb and fore-finger.

Helen takes a breath, steadying herself. "Will you sit with me for a moment?"

"I should—"

"Please, Juliette?"

Juliette lowers herself onto the bench. Helen breathes in deeply, the ivy leaves behind her shimmying in the breeze. She shifts and straightens, as though steadying herself.

"I said that I had never seen it. Happily ever after."

"I remember," Juliette murmurs, looking away from her. It is enough to be this close to Helen, to see the skin of her legs below her trousers and above her patent leather ballet flats, the movement of her hair out of the corner of her eye; to feel the warmth of her body right there.

"I'm still not sure it is for me. If it is possible."

Juliette looks up then. Helen's eyes are round and dark. She reaches out and takes Juliette's hand. Her skin is soft and cool, and her fingers lace with Juliette's easily.

"But I'd like to try."

"Helen, I—"

"I know it took me too long."

"It's not that—"

"I was terrified, Juliette. But I've thought about it a lot. There's no curse, no poisoned arrows."

Juliette runs her thumb along the side of Helen's hand. She marvels at the way her skin feels and at the combination of peace and buzzing, racing joy she feels flooding her chest.

"I know it might hurt," Helen whispers. "But I'm not going to change my mind."

Juliette nods.

"At least come to the wedding," Helen urges, gently squeezing Juliette's fingers. "You have to see Nina—she looks so beautiful. So well. She wants you there and Lars does too. Sophie, Rosie . . . All of us, truly." She glances at their hands. "It wouldn't be the same without you, Juliette. That weekend changed us all."

Juliette knows it did; she had felt it too, an unraveling that meant rearranging herself in a whole new way, weaving the threads together differently. It had been that way for all of them; there was no unbinding them now.

"Please?" Helen's voice is light and sweet.

Juliette meets her gaze again.

"With me?" she adds.

"Okay," Juliette whispers.

Helen shifts closer and leans her head against Juliette's shoulder. She exhales. Juliette looks down at her face, her soft lips, her hand still tightly woven with hers. Like a gull stretching out to ride the invisible currents in the air, trust in its pointed wings, Juliette feels hope broaden within her. She looks up for a brief moment at the pale, cloud-veiled spring sky and smiles.

A French Wedding

LARS JOHNSSON AND NINA WRIGHT,

TOGETHER WITH THEIR DAUGHTER, SOPHIE,

WARMLY WELCOME YOU TO THEIR WEDDING.

Processional song:
"Landslide" by Fleetwood Mac, performed by
Claudine Moreau (singer) and Etienne Reynaud (violin)

Reading:
"[i carry your heart with me (i carry it in]" by e. e. cummings,
read by Rosie O'Connor

Recessional song:
"Wonder,"
written and performed by Max Dresner
Every thing you gave me, saved
Every word, every gesture
Is a treasure
Lock of baby's hair
A wisp, a curl
A thing no longer
Makes you wonder—
What a wonder
To wish you well
To wish you better
To be better too—
What is left
After the notes have faded
A Nothing Something
Riches of Nothing Somethings

A wisp, a curl
A thing no longer
Makes you wonder—
What a wonder
To wish you well
To wish you better
To be better too—

JOIN US FOR EATING, DRINKING, DANCING, AND LAUGHING

AFTER THE CEREMONY.

TAKE YOUR SHOES OFF.

LET YOUR HAIR DOWN. STAY AS LONG AS YOU LIKE.

THANK YOU FOR SHARING THIS DAY WITH US

AND THE DAYS BEFORE

AND THE ONES THAT WILL COME AFTER.

WITH ALL OUR LOVE,

LARS & NINA

Acknowledgments

As always I am indebted to a great many people for their contribution, kindness and support, without which this book simply would not exist.

So much gratitude to: Veronique Guilloteau, Sid and Monique Nedjar, Agnes and Claude Francois, Marie Chesneau, Mahé Correlleur, and the people of Douarnenez, Brittany, for sharing their magnificent country and language with me; the generous, gracious, and dedicated team at Doubleday especially Melissa Danaczko and Margo Shickmanter and my agent Catherine Drayton for essential and tireless hard work; Brianne Collins, Elizabeth Ireland, Ria Voros, Karen McMillan, Glenys Tunnicliffe, Kendall Stewart, and Lucie Geappen for reading drafts and providing encouragement; Alayna Wilton, Sam and Jo Hallinan, Dionne Martyn, and many others for research assistance; and Moana Salmon, Tunnicliffes, Ballestys, Wattses, Olds, and Stewarts—the family who make up the very best team of cheerleaders a person could wish for. Plus, of course, a huge serving of appreciation and adoration for my girls: Wren, Noa, and Bonnie, who save me from too much selfishness, solemnity, overthinking, and going to the bathroom without company; and my guy: Matt—comic, enthusiast, protector, co-ringleader of this crazy circus, and true love. Life is a beautiful, madcap adventure with you four to enjoy it with.

Finally, this book is dedicated to my parents: Robert and Glenys Tunnicliffe, for sharing and reading so many stories and, most importantly, giving us the love and courage to write our own. *Merci mille fois.*

ABOUT THE AUTHOR

Hannah Tunnicliffe is the author of two previous novels,
The Color of Tea and *Season of Salt and Honey.* She is founder and
coauthor of the blog *Fork and Fiction,* which explores her twin loves:
food and books. She currently lives in New Zealand
with her husband and three daughters.